The BLACK HORSE
Chronicles

BY R.D. EAKER

BOOK ONE

THE BANA-BHUIDSEACH

Copyright © 2013 by R.D. EAKER
First Edition – December 2013

Cover illustration by Geraldine Cruickshank
Edited by Candice Eaker

ISBN
978-1-4602-0718-5 (Hardcover)
978-1-4602-0716-1 (Paperback)
978-1-4602-0717-8 (eBook)

Produced by:

FriesenPress
Suite 300 – 852 Fort Street
Victoria, BC, Canada V8W 1H8

www.friesenpress.com

Distributed to the trade by The Ingram Book Company

What an excellent horse do they lose, for want of address and boldness to manage him! ... I could manage this horse better than others do

Alexander III of Macedon

ACKNOWLEDGEMENTS

My profound thanks to my wife Geri, and my daughter Candice, for showing me the strength, determination, and courage all women possess in spite of the obstacles this world shoves at them. A woman's heart has been my inspiration.

And thanks to Bill Mowat for being the only person brave enough and patient enough to read a beginning writers first horrible draft. In this deed alone, he has proven himself to be my most valued friend.

Acrowd gathered on Chanonry Point where a huge cauldron of boiling tar bubbled above the flames. A man known as Coinneach Odhar was shackled and forcibly pushed toward his intended demise. Lady Seaforth exultingly declared that his soul would burn in hell forever, for the lies he spewed about her husband. The seer turned his gaze upon the lady, wherewith his one blind eye glowed, causing her to step back before he spoke.

"I shall happily go to my death in the knowledge that heaven awaits me with joyful tears and open arms, but you woman have angered the gods themselves to a provocation beyond forgiveness; and this will be a sign whereby you can determine whether my condition after death is one of everlasting happiness or of eternal misery. A raven and a dove, swiftly flying in opposite directions will meet, and for a second hover over my remains, on which they will instantly alight. If the raven alights first, your condemnation of me is true and just, and my eternal suffering will comfort your dreams. But if the dove touches down afore the raven, all you prayers and repentance will not save you from eternal damnation." Coinneach smiled and lifted his face to the heavens. His body became almost translucent, and then he lowered his head and slumped to the ground.

The seer was picked up and dropped into the boiling cauldron. He never screamed nor struggled. And when the flames had consumed his mass, the contents were poured onto the beach, where the sand soaked up the tar and exposed the charred bones of Coinneach Odhar.

His last prophecy came true almost immediately; when a raven from the west met a dove flying east. They hovered and dove down to the remains. The white dove landed first.

To this day a stone stands marking the spot of his demise; a few yards east from the road leading from Fortrose to Fort-George Ferry, and about 250 yards north-west from the lighthouse, which is still pointed out as marking the spot where this inhuman tragedy was consummated, under the eyes and with the full approval of the highest dignitaries of the Church.

On the west coast of Alba, a small 'baile' called BlairMor, lay nestled beneath a towering sliver of the highlands, referred to as the 'Starry Mountains'. The village, separated from its nearest neighbor by more than a hundred miles, existed in almost complete obscurity. BlairMor was accessible only from the gale shaped shores of Muireann; a natural harbor for seagoing trade with one single rutted road that steadily inclined into the hills and crossed the river Morag into the borderlands of Odhar.

To the north, northeast, and northwest; people hunted, traded, built homes, and grew crops. But to the south and southeast no one traveled. The subject of what lay between the village of BlairMor and 'Sliabh Dubh' (the black mountain) is shunned by even the most stout hearted.

Centuries before, ancestors fought an ancient evil spewing from the dark woods of the south. Many died trying to stem the flow of the iniquitous devilry that transgressed those boundaries. Some of the survivors unknowingly became victims of enchantment. Ignorance of their afflictions caused many generations to suffer for the curse on their parents.

A primordial steading overlooked the village. The farm, owned by the family Odhar, encompassed everything to the north, east and west of the river Morag. Seanáthair Odhar had granted the village below to the inhabitants. The rest remained with the family. This family suffered most from the curse of iniquity. Their children died, wives went mad, and fathers lived to bear the burden.

Years passed and many thought the threat no longer existed, until a pack of wolves attacked the livestock and killed several children. The villagers breached the boundaries of the wood, killing as many beasts as could be found. The cost of human life was great. The spilling of human and demon blood created a barrier, and the forest was sealed up once and for all. Some say the stockade, built higher than a man and twice as thick, surrounding the wood from peat bogs to the northern canyons, allowed nothing without wing to pass. Others said the thorny hedge, thick with rowan, planted this side of the barrier and using the ground bones of the fallen as fertilizer, would turn 'all' evil away. But most believed it was the black magic of Eilidh, the wife of Seanáthair, holding the demons at bay. It was no secret she had the power to heal, but her darkest powers escaped comment for fear of retribution.

With the barriers in place, the village tried to assume a normal existence, ever mindful of what lay so close. The full moon had not appeared twice before Eilidh's eldest son lay slaughtered near the boundary. His throat and heart ripped out. Eilidh began to keen. She bit her lips and clawed the door of her murdered son's bedroom until the blood flowed freely. Her shrieks echoed down into the village below. Children moaned and shivered in their beds while she wailed. Finally, on the seventh night, mad with grief, Eilidh disappeared into the forest. On the full moon thereafter, her keening could be heard beyond the barrier.

The people of the village turned to religion, out of fear and in hope something would protect them from the evil so close to their homes. They built a church and made sure every man, woman, and child attended, all except for Seanáthair. He never showed his face in the village again. His family remained reclusive, his friends few, and his enemies silent. When he died, he took many dark secrets to his grave. Secrets about his land, the valley, and his wife remain untold. Generation after generation of his family bore the brunt of intolerance and fear. They all quietly accepted their lot as peaceful hard working tenants of the Odhar estate.

Then the raids began again. Sheep and cattle went missing. Their carcasses discovered just outside the wood. Many men brought weapons to bear and went into the forest to kill as many wolves as possible. Lailoken Odhar led the warriors in. When they returned, only four had survived. Lailoken was among them. He fell into a fever and began ranting about demons, ghosts, and something more horrible that was imprisoned within the wood. He grew frail and died. His wife 'Vika' and son 'Fearghas', were left to fend for themselves. A few neighbors offered help in keeping the farm going. In return Vika granted them land on the ridge below the Odhar estate.

Three generations later Arthair Odhar married Gavina Cruickshank. Finally a descendant of Odhar seemed to have found happiness, but when his wife gave birth to their only child, she died. Arthair raised his daughter alone. She grew into a young woman of age. His daughter was named Cailleach, and this is where our story begins.

The words of Chleirich Fiosaiche,

Six days after the execution of Coinneach Odhar

"The monster planted his seed within a common girl of tender years. He left her to beg and scrape for everything she needed. His absence heaped shame and ridicule upon an innocent of the sweetest nature. That heinous act forever changed our world. It brought about a reckoning generations will long question. 'Which was truth, and which was a lie.' For you who survived this tempest, tell your children, tell them to tell their grandchildren, that reality and fantasy are barely separated by the thin veil... of a dream"

Cailleach's life had come to an end. She walked down the path of her childhood farm toward the village below. It was raining and cold on this early fall morning, not unlike the inside of her soul.

Cailleach would not be considered an attractive woman, nor did she ever consider herself such, with heavy brow, strong jaw, and a body firm and hardened. She had long black hair plaited below her shoulders, with thick bangs barely exposing her deep dark eyes. Cruel people had called her hag to her face. Once everyone knew her to be pregnant and unwed, far worse names had been used.

Cailleach was a kind and caring person. She made the mistake of desiring a man who cared nothing for her. Her need to be loved blinded her to the harsh truth. A rogue with no morals allowed her to believe they would soon wed. His real ambitions proved to be dishonorable.

She never thought to be married, or to ever experience love. Yet within a dreamlike moment, she gave herself to him before marriage. She would now have to live with that decision. Tears streamed down her face as she passed beyond the boundaries of her farm.

Throughout the village, a few chimneys threw sparks from the new morning fires. She moved past them, hoping none would venture out.

She planned to disappear into a place where no one would dare to go. A place called the 'Dark Wood'.

The stories told of an evil place beyond the great glen, in the shadow of 'Sliabh Dubh'. These names are not spoken aloud among the fearful. What better place to hide her shame.

Cailleach came to the river at the southernmost boundary of the village. She crossed the bridge and glanced to her right. She barely made out the white steeple of the new church in the mist. Her last hope of repentance died there.

She did not believe God lived in that church. In fact, she believed exactly the opposite.

When her heart was torn and broken, she went to confess. She was severely chastised for her trouble. Instead of offering help, the Sagart offered condemnation and punishment. Then she understood how severe her situation had become, and what she had to do.

Beyond the bridge, the road continued west toward the sea town of 'Muireann'. This is where Cailleach stepped off the path. She crossed into the valley that led to the black mountains. The night was still upon her, and her chosen course remained obscure and foreboding.

A thick gray hooded cloak kept her clothes underneath dry. Old worn leather boots, sealed with beeswax, kept the black mud from soiling her feet. The weather couldn't have been more miserable, and in spite of her wrappings, she felt the cold wetness creeping in. Her woolen sack of scant provisions hung heavily on her shoulder. It contained only a knife, a small beaker, and some meager portions of food. The sack became heavier as the rain soaked in. She trudged through the valley with no sense of anything in front of her.

Hours passed before the rain eventually subsided. The wind died down. A faint glimmer of sunlight illuminated the clouds above as dawn approached.

Waves of fog and mist rolled into the glen. Walking blindly, she still perceived nothing more than a few feet ahead, but the light took away some of her fears.

To her right, she heard the sound of water over stone. A memory gave her hope.

A burn she remembered from childhood meandered through the center of this glen. The sound of it now guided her to its bank.

She remembered the stream flowed in a straight path for many miles toward a stand of silver birch. Past the trees, the creek would veer to the extreme right, away from the dark forest. That childhood journey was the greatest distance she had ever been from the farm in her lifetime.

She followed the stream for miles. The mist began to dissipate and she could see patches of sunlight streaking through the clouds. Her path, and the stream she followed, became clearer.

The water flowing in the burn was brown from the peat bogs. A ray of sunlight touched the water's surface. The cold liquid shone like molten gold flowing between the rocks.

Overhead an eagle screamed, startling Cailleach and causing her to stop to look up. The eagle swooped down on the valley as the light invaded the mist. A rabbit had been spotted. Cailleach watched in fascination as the eagle took the rabbit in one fluid motion. No noise or scream, just a disturbance of the wind as it passed. She continued on, strangely fascinated.

The creek turned to the right as she remembered. The stream flowed into a distant valley, then further into the mountains, until its ribbon-like shape diminished.

She sat down by a silver birch to take a moment of rest. Across the bank, cedars exuded a sweet perfume. The evergreens stood tall beside the huge yellow and orange larch. Together they dotted the hills and created a beautiful palette of autumn colors.

At the base of the birch grew a patch of brown mushrooms. She knew them by sight, 'golden stewables' her father called them. Perfectly editable, so she gathered as many as might fit into her sack, and as soon as a fire could be made, she would roast them.

Beyond, patches of forest spread out in every direction; mostly sparse, but further in, a darker and denser wood awaited.

The wind began to pick up, blowing bits of spray from the burn to her cheek. The sensation awakened her spirit. She walked to the bank and scooped her hands into the cold water and splashed her face. The chilled exhilaration ran down her neck. With renewed strength, Cailleach gathered her courage and continued. She reluctantly advanced toward the wood. She remembered the horrible stories. She tried not to think about the foolishness of this journey.

The day passed and her destination loomed in the distance. A giant hedgerow surrounded the forest. There was a story of how the villagers killed hundreds of wolves here. They built a fence and planted thick thorny bushes as a barrier to keep any future hordes from getting through. That was so long ago. Now it seemed impenetrable.

The sun began to set when she came upon the hedge. She looked for a way in, but nothing like a path or natural opening allowed entrance. This was certain to be hard going, and with no light, she gave in to her weariness. She felt cold, damp, and bone tired. Cailleach decided to make camp in the thicket.

The hedgerow did at least offer some shelter from the gales. She parted the brush near the bottom and drew herself under. With her cloak clutched about her face and her sack close to her chest, she made her bed on the moist ground. She heard the wind whip the branches above. Within the darkness she sensed movement around her. She gave thought to going back home at first light, but she knew her life there was over and her only option was to flee. When morning arrived she began looking for an entrance.

After hours of searching she found a thin spot, and with great difficulty, pushed herself through, managing several deep scratches and torn cloth for her trouble. The ancient wooden fence was now only rotted post barely inches off the ground. Cailleach stood within the barrier and marveled at a living forest, which appeared to be dead. She toiled through the thick scrub full of brambles, bracken, and ticks. Cedar rosin smeared around her ankles worked well enough on the ticks, but the thorns became a hindrance, and blood trickled down her arms and legs.

Once past the first hedges, all bird song had ceased. Only to be replaced by phantom sounds of hissing, slithering, grunting, and flapping from every direction. She saw nothing and yet the damp earthy smells of rot and decay overwhelmed her senses. Musky odors in various pungent levels of intensity assaulted her nose.

The thick canopy of limbs and vine choked out the sun, making her path eerily dark beneath the trees. The precious light getting through appeared trapped, creating small living gardens within its rays. Those green pockets lay surrounded by dying plants and rotted forest. Even so, the thick briers held onto a sinister life within this black coppice. Tracks and droppings of a variety of animals made Cailleach fully aware of her peril. In spite of these fears, she took time to gather long tufts of hair hanging from brush and tree. With so much scattered about, she reckoned she'd find a use.

She came upon an open graveyard of skeletons strewn across the ground. Some lay sticking through the earth. Others had been smashed against the rocks or hung in the trees, as though an orgy of death occurred here. Bones larger than Cailleach's entire body fascinated her, while at the same time urged her to move on quickly. The hairs on her neck stood as if danger followed her every step. Fear kept her curiosity in check.

About midday the forest opened up. This made for easier maneuvering and gave her a wider clearer perspective on the possibility of whether she was, in fact, being followed. The air also seemed less offensive. Fewer thorns and scrub impeded her path, but many more stones became obstacles. Stepping over rocks proved difficult, and then further in, they got larger. Giant boulders appeared from nowhere. Some so incredibly huge, she had to go around, instead of over.

Cailleach remembered stories from her childhood about stone giants roaming these woods. Tales of how foreign warriors sought to enslave them for the purpose of battle. One such giant escaped and walked between the causeways of the islands like a man wades through a river. Later killed on the mountaintop, its form still remains. Her father told her this story. He seriously believed without question. Cailleach did not.

But here these massive boulders littered the landscape. They seemed out of place, as if someone had indeed dropped them. She remained cautious and took careful notice of her surroundings.

There appeared strange 'striations' marking some of the stones, runes perhaps. Definitely a form or symbol had been chiseled into quite a few of them; possibly a warning, or maybe method to show intended use.

She understood nothing of them. She continued around, being careful not to lose her way, when up ahead appeared another obstacle. The entire forest seemed to completely merge into blackness. Cailleach crept closer until a dark form began to take shape.

Massive carved stones, forming a huge fortification, swallowed all light from what little remained available. Covered in vines and moss, the walls created a perimeter hundreds of feet in each direction. She had no choice but to walk around its edge.

This ancient fortress was immense. The facade was gigantic. Nothing was visible beyond it. So completely grown over, the strongholds existence remained undetectable until well on it.

An archway at the center gave access into the keep, and she approached the entrance hoping for shelter. She found iron bars blocking the way and the door secured with heavy chain and lock.

Above the arch, runes chiseled into the stone appeared to be a warning. More strange writings without meaning, yet their existence seemed a portent of evil. Was the shackle meant to keep people out, or something in?

The inside court contained weathered statues of warriors staged in various forms of battle. Some depicted in agony lying on the ground. Others are leaping with furious venomous faces as they hacked their enemy. All of them appeared foreboding and ominous.

In the center of the court was a monstrous stallion rearing back on its legs. The eyes were wide and the mouth was agape in fury. The horse towered over the men in unequal size and girth.

Behind the steed, a gigantic obelisk of black granite rose towering over the battle, reaching through the trees. The solid polished stone spire stood ominous and grim, accessible only by the great oaken door at its base.

Affixed to the entrance, a large seal of purest gold hung encrusted with jewels. The entry had never been crossed. And in spite of the treasure embellished over its hinge, no one had ever tried to remove the precious stones.

To one side of the obelisk, a monstrous demon reached out towards the horse. On the other side, a Greek soldier stood with arms crossed surveying the battle.

"I've never heard tell of any such place," she whispered.

She felt uneasy being this close. She sensed a living presence within the walls. Something tortured and angry existed here. A strange awareness in her gut told her to move on. She listened.

Cailleach made her way around the stone. The distance proved much further than she anticipated. This had to have a story, but some things are better forgotten and this was definitely one of them.

The wall ended against a large rocky hill. A small gap was all that existed between the keep and the summit. She just managed to squeeze through. This wasn't a path; at best it might be considered a crevice. Still, the chasm was wide enough for her to maneuver, and she had no intention of returning back the way she had come. Unable to stand fully erect, Cailleach kept her footing by leaning into the rock. Each step put as much pressure on her fingers as it did her legs. She struggled for hours until the wall ended.

The day loomed late and her surroundings offered no safe haven so she moved on. The sun set and darkness swallowed everything. She stood motionless for hours, listening to every sound, watching strange eyes, watching her. When the full moon arose she continued. Sometime later, perhaps early morning, Cailleach walked into an open valley.

A new world emerged, brightly lit, by the moon's silver light. The valley appeared to be immense. The glen spread out between two enormous snow covered mountains. Down below, a still lake reflected the moonlight and the bright stars sparkling above. Beyond, the ribbon-shape of another stream meandered towards the foot of the mountains, passing a grove of trees. This valley was magical, and produced within her a sense of security she hadn't thought to ever know again.

"Here," she breathed, "I should make a home."

Cailleach walked to the grove. Under the trees, thick moss covered the ground. No brush, no bracken, no thorns, only lush velvety green moss. She chose a spot beneath a great Wych elm tree. A nearby stream gurgled with cold clean water flowing over stones. The soothing sound helped to ease her fears.

This place seemed right; located far enough away to provide a sense of distance between her and those who may hunt for her, yet close enough to hurry home if needed. This thought made her sad and she resisted an urge to cry. She was weary and depressed. She thought of nothing more, but to find a place to lie down.

The elm's trunk, hollow and dry, provided a cozy chamber. She crawled into the cavity where sleep came swift and deep. Her mind moved between the shadows of reality and the darkness of fear. She dreamt of strange men from foreign lands fighting over rights to a mythical stallion that would be free of all creatures, and in its fury, destroyed everything.

An impatient devil stood beside a pensive king watching for the outcome in this evil battle. Something else lurked in the shadowy mist of her dream. Another entity offered the prospect of good fortune, yet did not show a face. This small sliver of hope eased her fear and took away the nightmare.

She slumbered peacefully when first light fell upon her eyes. A new day with renewed purpose gave Cailleach the strength to get up. She was intent on creating her world.

Beneath the vast branches of the elm, a wooden hut began to acquire shape. Digging holes, Cailleach placed long wooden limbs about a foot apart. Once the basic skeleton of a round hut was accomplished, smaller branches interwoven with the standing poles created the walls. The hut took shape, but several days would pass before completion.

Birds sang in abundance in this part of the forest. Most of the small animals seemed not to mind her presence. In fact, most were quite curious. A red squirrel was especially anxious to help Cailleach with a gathering of nuts she had collected. The squirrel sat inches from Cailleach and enjoyed the treasure. She watched it happily munch through the whole lot. She had a new friend.

Indulging the squirrel made Cailleach hungry as well. She reached into her sack and removed some dried fish with hard bread. She walked to the spring to wash her hands.

The moss at the waters edge smelled lovely. Cailleach wanted to squeeze it between her toes, so she pulled off her boots and buried her feet into the lush carpet. Life was almost comfortable. She lay back to let herself enjoy a few moments.

All the animals gathered sustenance for the winter to come. High in the trees, nests took shape, nuts filled coffers, and the business of survival preceded every other need. Nature grasps Cailleach, calmed her fears, and soothed her sorrows with a surrounding tranquility. She allowed her anguish to fade and her doubts to dim. But then, her pragmatic sense took control. She pushed the thoughts of harmony away and embraced the practical thinking she knew from a life on the farm.

"I wish I had some help gathering the materials for this hut," she muttered under her breath.

She sat up to eat her food. The fish tasted tough and salty. The hard bread required a little water to soften. Her stomach reacted. Several days had passed since her last real meal. She could consume only a small amount. She lay back down for her belly to settle, closed her eyes, and fell into a gentle slumber. When she awoke the sun had set. The day had vanished leaving her lost in time. Moonlight filtered through the branches of the elm and only the wind sweeping down into the valley disturbed the silence.

She stood and stretched. The child she carried created new pains in her back and legs. She didn't know if this was normal or not.

Cailleach walked to the hut when she saw something, which made her think she must be dreaming. She rubbed her eyes, but it was still there. Beside the hut, placed in a neat pile, lay thin branches and long strips of bark. The perfect material for weaving her walls had been provided by an unknown hand. She looked around. She listened carefully; silence. She searched for tracks, but none existed.

'Well, if someone is helping me, they don't mean to hurt me.' She thought.

"Thank you!" she said loudly, almost scaring her from hearing her own voice.

The sound echoed through the valley and returned in gentle waves.

"I'll finish in the morning." Cailleach said aloud. She lay down to sleep, unafraid and full of hope.

At dawn she got to work finishing the lattice on the walls, then tying the roof by pulling the upper ends of the branches together and locking them into each other. Smaller vines interlaced the wood creating a fine woven cage to support the outer shell. She made a mixture of straw and mud to daub over the frame. The valley offered plenty of straw. The creek had mud banks further up. She dug a hole to mix the daub and proceeded to gather the materials.

She took off her boots and pulled up her skirt to cross the creek to dig out the clunch. The water, like ice, sent shock waves up her legs. She had never known anything but harsh winters and cool summers all her life, still it remained something she couldn't get used to. She shuddered from the pain.

Cailleach created a basket from some of the weaving, which she carried across the water under her arm. The opposite bank, although steep, offered good clay within reach above the waterline. This thick pure mud sustained good quality for mortar. Along the waters edge, a finer loam existed. Pottery may be formed from such. The possibilities presented themselves as her feet became numb. She filled the basket and turned to go back. As she crossed the stream, something caught her attention. On the hill, above the far bank, a doe and her fawn surveyed the stream. The deer stood staring with cautious interest. The baby stepped closer to the near bank. Large brown eyes gazed upon her with intense curiosity. The fawn was spotted brown with bright red ears.

'I've never seen a red eared deer,' thought Cailleach.

Cailleach smiled but didn't move. For a short time Cailleach and the fawn exchanged a mutual interest becoming lost in each other's gaze. The mother moved and the spell broke. Cailleach experienced something different in that moment. The deer turned and retreated into the valley. They walked away looking back every few feet. Cailleach remained still until they disappeared from sight.

'That fawn was special,' she thought. The encounter lasted seconds, yet a new emotion engulfed her. She could feel the love of her unborn child. She knew anything would be worth whatever she must endure.

In a few days the mud dried. She gathered suitable stones to lay a floor and stack around the mud walls. The mud and wood had created a sturdy frame. She laid them against the wall, stacking until they arched over the roof. With the placement of the last one, the entire structure became solid. Inside, flat smooth stones created a raised floor. In the center of the hut, she built a hearth, and for the first time, she built a fire. With flint and tinder, a flame nurtured from the sparks consumed small twigs. Soon, a roaring fire blazed and filled the room with heat. She placed the mushrooms onto a wooden spit and roasted them.

In the days following, she gathered more nuts, soft fruit, and nettles. The fruit was eaten for breakfast. Pine nuts ground and mixed with water for gruel. The nettles made into a soup. She would need strength to endure the cold winter. Kitchen tools she carved from hard wood. Baskets she wove from vines. Her bed she made from straw and the door Cailleach fashioned from the strongest oak lattice. She had built a home provided from nature; sturdy, strong, and with a brace affixed across the entrance, unassailable, at least not by anything without an axe.

She ventured further out each day. The surrounding area seemed safe but offered sparse resources for food. She was rubbish at catching fish and too fond of the animals to hurt them. She managed to stave her hunger; only just.

One day a reflection from the valley caught her eye. She took off to investigate. She was almost to the foot of the crags when she glanced something large and brassy. Cailleach walked to the place and discovered a shield. A shield still held by its previous owner.

A skeleton lay peaceful in the open field, propped up by the shield he still clutched beneath his arm. She carefully removed the shield. Inscriptions, similar to the ones at the fortress, embossed the edges of the bronze disc.

Cailleach gathered the remains and carried them to the hut. She buried everything near the stream. She placed a large stone over the burial to prevent any from disturbing him again. Not knowing the warriors name, she copied a rune from the shield. She marked the stone as such.

One bone she kept. From the longest bone of his forearm, a dagger could be fashioned. This would provide some amount of protection and small enough to be hidden for close encounters. She had always been 'a sturdy lass' on the farm, but here she seemed vulnerable. She intended to change that.

Cailleach took special interest in creating the dagger. The bone she chose had length, but not strength. The thin bone needed more substance. She sharpened the smaller end to a dangerous point. The marrow had flaked out, leaving a hollow core. So using some tufts of forest hair and knotting it together into hers, she laced the braid through and tied off on each end.

A yew tree provided thick amber to fill the core. She poured the blood red sap into the bone and laminated the entire dagger. She laid her contrivance near the flame until the sap became solid, with weight and strength increased. For good measure she carved a few selected runes on the thicker edge. Now, long enough to kill and stout enough to use more than once, her weapon could be hidden within the folds of her cloak. Each scavenging trip took her further away. Her dagger remained close at hand in case someone or something threatened her.

Beyond the site of the fallen warrior she discovered an apple tree. Its fruit, though small and ugly, tasted incredibly sweet.

"Like me!" Cailleach cackled.

She set about picking apples off the ground, and from the branches within reach. She gathered as much as would fit into her worn woolsack. When she had a sufficiency, she turned to go. Cailleach froze dead in her tracks. Many yards away stood the largest boar she had ever seen.

Red eyes focused on her with deadly intent. Breath, like smoke, came in heavy puffs with nostrils flaring in furious pulse. Long tusks covered in blood and dripping with thick saliva glistened in the fading sunlight. The beast surveyed its next kill. Her heart began pounding like a drum. She had nowhere to go.

Carefully lowering the sack, her slender fingers slid slowly inside the cloak, searching for the dagger. A slight chance, if any, would be to bury the dirk into the eye, forcing the length into the brain. So as unlikely such success might be, another plan did not present itself. She placed the butt to the center of her right palm supporting the shaft with her middle finger, index finger, and thumb. She majestically raised her hand into the air. The behemoth grew tense. The creature pawed at the ground, tearing away the grass.

Fear no longer held her captive. Something awoke within Cailleach. Her desire to protect her unborn child consumed any abhorrence. She visualized destroying this beast in a single movement, because that would be all she would get.

The boar shook with fury. With an aberrant lust for blood, the monster dug into the earth and screamed.

A storm seethed within the narrows of Cailleach's mind. Her chin jerked slightly as her arms filled with a strange bloodless liquid. Fire coursed through her veins. Her legs reached into the earth's depths and grounded her soul.

The boar lunged forward in a mighty charge that shook the ground. Time stopped with everything sliding between the beats of her heart. The creature moved as lightning strikes, covering the distance as she gasped. She smelled the blood on its breath. Eyes burning with fire captivated Cailleach's own. She couldn't turn away.

Her body began to shudder. She thought she might convulse from fear after all, when her hand pitched forward by an unseen force. A voice, from deep inside her, roared like thunder exploding, "Shaaaa Taaache!!!"

The dagger glowed and became hot. From the tip a blue flame erupted, striking the giant pig, killing the beast instantly. The forward momentum carried the lifeless body to rest at Cailleach's feet. Dust, silence, and thunder, reverberated throughout the forest. The blackened flesh lay motionless and smoldering. The animal, destroyed by a force expelled from a dead warrior's bone, crackled and spit.

Cailleach stood frozen. She was shocked. She stared at the dead beast. She held up the dagger. Her hand ached as deep dark red veins formed under the skin. How or what had happened she didn't know.

The sun began to slip behind the mountains. Night approached. Her shattered nerves caused her body to twitch. She shook her hand to rid herself of the numbness that had set in.

The boar might provide enough food for the winter, but its massive size decided her next action. An hour passed as she severed the meat around the hindquarter. She used a large stone to break the bone. She left the carcass beneath the tree.

Cailleach struggled back to camp. She closed her door tightly, fitting the brace for security. A fire soon roared to life. Some good portion of the leg she cooked that night. The aroma was incredible. Her hunger was ravenous. She ate her fill.

An examination of her hand revealed darker veins than before. Pain replaced the numbness. Her shoulder burned.

The markings on the dagger had somehow deepened. The weight seemed to have increased. The weapon, once light and brittle, now stout and strong, had a life force within the marrow. She felt a reluctance to handle it again. Using it caused damage to the wielder as well as the victim. Perceived by her to be a dagger, this was really a wand, and somehow, Cailleach knew... she was a witch.

Cailleach arose from a deep peaceful sleep, so desperately needed after the turmoil of the day before.

Plenty of meat lay on the table, enough for many days to come if dried and smoked. She inhaled the aroma and her stomach curled in, causing a sensation most unexpected. Maybe from the trauma of the night before or perhaps from a bit too much indulgence after so long without meat, either way she didn't want any for a while.

She stretched her hand and sensed the dull pain from her fingertips to her elbow. The red veins, visible beneath her white flesh, had faded since last night. She rubbed her hands together to bring back the circulation, and thought of the power arisen from the bone of a dead warrior. She wondered at the strange runes she had carved. She marveled how the blood sap of the yew tree bound such magic. She feared an unknown force risen from her belly into a deadly burst of energy. Although things seemed to exert a life of their own, she sensed another hand shaped the outcome of the boar-beast's fate.

This wand was too powerful and dangerous for herself or her child to chance using again. Only the direst circumstances would warrant any further interaction. Without thought, she stashed the wand into the innermost pocket of her cloak. She vowed not to remove the thing unless she had no choice.

She needed answers, and she would start with the carcass of the boar; providing the body still remained. Many hungry animals roamed the hills, so she assumed it was devoured, save for some scattered bones. Something about the pig and her wand had a relationship in all this dark magic. She wanted to know why and what happened to her.

The last throes of autumn endured against the first assault of winter and its gales. The days grew shorter and the frost began to consume the young buds springing to life; being fooled by a false spring. Cailleach opened the door to let in some fresh air. The approaching day offered hope. Clear and warmer than usual, the season struggled with the change.

She went to wash herself by the stream. A young fox bounced through the brush and scurried past her feet. The sun's light passed over the darkness of the demon forest. The shadows of the dark wood never faded even during the brightest hours of daylight.

Today a bright blue sky, devoid of clouds, lifted her confidence. The birds began to sing, and hearing them filled Cailleach with a gladness she had not known for a long time. The valley became special to her in so many ways, allowing her more freedom than at any previous point in her life. Nature connected with her at a spiritual level.

Her first chore required stripping the shank of all usable flesh. The skin and extra fat, she placed on the shield. These would be cooked down and used for lamp oil. She laid the cleaned bone on the hearth to dry. She put the strips on a split high enough over the coals to feed the low flames, without creating a larger flame and burning.

Once sure she had the fire controlled, she packed her things. She took the beaker filled with water; strapped the basket to her back, grabbed the knife, and stashed her wand. With renewed strength and gathered courage, Cailleach secured the door and set off for the carcass.

Her father would be appreciative of her accomplishments. He always seemed to be proud of her no matter what she did. Now she wanted to hug him. She needed tell him not to worry.

Cailleach realized that she existed in a different time than before when she would have been cleaning stalls, washing clothes, or mending fences. Today she journeyed out into an unknown wilderness, in search of answers about a dead monster and magic wands made from bone.

'How different could two worlds be?' She thought.

With this, she realized she had been walking while taking no notice of her direction. These were strange surroundings, so she backtracked looking for something familiar until she corrected her path. How easy to get disoriented in such a place, what with everything being similar. She made a promise to herself she would not make the mistake again. A few steps in the wrong direction and not paying attention might result in tragedy. She marveled at how she had lost her way. This was a strange land she had come to. Cailleach wondered if something else had a hand in this matter. She traced her steps back to the apple tree veering towards the place where she found the warrior.

In the open field, she raised her hand to her brow to shield the sun. She knew the spot rest somewhere near the far edge before the scrub and crags' began. There being little evidence of the place where he had died, and she had not made any marker in order to return to it.

After maybe an hour or so of panning back and forth across the field, she walked up on an area where the grass lay dead and flattened. She realized here he had fallen. She removed her burden and sat down on the cool ground of his death spot. She wanted to get a sense of everything. She looked in all directions, taking in every detail, trying to experience some idea of what this man saw before he died.

Towards her camp, fields of grass spotted with trees and rocks extended several miles into the distance. To her left, snow-covered mountains rose out of the valley forming a majestic arc. Here, eagles flew high in the air. They hunted the lowlands, but made their nest in its peaks. Behind her, bare rock cliffs bordered a heavy growth of bracken, scrub brush, and a few larch trees. It would be hard going for anyone caring to explore. To her right, where she had met the boar, were grass, large stones, open fields, and an apple tree. Beyond that, she didn't know.

Sitting here in such a peaceful place, the violent death of a warrior seems unconscionable. A soldier killed and left without a sword.

'Hmm, maybe the man came unarmed, or perhaps his killer took the weapon as a trophy of battle.' She thought.

"Why was one soldier alone in this wilderness in the first place? What reason or purpose would draw him here?" She said aloud.

She'd heard tales of the Vikings traveling many miles from the coast looking for cattle to steal or riches to plunder. Women were kidnapped, villages looted, and some burned. Pirates rarely needed a reason for violent behavior. But one man, alone, unarmed, at the foot of the mountain had died, and she had no rational idea why.

She stood up and stretched her arms. The pain in her hand still throbbed as the marks writhed near the surface. Magic endured and stained deep into the flesh.

She dreaded the path ahead. Her eyes searched above the trees to find only the jackdaw and occasional robin. She fully expected to see vultures filling the sky. She considered the possibility of dangerous animals roaming these woods and didn't want to foolishly disturb their meal or risk confrontation. Stealth, measured with caution, would be most advantageous to her purpose, and her well-being.

Cailleach gathered her things. She turned to leave when a glint of sunlight caught her eye. Something buried here below the surface had reflected the bright sun. She fell to her knees and scraped at the dirt with her fingers.

With only a few strokes she unearthed a ring of gold. It must be the ring of the warrior. Perhaps falling off his finger as the flesh rotted from his hand. This ring bore a finely crafted crest of an eagle with a blood-red jewel for its eye. A sword of emerald and silver lay clutched within the claws. Strange markings encircled the eagle as well as adorning the interior lining. Something more skilled than runes, its delicate lines and flourishes fascinated Cailleach. The jewels lay perfect and firm with no obvious setting amidst intricate carvings in lifelike detail. She closed her fingers around it.

'This may be the means by which to give her child a chance to start life without the burden of poverty she had always known.' Her thoughts took shape.

With an exhilaration of new hope, she imagined living among people of means. She envisioned her proper education, fine clothes, and respectful surroundings. Her child would be a scholar.

They would live among the finest of society. She may even find a suitable husband from the many suitors who would come to share her fortune.

A beautiful destiny spread its wings inside her mind, making her glow with a warmth of comfort she had never known.

The vision faded and turned into a darker future. She imagined people being hateful in spite of, or because of her fortune. Their cruelty increased because now they couldn't stare down upon her as the lowly beggar they had enjoyed reviling before. She heard the voices of children taunting her child, calling cruel names. People were distressing every moment of their lives out of envy, covetousness, and rivalry. Everywhere she turned, someone haunted her steps with ridicule and bile. They cast aspersions on every facet of her life. The tears of her child became unbearable. Eternity stretched out into endless days of longing for the comfort of a friend. The mask of fantasy crumbled into dust. True nature no longer hid behind smiling faces.

These thoughts, distressing and confusing, seemed to be coming from everywhere and yet, from nowhere. Two opposing destinies competed within her mind for the right to rule. When only moments before she found the ring, she knew full well how she would move forward with her life.

This ring had power and its 'will' sought to control. This valley held dark secrets with immense power, and the surface had only been scratched.

Cailleach folded the ring into her cloak. She stepped away from the spot, turned toward the path. She walked away and struggled to clear her mind.

The path proved difficult. Cailleach marveled at how she had managed to bring home the boars' leg. Her recollection of the night's events did not include the labored steps she was now taking. Several miles later, the apple tree came within sight. She decided to drop her burden for a more silent approach. The air still smelled of burnt flesh. She expected to find the area marked by predators, but nothing appeared disturbed.

No sound of any kind, birdsong or insects, nothing whatsoever existed around the tree, including the carcass. She cautiously maneuvered her approach among the surrounding stones in order to keep a low profile, hoping for a quick escape if needed.

After a few moments she decided to proceed into the open, keeping her hand inside her cloak. Her fingers touched the wand should something threaten. The area was clear with no sign of the boar, indication of its death, or evidence of the body's removal.

She thought back to the scene in her mind. She did not remember any blood from the beast. Perhaps the flash of energy had stopped the bleeding. She found her tracks, as well as the boars, but nothing else. The body had vanished.

Strange and beyond reason, the boar had disappeared without trace, as if something with wings had lifted the corpse. Such a creature would cast a huge shadow, and those bones she had seen in the dark wood made anything seem possible. Her eyes moved to the heavens in fear she might discover the truth. The blue skies held no horrors save a few wispy clouds moving in the wind. She breathed a sigh of relief and went back to gather her things. She decided to go a little further before returning.

Not yet midday, she had enough time to explore another mile beyond the tree. She came across the ruins of an old single room steading, minus the roof and most of its stone. A fragment of chimney holding barely at an angle still remained.

Close to the steading, a cleared area, once a garden, lay overgrown in bracken and scrub. Evergreens bordered the southernmost edge, with the rest outlined by the rubble of an ancient fence.

Further down the hill, a small creek bubbled up from a spring. Rocks, piled into a mound, formed a shelter where the water gurgled from the earth. She ran over, hoping it would be good to drink. The spring looked clear, so she sat down and cupped her hands to sup. The water tasted sweet, quenching her thirst in an amazing way. The pain in her hand subsided. The veins faded. Her legs gained strength. She was renewed. The uneasiness in her spirit was replaced with new determination. Cailleach pulled out her beaker of water, emptied the contents, and filled it again from the spring.

'So many unknown things here in this wilderness,' she wondered. 'What might materialize around the next hill?'

She drank her fill and fretted over the fact she only had the one beaker to carry the water. The thought seemed silly. She knew where to come. She would return often.

She wanted to explore even more now, but the day had passed, and little time remained before darkness fell. She pushed the lid onto the beaker and walked back to the ruined house in case anything useful survived.

Near the fireplace, an iron handle protruded from a pile of dirt. She began to dig and pull, until her efforts produced a large pot intact; exactly what she needed to make soup. A pot kept food for days or even weeks with the right amount of heat and herbs. This small treasure made her much happier than the ring she had found. She searched the garden next. She did not find any more tools or utensils, but did manage to locate several herbs. Some pepper plants still thrived among the weeds, as well as one healthy potato plant and its neighboring six onions.

'After my child is born, we will come back here and create a home from this ruin.' She thought.

She packed her good fortune into her sack and headed back towards home, giving the apple tree a wide berth.

Darkness came as Cailleach reached her hut. A small glow of fire still lingered within the coals. She removed the pot and took it down to the stream to wash. It was in perfect shape. She carefully cleaned away every speck of dirt. Back in the hut, she put the pot close to the fire to dry. She smeared fat into its belly to season and keep the rust at bay. Next, the vegetables needed to be washed and stored.

She carried several flat stones from the creek, stacking them on top of each other to form shelves, which dried quickly from the heat. She placed the clean vegetables inside the inner shelf. She gathered the long stiff fingers of flesh, which lay shrunken on the wooden split, and placed them in a bundle on the top stone. The pot dried, and the grease smeared inside made a slick shiny black surface. She coated the outside as well, sealing the iron against further decay.

Taking the knife, she cut up two potatoes, one onion, a pepper, some fresh herb which smelled like coriander, and a sliver of boar fat. She added enough water to create a stock, and positioned the pot onto glowing coals so the contents cooked slowly. The hut filled with a hearty aroma. Her stomach once again seemed ready for food.

She sat down on her bed thinking of all she had seen in the past few days. It didn't seem possible that so much could happen in such a short span of time. Most of her life had been spent in the monotonous repetition of farm chores. She thought of the endless housework and how it all felt unrewarding. Now, in only days, everything had changed drastically, with little or no intention of her own. She needed time to take in all these new strange occurrences.

She lay back to rest her head, she watched the smoke drift through a small hole in the center of the roof. Her arms and legs felt heavy. Stretching them relieved some of the tension of the day. She closed her eyes. A peaceful sleep engulfed everything, and brought dreams of giant eagles carrying Cailleach to a place where people shared a love of life, with a deep respect for all things natural. She envisioned strange people of a tribal nature. They revered the land and the heavens. Unseen forces, to every stone, blade of grass, breath of wind, and drop of water, connected them. They invited her to live among them. They offered to share their secret of life, where simple pleasures relished in the fascination each moment brings. Safe and comfortable feelings surrounded her fears. These people accepted her.

Her dream continued as layers of blue and green cloth enveloped her body. A red-jeweled belt of silver chain hung loosely from her hip. Her feet were wrapped in soft yellow leather reaching up to her hips. In her hand she found a mirror, showing the reflection of her face as far more beautiful than ever before. Her hair changed from black to brown to gold to red. With renewed life and altered appearance, Cailleach danced in circles while clutching the mirror at arm's length. She couldn't help but admire herself. She wanted to stay here forever. She belonged in this wonderful world. A place unlike anything she'd ever imagined. But when things seemed the most real, the mirror vanished, the clothes turned to rags, and she awoke clutching at her dream as everything disappeared into a fog of bitter disappointment.

Her eyes were still closed as the heat of the fire against her cheek brought her back to reality. She wondered if the stock had boiled over causing a blaze from the fat. She rolled onto her side and opened her eyes. She looked to the fire.

Seated beside the fire, the ghostly figure of a bearded man wearing a silver robe, sat staring into the pot. His hands folded in front of him in a reverent manner befitting a priest. Cailleach stifled her cry before it escaped. The ghost didn't look up. He raised his finger to his lips, and spoke.

"Do not be fearful of me my child, I've no desire to cause you distress." He cleared his throat. "We must talk of many things. I don't think you understand the weight of your decisions of late, or those yet to be made."

"Who are you? Cailleach asked, sitting up. She rubbed her eyes.

"I'm Elrick. Twas my body you buried near the stream, although not quite all of it, I might add." He turned his head to stare directly at her. She thought the green of his eyes flashed, as if fiercely confronting her.

Before she replied, he spoke again.

"No matter, your actions speak for themselves as you destroyed the beast and vanquished the puppet of my tormentor. I am in your debt for releasing my spirit from those demonic chains. However, I must guide you on this matter of the ring you now possess. Such is neither to be discarded nor sold without dire consequence, and never to be worn except by its intended." He reached for a ladle and stirred the soup.

"You're the warrior I found in the field? Your bone became my wand? The ring gave me all these conflicting ideas? The boar tormented you?" Cailleach's pitch steadily increased with each word.

"Yes to all your questions and yet each answer deserves much more than a simple yes. We must carefully look at each aspect of these events to fully construe their broader meaning in all this. I dare say any person might accomplish one thing, but only the correct succession of events and successful completion of each task could have brought about the current flux of matters as they now exist, and they are truly marvelous. I must say bravo my dear! You are to be exalted for your tenacity!" Elrick smiled as he made a broad flourish with his hands and bowed his head slightly.

"I wish I could smell!" He said sniffing the pot.

"Well, I don't understand any of this, but having a ghost sit by my fire, after everything I've gone through in the past few days, doesn't cause me the concern it would have a month ago. I'm willing to accept the possibility that I'm not still dreaming, and you do exist. I'm willing to accept that I've somehow completed a manner of quest in proper order, which brought us to this crossroad. I still must ask one question?" Cailleach said breathlessly.

"And what would that question be my dear?" Elrick gallantly asked smiling.

"What are you talking about?" The confused and strained look on Cailleach's face finished her question.

"Let's take these things one at a time, as I dare say we haven't even mentioned the spring you drank from!" He paused.

"The spring is another part of all this? What was in it? Am I going to be all right? My baby! Is my child safe?" Fear crept into her voice.

"Absolutely fine and better than before, you seem to be destined for greater things!" Elrick said. He smiled again and she thought his eyes twinkled. He turned his head raising the spoon to his lips. He feigned an attempt at tasting. His smile became a frown. He dropped the spoon back into the pot.

"Alright, one thing at a time, you tell me where we start. Tell me how it fits together. I don't understand any of this." Cailleach relinquished.

"I've no notion of why or how you became a part of this, except to say you've found yourself in the proper place, making the right decisions, saving your life and your child's as well. On top of everything else, you freed me from a world beyond evil imagination." Elrick said calmly.

"I will tell you this; your gentle nature has given you the attention of friendly spirits here in these lands. Their good feelings toward you have played a role in your good fortune. One spirit moved to help you on occasion, such was the physical manifestation you experienced." Elrick paused to see if she understood.

Cailleach's face lit up, "The wood for weaving the hut appeared out of nowhere!"

"Yes, yes quite true. The spirit seemed compelled to do that for you, yet I can't see the face. I'm quite confused as to who did such a deed. Most things are so clear in this spirit world. No matter, it decided to help you, and you are all the more fortunate." He paused again.

"To continue, your first real moment was in finding my bones. I dare say most would have steered away from them, yet in your need and desire to provide for your unborn child, you simply chose to make use of any resource you came across. Using my forearm as a weapon against the boar was a brilliant stroke of fortune. Not only did you choose the right bone. You fashioned everything in a way, which bestowed much power by emptying the marrow, pulling knotted boar hair mixed with your own through the core, winding it on each end with the exact number of twists, and filling the hollow with the blood sap of the yew tree. It is a process known to few. My goodness girl, there are many wizards in this world who never accomplished such a thing. The final act of carving precisely chosen death runes on its shell delivered a weapon of immense power, which I know you are now aware of, as well as the consequences of its use." Elrick seemed pleased at his explanation. He poked his finger into the fat lying on the shield and tasted. His face again seemed disappointed. He wiped his finger on his robe.

"I dare say that shield is of much better use as a larder than it was in protecting my life!" He remarked angrily. He now turned his full form towards Cailleach.

"But I must warn you about the wand, because it is human bone, it retains life, and desires to be covered in flesh once more. If you use it more than once you will find it embedding itself into your arm. Use the wand too many times, and all its sinews become bonded to your bones within. The weapon will remain there; never to be removed. Even the slightest motion of your hand might be destructive, regardless your intent." His face was serious at this point.

"How do you know this, if such a thing is so rare? Who would chance such fate and allow a wand to bond to their own flesh?" Cailleach asked.

"Once, many hundreds of years ago, Myrddin, a wizard of immense power, fashioned such a wand among many powerful talismans he had created for his dark magic. Within a matter of days the wand had disappeared into his arm. He was able destroy with the wave of his hand. But he discovered this power was not easily controlled. He realized he may let loose the energy in some unexpected way and fashioned a metallic glove to protect the innocent. So you must understand, even Myrddin did not assume complete control." Erick's voice had changed.

"I don't think I shall ever use it again no matter what, but I will say I thought the effects were permanent until I drank from the spring," Cailleach replied.

"Ah yes the spring!" Elrick lit up.

"Such a thing has always been spoken of. It's been eagerly sought after, even killed for, yet no trace of such a marvel has ever been found!" His voice rang out with new feeling.

"But the spring was right there near the old steading, and clearly marked by stone. Surely the inhabitants of the house knew what existed in their own yard!" Cailleach said.

"True my dear. What better way to hide a thing than by leaving all in plain sight? Its simple appearance fooled all those who expected the treasure to be hidden in some glorious manner. Many would kill to know the secret." Elrick's eyes brightened.

"Those people must have known all too well what they had discovered. Any hint of such power would've brought certain destruction to them! They chose to remain deep in these forgotten lands, keeping their secret, never growing a day older or weaker." Elrick reached into his cloak and pulled out a long pipe. He proceeded to light it with a selected coal.

"Where are they gone Elrick, if they never grew old or died?"

"Oh my dear, I never said they couldn't die, just not by old age, anything else could take their life just like normal folk. And to your next question," He paused, inhaled, then blew out a thick blue circle of smoke.

"Yes they all died. An adder bit the mother when she was gathering apples from the same tree you found. Her husband buried her body far inside the wilderness. His grief was overwhelming. He took his children and left the steading, never to return, growing old, dying in usual fashion. I had watched them all those years. I only saw them from afar. I grew fond of their presence. It's been lonely since. I never understood the source of their youth until you discovered the water." He looked distant and puffed again on his pipe, which had gone out.

Cailleach sensed his sadness. She asked a different question.

"What about the boar? Was the beast here all along, tormenting you since the day you died? Weren't those people in fear of their lives, living in such a place?"

"For reasons I can't divulge, the steading occupies a special place which doesn't tolerate evil. There are many magical secrets within this valley." Elrick smiled.

"The boar on the other hand, was a manifestation of another's evil power. A demon created it. You're lucky it was only a shadow of the monster himself. When I met him, he was a wolf and totally present in his form." The agitation returned to his voice.

"He ripped out my throat and watched me bleed to death. I've not seen him since he slaughtered me. My death left me bound to this wilderness, as I was unable to atone for the theft of the ring. Thank goodness only his magic existed within the pig. Had the monster himself gotten close to you, we would not be having this conversation. Whether magic or sheer luck, your appearance caused an outcome he certainly did not foresee. I dare say the ramifications of this turn of events are yet to be understood!" He lit his pipe again.

"So the meat I ate, is demon meat?" She asked looking sick.

"Absolutely not! It was exactly what it was supposed to be, a pig! The demon is a spirit with no flesh whatsoever, the flesh form was in fact what you saw and ate. I am quite certain he brought the beast from a faraway land, as I have never seen the like in these woods!" Elrick said as he blew more smoke rings.

"Next question, what happened to the rest? The body was gone today, with no evidence it ever existed?" Her eyebrows arched.

"I have no idea child, very strange that, yes, strange indeed." Elrick seemed preoccupied.

"But I will venture this, things conjured have a tendency to return from whence they came once the spell is broken. There might be a giant

three-legged pig galloping about in some distant land, extremely disheart-
ened at its inability to frighten more than a feeble ground squirrel or vole!"
With this, a broad grin crossed Erick's face.

He inhaled deeply from his pipe and expelled a marvelous blue smoke, in
the form of a clumsy looking three-legged boar, which grunted and hobbled
out of the hut, as if affronted by the ghost.

He and Cailleach began to chuckle at the image he had conjured.

They almost calmed down several times, but when the moment arrived, a
snicker from Elrick propelled them back into fits of laughter. This continued
for some time. Erick's charm was great, even in death. His words could both
hypnotize and intoxicate, this too would continue for some time.

CHAPTER THREE / THE FATHER

Over the village of BlairMor, the first rays of early morning sun painted the horizon a milky crimson. Mist rolled down from the hills, covering the lower regions from the blacksmith to the bridge, giving the impression of an island floating amidst a sea of white.

Roosters announced the new day in their usual manner, with cows bellowing for food, and needing to be milked. Brown smoke drifted from chimneys flavoring the air with a rich earthy aroma.

After raining for several days, the paths were mired thick with mud and the fields lay deep in water. A few farmers drove their wagons out hoping to gather what was left of their crops. Winter's brutal winds had come all too soon this year.

Near the river stood the village church, where most people attended on a more than regular basis. All the attendees made sure to give a large tithe of their monies if they wanted to stay in the good graces of Father Mackenneth. Those foolish enough not to attend became the fodder for sermons slandering their name, calling for their expulsion, and in a few cases, declaring their property forfeit by 'God's' law.

His notorious reputation preceded him, as Father Mackenneth had vigorously prosecuted witches. He subjected them to horrible tortures. Some were burned alive. He happily boasted that he personally applied the taper.

In the eyes of the fearful, he was a crusader of 'Truth', sorting the angelic from the demonic. His rule of law robustly encouraged by religious zealots whose inclination was to pick and choose which words of 'God' are to be enforced. Most notably the laws that persecuted women over men, giving them few if any rights greater than mere possessions, were highly favored by the clergy.

The church had been struck by lightning last year. Father Mackenneth proclaimed the sin of the congregation as reason for the divine wrath. He commanded them to build a grander church and offer more in order to appease a jealous God. People being the superstitious lot they were, allowed this state of affairs to exist. They relinquished control of their village, and of their lives.

The town had been full of slanderous talk lately. All focused on one family in particular; the farm outside the village boundaries. Visible to everyone as it stood on the highest ridge.

Well known for the dark cloud that seemed to linger around the owner. His bad luck caused many to remark he was cursed. Some whispered he had made a pact with the devil. Such was believed to be the reason why he controlled the high ground and owned the largest property. Satan's mark surely explained his massive size. He was a giant. The cowards even called him a demon in the flesh, but not to his face.

Mackenneth stirred up this entire falsehood of course. The handful of people who actually were friends of the man knew of none more honest or moral.

This farmer lived in an ancient estate with several steadings attached. A fence made of flat-stacked stones reached far into the hills and bordered the house. The land stretched to the river Morag, and was the largest property in the valley, existing long before the village itself.

Certain leaders who thought he didn't give enough of his resources to the church subjected the giant man to an undeserved scrutiny. The truth be told, given reason to pitch in, he did the work of three men. If someone needed help, he was always the first to react.

'The man never attended church.' Some said.

Only a few offered any help during the darkest days of his life when he buried his wife on the hillside. He still helped others as needed. He accepted nothing in return.

His child had run away because she didn't want to shame her father, or watch anyone ridicule him. When she told him of her state, she expected to be harshly dealt with. Unmarried mothers were seen as the lowest of the low.

But her father smiled. He said the world would be a better place when his grandchild came.

The young man of her choice was not her father's of course, few ever are. In this case, the nephew of the Sagart (priest) was said to have fathered the child, and even though he had long before asked for her hand in marriage, a date for the wedding had not been set.

The husband 'to be' was considered quite a catch in the village, but something about him and his demeanor didn't sit well with the father of the bride. Too many stories of loose women and drunken brawls were told of him in hushed whispers.

It wasn't considered a good thing to speak ill of the Mackenneths. When the 'would-be' husband was given the news of his child, he publicly denounced the daughter. He declared her to be sleeping with other men. He offered a list of the offenders, mostly paid henchmen, who would stand forth, if called upon to do so.

The girl was devastated and could not be consoled. The father became enraged. He vowed to kill the boy. A fearful daughter begged him to let things be and not be damned by making his grandchild an orphan. The sad father relented. He promised to do as the girl asked. Days later she disappeared without trace. She left her poor father a note asking him not to search for her. His world fell apart.

'A day would come when a reckoning would settle all matters.' The father lamented. He tended his farm. He waited.

Cailleach's father started his day bringing straw to the livestock. He had two cows, two horses, and one bull. He was empty inside, and in spite of his stature, or the fact that he could lift that bull with his arms, he felt as helpless as a child.

Arthair's daughter was gone now for over two weeks. No news of her had been spoken beyond the harsh speculation of busybodies in the village. He thought of going out to find her, but his crops would be lost with only a few days absence. If he might provide anything for his daughter and grandchild in the future, this farm had to survive.

Today the sun came out. He knew he should make haste bringing in the barley from the fields before everything became rotted from the rains of late. Water still stood in low spots. He realized he would probably lose most of the crop. Arthair had never been alone on this farm. His strength seemed to wane with each day.

The cows were upset. Some had stopped giving milk the day she left. Most farmers would butcher the animals, but these creatures were family. They were friends. Even if it meant supplying them food and shelter with nothing in return, he would do nothing less. He would suffer any inconvenience when his daughter and grandchild might be suffering more.

He leaned against his pitchfork. His eyes began to tear up. His lip trembled and he thought he may break down right here, but noise of someone coming up the path brought him back. He quickly dried his eyes. He focused his thoughts.

A lovely middle-aged lady with bright blue eyes and long brown hair, (that she tucked beneath a scarf) made her way up to the shed. She wore a long woolen dress. Her muddy boots stepped with a determined pace. She had the strong body of a hard-working woman. Few men remained stout or confident in her presence. She did not suffer a fool lightly.

"Arthair are you in here?" Betrain inquired. She owned the farm below.

She understood about losing loved ones. She had lost three sons in one year to fever. Her husband died the next year in an accident while trying to save a neighbor's' cow, which had fallen into a ravine. They had hoisted the cow up, and then the rope broke. Her husband found himself standing in the wrong spot.

She only had her youngest daughter to help her. She never took one bit of charity. Betrain, being the kind of good-willed person she was, stood as a role model for anyone who thought they had things tough.

"Arthair, I've been looking for you! She smiled as she walked up.

"I don't mean to be a bother but I've got a problem. I have way too many potatoes and cabbages piled up in my cellar which will no doubt go bad if you don't help me by removing some. The onions make such an awful smell if they rot. I couldn't bear it. We'd have to leave home. And while you're helping me clean out, I should insist you take a fresh baked pie for the trouble, the apples are so delicious this year …" Arthair politely interrupted her.

"Please Betrain; I understand what you're doing. My pantry is adequate, since it's only me. I've no need to store anything. I know how wonderful your pies are, but my appetite is gone." He smiled and pulled out a handkerchief, acting as though he wiped away sweat. He wiped away tears instead.

"Of course Arthair, but we're friends. I know what it's like. Please allow me to help in some way. You and Cailleach never forgot us, especially when things were so bad. I'd seem ungrateful if you didn't let me do something." Her eyes filled with tears. She tried to smile.

Arthair smiled for her and put his hand to her cheek,

"Betrain, your spirit is always as big as the sky. What you're trying to do is so special, but nothing will fill the emptiness in my heart. Friends like you are a blessing. I'm not one to forget things. In return for your kindness, I must insist you allow me to milk your cows each morning as mine are dried up, and I'm up every day several hours before the sun. I'll come round and make sure they get good care. I'll take a little milk as needs be, and maybe even take some of those rotten vegetables off of ya, them being a nuisance and all smelly like, " His face burst into a smile. Betrain gave him a strong hug.

He was a good man. Betrain often gave thought to their concerted efforts in a more marriage like way, but the man had only room for two women in his life, one being his missing daughter, the other buried on the hill. Betrain had enormous respect for such love. She never made mention of her thoughts. He was such a pleasure to be around. Knowing him and his family gave her strength. Stronger than an ox, he made two of any other man, yet he was as gentle as a lamb. She had never known one derogatory word to come from his mouth in all the years she knew him. Life must be so hard to be alone like this.

'If only that scoundrel Cadno Mackenneth had left his daughter be. That fox with the talk of marriage fooled Cailleach. Poor girl realized her chances of finding a man here were slim to none. He played her heart strings like a fiddle.' Betrain had a mind to take matters into her own hands concerning Cadno, what with his uncle being the Sagart, and held in high esteem among the pointed nosed majority of the hypocritical religious cult that condemned anyone who didn't join their circle. Some, pious enough to proclaim her a witch, said she enchanted the young man into obeying her insatiable will. What a load of shite!' thought Betrain.

"Alright, you win. We'll barter for each other's services and pay as paid, so now, tell me what news of Cailleach?" Betrain asked.

"None I'm afraid, nothing since she left. I fear for the worst with each passing day. I can't leave yet. When things are stored..." His voice trailed off.

"Do you think she traveled to the coast? Maybe she found some passage on a ship, or took up with a commune on one of the islands?" Betrain asked.

"The monastery is only a few days away." She added.

"I talked to the traders from the harbor, they know pretty much all the going's on west of us. There's no news of any young woman, of any sort, either coming their way or booking passage. Cailleach endured much at the hands of these 'religious folk' here in town. I think she's had enough of that sort. She'll be well rid of them." He said.

Betrain shook her head.

"No I guess not, she has a strong will that girl does. She wouldn't travel north through the mountains, not at this time of year, and east over the bogs is impassable until the hard freeze. Trying to cross them now would be certain death. She either went west to the coast or south into the dark wood, and though I know she has the heart of a man, even the bravest man would not care to walk those woods if at all possible, what with the horrible stories." Betrain seemed lost in thought as she spoke.

"So, she's gone west. Word just hasn't reached us as yet!" With this she feigned a smiled.

"She'll be all right Arthair, she's made of strong stuff, you gonna see her again and that fine child she brings will have a big bear of a grand poppa twisted around its finger," She smiled for real.

"I hope your right Betrain. I couldn't bear the thought of losing her. She's all I have left. I'll wait till the grain and crops are in, then I'll go to find her." He sighed.

"When that happens, I'll have to ask another favor of you. I promise I'll repay in kind. You can be sure." His eyes were serious and focused on hers as if their bond of friendship held stronger than a sworn oath. That's because it did.

"I'll tell you this Arthair Odhar, no matter what things transpire in light of this, you are the best of the best. Your simple ways are better respected than all the flourishes of kings and popes. Honor is not a right bestowed only upon the rich and privileged. It is the gift that one is given when he places others before himself. You Arthair are such a person, and any man, priest, or even king thinking to take it from you is already defeated by his desire to do so. You will find your daughter and everything be restored as before... anyway... such are my prayers every day until it is so." Betrain lowered her gaze thinking she may have said too much. She let too many feelings show, but it had been said, and she could not take it back. They stood quietly looking to each other, a bit lost for words, until Betrain could stand the silence no longer.

"I should be going now Arthair. I'm sure you have much to do besides listening to an old woman blether on so." Her hands were shaking.

Arthair took her hands in his and kissed them. He gave her a mighty hug that stole her breath away. The sheer joy of feeling his embrace was well worth those airless moments. He gently released her. She lost her ability to speak, so she turned and quickly walked away. She silently cursed herself as she did so, because she felt something should have been said.

Arthair finished in the shed. He gathered his horse and buggy for the fields. He went to gather the grain. His ride up the hill gave him time to reflect. For a man who liked things so simple, he couldn't have found them to be more complicated.

Betrain made his heart feel young, but he knows now is not the time to explore any feelings they might have for each other. He didn't trust his heart now. Anything short of finding his daughter would only distract him. Besides, one more problem had to be dealt with secretly. He accomplished the work a few hours before dusk. He washed up, put on his best clothes, and went to pay a visit to the town smithy.

Near the southern edge of the village, before the bridge crossed the river 'Morag', several huts were joined together with plank and rope, creating small stalls in a clumsy attempt to form a single structure. A business had grown and eventually absorbed the less successful neighboring huts. A family of blacksmiths going back four generations had labored here.

It began with Arden Monroe. He learned his trade in the wars against the invading Gaul's over three centuries ago. Business was always good because of a superior family reputation, and they were the only blacksmiths for hundreds of miles.

Today Luthias Munro worked on several sets of shoes for a Clydesdale horse that Hamish Anderson had brought from across the islands. Hamish had found lodgings in the nearby pub. He awaited Luthias' work to be finished by next day.

Luthias glanced up to see Arthair Odhar standing outside his doorway watching him. He stood with hands in his pockets, looking rather boyish, and full of mischief.

"Well come on in Arthair, yer no gonna learn inna thing so far away," Luthias threw the shoe into a tub of black water, boiling as it hit. He pulled off his gloves and reached for the giant hands of his friend Arthair.

"Is good ta see ya lad, I's worried you might go off and not say goodbye to yer ol noush!" Luthais grasped his hand with both of his.

"I'm not leaving yet Luthias, but I do need your expertise in a matter I think you are aware of. You've always been a true friend. I wouldn't ask for favors if there was any way I could do this myself. Let's sit down. I'd like to discuss some things if you don't mind," Arthair said.

The two men spoke softly for a while, with much nodding of heads and audible gasps. Their conversation grew slightly louder, and just a bit agitated, when Luthias stood up. He scratched his head and looked confused. He walked a few paces, then turned and rubbed his forehead in frustration, as if trying to make sense of it all.

"Are ya sure of this Arthair, I'm not exactly understanding what you intend to do with such a thing, but it seems to me your feelings about what's happened to yer daughter are playing on yer emotions a bit eh? Now me, myself, I would be hard pressed to be as kindly as you in all this, and I can't think of any man who would blame ya fer beaten the lad to a pulp, Hell! I'll even do it fer ya, but I jus don't know bout these sorts of things, what would come as a result. I'm sure some law would be broke in some manner, I would be certainly implicated because, well just because!" Luthias said frustrated.

"An besides, this kinda work ain't cheap, I'll be working on this for several days on end. What am I gonna tell folks. What if someone asks me what it is? There are so many things we gotta think about!" Luthais argued. His voice had become thin and stressed.

"I understand Luthais. Just consider it a job like any other. If someone sticks his nose in tell him you're making some special contraption to catch a wild animal, or tell'em that's what I told you it was. I've got money in advance, if it cost more I'm good for it. I'm at my wits end. Doing nothing is hard enough, and this'll put an end to the evil that needs comeuppance!" Arthair said.

He folded his hands together as he stared up at Luthais, he was honestly begging for help. Nothing was said for several minutes. Luthais paced back and forth. He heard the silent pleas as if shouted. He had a soft heart and an understanding for vengeance in manners of honor. This man had helped him many times before. Not once did he ask for anything in return.

He didn't think he would be able to help him in this though, but he didn't want to say flatly no and have it done in such a way. They'd do better easing their minds over a drink. They needed to lighten their mood before he refused him outright.

"Aye Arthair, but would be good if we thought this out eh? How about you and I go down an git a pint over at Bob's. We'll share some stories like old friends. I think we kin figure this out in a better way which don't create as many problems fer us?" Luthais smiled. He placed his hand on Arthair's shoulder. Arthair seemed lost, but shook his head and agreed. Luthais went to wash up. Arthair had a look around; curious as to the ways in which iron was wrought. He picked up a yoke made for oxen. He stared at it, wondering at the possibilities. Then he heard Luthais coming round and laid the yoke back in place.

The lights shone through the single window of the tavern as Luthais and Arthair walked up. It was the only true glass window in the entire village. Many a drunk had spent time looking through, marveling at the transparency. Although transparency was a trait uncommon among its patrons, as many a lout could usually be found gracing these doors.

Tonight was no different. The pub was full of men; mostly strangers passing through, some traders, and assorted rogues, but if they had the price of a drink, Bob allowed them in, at least until their money ran out, then they were quickly shown the door. Tonight, more scoundrels that usual filled the tables and drank their excess. The bulk of the debt they incurred got paid by the loudest drunk in the bar and his money never ran out, so Bob let things be for now. When he saw two honest gentlemen walk through the door he quickly ran to their side. He ushered them to the bar up front so as to keep them separated from the lowlife.

"Aye gentlemen please, please sit yerself dun and an tell me whatta ya ave fer yer pleasure?" O'l Barrel Bob asked in a jolly tone.

Bob was short, fat, bald, with two belts, one at his waist holding his trousers and one at his chest holding his apron, thus the name Barrel, plus the fact he looked like one. But not to mislead, Bob was as stout as any man. He capably wrestled three or more men, as seemed necessary if the clientele became a bit too enamored with his whisky.

The two friends sat down at the bar. They ordered whiskies with a pint of cider each. The tavern's dark atmosphere of smoke and sputtering lamps provided darkness for those who wanted to remain unnoticed amid the crowd. The tables barely contained the cards and whisky of all who threw their money to chance. With so many loud voices in such a small place, one had to talk above the fray to be heard. The whiskeys came first. Luthais loudly proposed a toast to Cailleach.

"To the lovely Cailleach, Daughter of my dear friend Arthair; may her child be born strong, with good health, fortune, and joy in abundance for all the days of their lives!" They clinked their drinks.

"Aye, an to you great Luthais, may your family never experience a moment's sorrow, and your business continue to support your children for many generations to come!" Arthair grinned for once as he winked.

Their tumblers clinked. They swallowed down the amber liquid. A man approached from the back of the room.

"You'd do better toasting a mongrel's arse than the likes of that daughter o' yers… sleeping around like some harlot, and trying to lay her sin on an honest man!" A drunken voice shouted loudly from behind them.

It was 'him'.

Cadno was very drunk and clearly in need of self-restraint. Arthair gripped his tumbler. He thought of his promise to his daughter, not to make her child fatherless. Luthais jumped into the face of Cadno and with steely eyes spoke inches from his nose.

"Arthair might let you live to spill your filth like a wagon overloaded with shite, but I've never made any promise to spare so much as a hair of yer arse, nor the blood of it!" Luthais was seething.

"Oye now gentlemen, let's not come to blows here! Not in here!" Barrel Bob moved quickly to sort things out. Standing just behind Cadno, Bob gripped a short club behind his back with which he used to make quick work of these type problems.

Cadno took a swig from his mug. He smiled drunkenly and then spat on the floor at Luthais' feet.

"Was me that was wronged!" he bellowed.

"I gave that hag a chance to become an honest wife… cause no one else was gonna have her!" He slurred. The room became suddenly silent.

Arthair's tumbler shattered in his grip. Blood oozed from the wound, and just as it looked like Luthais might raise his hand, Arthair grabbed him by the shoulder pushing him to the side so that he stood chest to face with Cadno.

Bob swallowed his spit because this was getting out of hand. He might be able to control these two, but Arthair was another thing entirely. Arthair was more than any man could handle. The insolence of Cadno sprang from his notion of being untouchable because of his status in the village. All the whisky he had consumed only made his arrogance worse. For a moment Bob though he might just have to let this one happen. Now it was Arthair's turn.

"As God as my witness, I vowed I wouldn't kill ya, but it leaves a mighty lot o' things I didn't promise. You shall regret the day you ever spoke of my daughter in this way, and a hundred times more you'll regret crossing me!" Arthair's veins bulged on his neck. His massive arms looked to burst the seams of his sleeve, while Cadno's blurred eyes stared straight into the chest of Arthair Odhar.

Cadno's eye's slowly found their way up to meet Arthair's. Luthais moved between the men in a feeble attempt to avert the inevitable. When some woman shouted from the back,

"Com'on Cadno, your moneys only good for the next hour! I'm sure it'll take you that long to find me..."

The drunken crowd exploded into laughter. Cadno stumbled toward the voice. Arthair stood seething as he watched the young man retreat. Luthais placed his hands on Arthair's shoulders. He motioned him toward the bar-stool. They both sat down. The crowd settled down to loud talking and laughter. Arthair was livid. He drank his cider in stony silence. Bob went back to bar-tending his patrons, all the while keeping his ears up for more trouble. He could see Cadno sprawled out with the winch in the shadows, oblivious to any and all around him. The boy and his kin made Bob's skin crawl.

When things returned to normal, one drunkard quickly ran for the door.

"Hey! You ain't paid yet Scuigin! Give me three shillings or I'll take it outa yer hide!" shouted Bob.

"Cadno's paying fer mine, besides I'll be back. You ain't seen the last o' me." Scuigin replied.

"Too bad, I could do with less a yer kind." Bob muttered to himself.

In the shadows Hamish Anderson sat drinking his beer. He watched the drunken Cadno fall into his seat between some shady looking fellow and a woman of "ill repute" to put it nicely.

He had acquaintance with Luthais for many years. If Luthais found need to confront this drunk with so much venom, then Hamish wondered what evil this braggart had accomplished. Not really given to sticking his nose into other people's business, he'd learned a heads up was always good practice to stay clear of such trouble.

The scoundrel beside him seemed friendly enough with Cadno, so Hamish decided to fish a while. What he found raised his blood and made him swallow his anger for fear of showing it. He would have much to relate to Luthais on the morrow.

When Luthais and Arthair finished their drinks they paid Bob adding a generous tip. They apologized for the trouble.

"Now lads I don't blame yew's one bit fer being rough. If I wasn't afraid a getting shut down by them Mackenneths, I wouldn't even let the boy in here, but truth is, he spends more money than I would care to live without, so my shame is on me fer doing such. Please come back again and I'll make sure no one will trouble ya." Bob seemed embarrassed by it all.

He accompanied the men to the door. He held the door as they walked out. Someone in the back tried to shout something but was quickly muffled. Bob looked sternly in that direction. He shouted chosen words in a much darker language than he was known for. No one replied.

Once outside and well past earshot, Luthais turned to Arthair. He looked him dead in the eye. His blood was boiling. He could barely keep his voice down.

"I'll start on it tomorrow!" He said. Then walked several more determined steps and swung around to face Arthair again.

"And it's free!"

CHAPTER FOUR / THE GODDESS

Cailleach awoke from sleep, dimly remembering Elrick from the night before. Not sure if all had been anything more than dreams trying to comfort her loneliness. And yet his presence was as real as any waking moment.

'But if he had been real, why didn't she remember him leaving, or her falling back asleep?' She wondered.

The pot on the fire emitted a wondrous aroma giving her reason to rise. The broth had reached a perfect form of chunky vegetables in milky brown soup, with just a slight luminescence of oil floating on top. Using the ladle, she ate right from the pot, barely able to savor each bite before she swallowed and dipped in for another.

With the soup half eaten, she slowed, because if she wanted to keep enough for days to come, she would need to add water, fat, plus whatever else she had to retain some semblance of the present hearty form.

She opened the door. Cold wind blew wet leaves into the hut as rain had started to fall, and judging from the skies, bad weather approached. Her stores would last several days before needing to be replenished. Most necessities were close at hand. Her beaker had half the contents of the spring water left. She remembered the ghost telling his story and its life giving properties. Even if all was a dream, this water had indeed some type of restorative ability. She would use the precious fluid only when needed. The nearby brook could sustain her for now.

The dried wood she had, dwindled and she needed to gather more. She pulled on her boots, wrapped around her cloak, checked the inner pocket for the wand, placed a few small branches on the flames, grabbed the pot, and stepped out into the rain.

Wind from the west began to gain strength, blowing the rain sideways, and making it hard to stay dry when every opening allowed in the moisture.

Cailleach dipped the pot into the brook. She gathered just enough water for another day's broth. She carried it back to the fire, added some fat with a few herbs and stirred the coals to life. Wood was her next concern.

First she gathered small nearby branches. She laid them close to the hut under the dry of the trunk. Cedars, yew, and larch all burned too quickly. They were better used to start fire, whereas ash, birch, and oak lasted longer, creating beds of coal to burn throughout the night.

The direction she assumed offered a chance of oak was not at all her first choice, but the dark wood seemed her best bet. Cailleach pulled a sled she had made by weaving yew with oak. Longer than the height of a man, dragging the sled allowed for greater loads to be managed. The harness fit around her shoulders, giving her good purchase when pulling large dead weight.

She was now completely soaked. The chill of winter settled into her bones. The rain stung her eyes. She had limited visibility of anything more than a few feet ahead. Rotten pieces of wood were strewn throughout the bracken. They didn't offer much to pick from. She kept walking toward the forest in spite of her fear.

Up ahead, a strange mist hovered near the edge of the dark timber, forming a barrier between two worlds, floating untouched by the wind and fierce rain. Prone shapes like downed trees appeared to be a few yards away. She drew closer. Two large fallen oaks lay on this side of the mist. Cailleach cautiously maneuvered the sled alongside several pieces small enough to handle. She quickly loaded them.

Lifting the harness, she heard footsteps coming from the wood. She turned around seeing nothing, but the crush of leaves was undeniable. The urge to run almost overwhelmed her. Her fear rose in her throat as her hand reached for the wand. Power surged through her arm with only a touch and the shock restrained her from pulling the bone out. The footsteps stopped.

She leaned into the load. Nothing moved. The sled sat stuck in the mire. The wind and rain increased. Cailleach gave her all in a thrust forward that freed the sled from the grip of the mud. She pushed with all her might in panic of something unseen. She struggled toward the hut until finally she came within view of the elm tree. Her legs were on fire. Her shoulders were raw from the exertion. She left the sled near the door and collapsed onto the bed.

The beaker of spring water lay close. She drank in controlled sips, being careful not to deplete the contents. Her strength renewed and the blisters on her shoulder began to heal leaving neither mark nor pain. With only a few minutes rest, she was refreshed.

The pot looking robust again, beckoned her tummy for another taste, but Cailleach thought the broth needed more substance. The bone lying on the shield should suffice to provide enough for several meals. Cailleach picked up a stone and managed to knock off just enough to fit into the pot. Having done so, she removed her clothing and laid them by the fire to dry.

She sat naked, rubbing her skin in an effort to bring back the warmth. She gazed at her stomach. The baby was growing. Still passing for slightly plump, she realized that it wouldn't be long before this might be a problem. Her supplies needed to be gathered soon. Food, wood, and water were essential. Surviving the harsh winter would be a daunting task for anyone, much less a pregnant woman alone.

The rain became torrential. Thunder rolled across the valley. Cailleach put her dried clothes on and glanced outside wondering if the burn had risen. It had. Water neared the bank. Her hut with raised floor kept everything above the damp for now.

Beyond the brook, the fawn with red ears walked aimlessly in the storm, distressed and frightened. Cailleach opened her door full wide. She called out.

"Come on…over here!" she cried.

The fawn looked at Cailleach and froze, not knowing what to do.

"Come on sweetie…it's alright!" Cailleach pleaded.

A tremendous clap of lightening struck. The fawn raced over the brook and ran frantically into the hut, shivering and scared.

"Oh baby, it's all right…I'll leave the door open …you're all right sweetie…be calm," she soothed.

The fawn stood in the doorway, facing out, shaking, moaning, and looking for its mother. Cailleach sat on her bed, giving the baby deer plenty of room. The gale lasted for hours, and eventually, the fawn lay down and went to sleep. Cailleach kept her distance. She was concerned about the mother. A storm like this would terrify anything. Hopefully the doe was not too far away. Cailleach, overwhelmed by the weight of the day, fell into a light sleep.

She awoke when something wet pressed itself against her cheek. She opened her eyes with the young deer's nose merely inches from her face. She lay perfectly still in amazement, wondering what would happen. She smelled the fawn's sweet breath, new like the fresh rain. Outside a noise broke the spell.

"Beauuwaa!" The mother was bellowing for her calf. The fawn looked away and then back to her. Its eyes widened before doing something amazingly odd. It nodded its head at Cailleach.

Before she understood, the fawn bolted out the door to reunite with the mother. They crossed the brook and headed into the scrub. Something special had just happened. That nod seemed human and familiar. She wasn't sure what this meant, but she realized her heart had been touched. Sadness overwhelmed her because the fawn had gone. The result left her curious and empty.

The next two days remained wet and miserable. Cailleach had time to fashion pottery from the creek mud. She created several jars, a cup, some plates, and bowls. Not perfect, but they were usable nonetheless.

She had taken the hide from the pig leg and dried the skin enough to scrape off the remaining meat. Once accomplished, she heated some water and soaked 'oak' leaves to draw out the tannin. She used the tannin to cure the skin. This created a large brown hide that she intended to sew into a water sack. Her clothes were becoming threadbare and something would be needed to survive the cold. For now these had to last, as she had no alternatives.

She wove some small animal bones with the tufts of hair she had gathered into a necklace-like-breastplate. She did this more out of boredom than necessity, not having any real use, the design satisfied her need for something feminine to hang about her neck. She slid the necklace on and placed her hands against the choker. The design against her skin she reckoned was a good fit for a woman of the wood.

She thought of the ring and pulled a wad of cloth from her sack, all the while being careful not to touch the band for fear of its power to overwhelm. The ring glistened in the firelight.

She wondered if the dream of Elrick might have been a vision, and how much truth his vision spoke. Regardless, she wasn't keen to try again until she had some idea of its true origin. Nothing fit into any normal reality, and all her senses told her much more remained unknown.

On the third morning the rain stopped. A thick fog blanketed the lowlands, limiting visibility to only a few yards beyond her door. She ate her breakfast of nuts with dried fruit, as she waited for the haze to lift. Birdsong started early this morning. She was eager to get out to forage for 'what needs be'. She finished, washed up, and dressed. Ready when the clearing began, she took off.

First the mist dissipated, and then clouds gave way to blue sky. Cailleach walked into the sunshine soaking up the warmth.

'There is nothing like a new day to lift the spirits.' She thought. Today she would try a different direction. The fawn and its mother had gone into the briars below the crags, so she decided to start there. With her usual belongings for foraging, she headed toward the rocks beyond the edge of the valley.

'What a stunning day!' She remarked, as she made her way west past the Crystal Lake. The crags were steep and the foliage thick, with little or no access through the brambles. Further down, a rainbow had formed. She walked towards it, finding to her delight, the colors became more intense as she approached. It touched the ground just outside the scrub, then lifted up, and arched into the cliff face near the top.

Rainbows were plentiful in her village. She never ceased to marvel at them. Most would disappear as you approached, but this one seemed to grow more vibrant with each step she took. Finally, standing at the base, a small opening into the thick brush presented itself. She stepped into the path, becoming completely bathed in colour.

Hues of blue, red, and purple, plus many shades that she had never seen before, surrounded Cailleach. These colors had substance. A soft silky sensation encompassed her body and touched her skin. She inhaled the warm fragrant air, filling her with an unusual vitality. She seemed lighter, as if she were floating inches above the ground. Her eyes told her that her boots were touching, but the weight of her step no longer existed. She walked unscathed through the scrub until she came to the edge of the crags. At her feet, carved steps led the way up until they disappeared from view.

Without hesitation, she stepped onto the stairway and climbed. The floating sensation left, and her full weight pressed on every stone. She ascended
the stair marveling at the incredible effort taken to hew each step. Higher and
higher she scaled beyond any height she had ever experienced before. Hours
went by as the ground dropped further away. She stopped a moment to gaze
upon the landscape. The valley below stretched out into a patchwork of
rolling hills. The land, framed by woodlands to the north, rivers to the west,
and mountains to the south, spread before her in an unfamiliar pattern. The
dark wood encompassed the northeast, where knolls of rock broke through
the black canopy like stepping stones of ancient giants.

Cailleach wasn't afraid of heights, but sheer steep stairs, with nothing to
hold on to or grab if misstep happened, gave her cause to hug the face of the
cliff. She carefully leaned in. Water trickled over her path as she neared the
top. The next few steps were deadly to traverse. She managed with her heart
in her throat. Now approaching a great height, she wondered if she should
reconsider this dangerous climb. Eagles from the mountains were almost
flying at eye level. Looking out made her dizzy. She kept her gaze to the
stone steps ahead.

Cailleach looked up to see the rainbow bending into the mountain. The
top wasn't much farther. She mustered her courage to continue. Within a few
more steps, a landing appeared between two large walls of stone. Cailleach
pulled herself up. A short rest gave her nerves time to sort out. The rainbow
faded, as only wisps of it near the ground remained. She stood and climbed
the stair until it ended on a plateau.

A path led into some brush, then through a natural arch. She ascended
and walked through. The passage preceded a cave, where near the entrance,
someone had carved the figure of a woman sitting sideways on a horse. She
touched the weathered carving in fascination, and cautiously stepped into
the chamber.

The sun filtered in from several gaps overhead, allowing shafts of light to
encircle a polished stone in the center of the cave. Paintings of a horse, an
eagle, and a woman adorned the walls. Unlike the carving at the entrance,
these appeared amazingly fresh, as if they had only recently been created.

On the glistening stone, carved runes gilded the outer edge. Each rune
glowed with an inner fire as light moved across them. Cailleach thought the

markings bore resemblance to those on the ring. She pulled it out, forgetting the power of its touch.

As soon as the gold hit her skin, she heard a soft voice speak her name. She wasn't afraid, and she didn't know why. There was something comforting in the sound, almost familiar, singing a song, laughing, and coming from everywhere.

Inside the circle of light, a form took shape. Kneeling with arms clasped over legs, with head bowed, the bluish figure of a naked woman began to appear. Her skin was perfect without blemish. Her hair was red. She kept her face down with eyes shut. Slowly her form became complete. The voice stopped. Around the woman, a shimmer of gold dust floated, reflecting a thousand stars onto the surrounding walls. She lifted her head, opened her emerald green eyes and gazed into the eyes of Cailleach. Cailleach fell to one knee, bowing in reverence to this goddess.

"Please rise my dear Cailleach. I'm touched by your honorable respect." The goddess stood. Her blue naked body shone like glass. Her fiery red locks fell beneath her shoulders. Her piercing green eyes illuminated the room. She was perfect in form. Cailleach had never before been so fascinated by another in her life. She tried to speak but found no ability to do so.

"I am Epona. This is a place of manifestation for me. I take human form on occasion when deemed necessary to enter your world. You are safe for now. Please accept my hospitality."

With this she motioned toward the wall, where many pillows, rugs and silken curtains of every colour and texture appeared. Floating torches burning blue, green, and purple lighted the room. Strange incense burned within a yellow smoke, which flowed like streams of water suspended in the air. The tinkling of many different chimes softly moved around the room with no evidence of their origin. Epona walked to the pillows. She sat down, motioning for Cailleach to do the same.

Cailleach sat down next to Epona. When she looked into her eyes, she saw kaleidoscope prisms rotating where her iris should be. The startling effect was hypnotizing.

"I am impressed with your sense of propriety in how you have chosen to survive when others would have damaged or destroyed their environment, you instead use only what you need. I saw you care for the fawn instead of killing the precious life for food and clothing. This is my land. These creatures are under my care. Those that have ignored this have suffered."

Epona smiled, cupping her hands where a bowl of strange fruit appeared. She offered the food to Cailleach. Cailleach took a round black shaped pome and ate. She had never tasted anything so indescribable. Upon swallowing, her voice returned.

"Thank you, this is truly wonderful. I have no words to describe how I feel other than, overwhelmed." She stammered.

"It is I who feels that your presence is overwhelming my dear, for you are rare among humans, and braver than most men. Your beauty outshines all around you." Epona touched Cailleach's cheek. A thousand warm feelings coursed through that touch. Cailleach almost came to tears.

"I'm a hag dear goddess. Such as I am, is the cause of my fate in this world, and of my unborn child. And though I do not have the sin of conceit, I do bear the sin of covetousness, for I wanted that which I couldn't have. I gave away my morals in hope of acquiring them." Cailleach lowered her head, ashamed.

"Do not curse yourself with these things, your beauty shines from within and summons those who possess the vision to your bright light. Many in this world, and the next, are drawn, as to a beacon on the shore. Your pure spirit will allow some to reach you, while casting others upon the rocks. For a few that are attracted to your light will try to extinguish your life. You must decide wherein the truth lies when so many will offer false compliments. All will seek to manipulate, though not everyone means harm." Epona warned.

"I fear for my child as my actions have brought me to this place without help, or hope of returning to my home. I have shamed my father. I have affronted many dear friends with my careless behavior. I would ask if you know my fate in all this and what I should do to keep my child safe." Cailleach's voice trembled.

Epona smiled, "I do not possess the power of foretelling your future dear one, but you alone have the ability to ensure the survival of yourself and your child. Others have foretold about the arrival of enlightenment and how one person would gather powers. It is a quest that many have tried and failed. The true enlightened one will parent a child destined to become a seer, the likes of which this world has never known and shall never see again. I think 'you' are this person who brings forth the child and you have already gathered powers."

"Powers?" Cailleach said, "I only have the ring!"

"You have the ring and more, but you shall decide what matters. I cannot tell you what else you need. You must find out yourself," Epona smiled.

Cailleach frowned and looked away in deep thought, "I do not grasp the meaning of this ring. The water I understand, but the effects of immortality are beyond comprehension. The wand channels a horrific power that frightens me more than death!"

"So far my dear Cailleach, your natural instincts and good spirit, have served you well. Trust them. Keep your heart free of desire. It is the undoing of all things. Selflessness on the other hand unravels desire and ultimately rules. Only one power is greater; love." Epona's face seemed to radiate at this word.

"I fear that your faith is misplaced in me. I pity myself too much these days to be selfless. Will you be here if I need you? May I come to you again? I'm so lonely, and more often afraid than not!" Her voice pleaded.

"Do not confuse pity with survival. One must know the depth of their situation if they are to rise from the depths. Your feelings give you guidance and are worth more to you than physical comforts provide. You have used the power of the rainbow to find me. Perhaps you shall again, but always this is not so. I travel to many places involving myself in the affairs of men should they forget the sanctity of women. There are times their arrogance makes them believe 'they' own nature, as if my resources exist for them to take and destroy as they deem fit. Then my fury is unleashed on all that seek to defile. Men discover their affection for Gods when their lives are at stake, even those that professed never to believe in them before. Such is my devotion to this world and the innocence concealed. It is why I cannot stay to care for you only. However, I will not leave you alone. I grant you the fellowship with one who is immeasurable in spirit and magnificent in strength. He is the last greatest eagle of the Elysian Raptors. He is older than the mountains. Dragons revere his name as their equal, 'Taliesin'. He is ancient and he is wise. When trouble arises, he will intercede. His advice is beyond reproach and must be heeded. His friendship is a comfort. His presence will give you strength." Epona motioned toward the entrance.

There, on the ledge, stood a huge golden eagle, many times the size of the largest Cailleach had ever seen. The bird bowed to Epona and cast its eyes to Cailleach. She did in fact feel the comfort of his presence, and the splendor of his power.

Taliesin's claw was larger than a horses hoof. His head towered over Cailleach by several feet. His feathers were like molten gold on silver, with shades of brown near the quills. His eyes were bright yellow globes floating in a pool of red.

Unsure of how to react, Cailleach bowed in respect of such a majestic creature. Taliesin bowed in return, and then cocked his head to one side. A voice inside Cailleach's mind spoke in deep tone, like distant thunder rolling through the hills.

"You spoke truly Epona. This one is special in every way. I have watched her since she came. I have found no fault in her method. Such will be my honor to watch over her and her child." The words of Taliesin floated on the air, seemingly from every direction.

"If you have need of me Cailleach, I will come instantly. My eyes can penetrate any distance. My wings deliver me as lightning before the thunder. If you desire my counsel, speak my name. My voice shall be in your head. Yours shall be in mine. By Epona's grace these things I vow. My word shall not be broken!" Taliesin's voice faded. He turned and ascended into the sky until his shape disappeared into the sun. Cailleach was speechless. She was stunned. When she turned back to Epona, the cave was empty with only the circle of lights flickering on the stone.

The walk down felt oddly dreamlike. The dizzying height seemed insignificant and without danger. Cailleach looked behind her. The stairs disappeared only feet above her, revealing the steep rock face. She calmly walked down until she stood on level ground. She found her way through the scrub, and was once again standing on soft grass.

Turning around to see from where she came, there was neither trace nor path to follow. The cliff face was solid, offering no foothold for climbing. The place she had been no longer existed. Time had stood still, and her journey occurred within the space of a heartbeat.

A loud screech sounded from above where the eagle passed over the mountaintops and dipped down, soaring towards the valley below. Her heart grew strong. Her legs planted into the earth. Something had connected her to all of nature in one moment. She heard the sound of many waterfalls, the singing of every bird, and the rustle of every leaf, separate or together as she chose. The sap of a thousand oaks' was rising up through her legs carrying a new kind of strength unlike anything she had ever known. She had the strongest desire to run, and she did, with all her might. Her arms fell to her sides. She cupped her fingers as if holding invisible banisters. Her torso leaned forward. Her knees rose higher as her strides became longer.

She was tapping the 'Gait of Power' and once tapped; she ran without tiring, without thirst, and increasing in personal power with every step. She took breaths into her nose and out through her mouth. Somewhere deep inside her a sound was developing. First sounding like a moan, then more guttural, rising from the pit of her stomach up through her chest and finally into her mouth. A sound fluttered in her throat rising and falling in pitch quicker than the wings of a hummingbird. A sound of nature from deep within her soul swelled up.

High above, the eagle watched as his gift was received. He circled until the girl finally stopped running. She fell down laughing and crying. The gait always had this effect the first time. He banked to the west, soaring higher into the heavens. Cailleach lay still on her back staring up into the sky until her tears and laughter subsided. Something was floating down in slow spirals. A feather lightly touched down on her navel, and deep calm warmth spread throughout her body. She lay there with her mind empty of thought, listening to all of nature feed her spirit.

After what seemed like hours, but was only minutes, she sat up and wondered what kind of magic would kindle such a flame. She was no longer sad or weary. She neither feared life nor death. She just wanted to experience all that there was. She wanted to make every second extend into hours. There was no hurry. There was no fear. She no longer posed questions. She just listened and became aware.

Cailleach got up and began walking back to camp. She had run a long way, but seemed oddly invigorated. The smell of fresh grass excited her nose and heightened her sense of smell. She saw farther and clearer than before.

An unfamiliar odor accosted her senses. A bitter, sweaty, musk-like aroma was filling her nostrils. And though she was still far away from her hut, she saw there was something strange standing just outside her door. An entity most black and foul moved with evil purpose around her hut. Cailleach felt no fear. With resolute steps, she calmly kept her pace and reached into her pocket for the wand.

CHAPTER FIVE / THE SAGART

Father Mackenneth sat behind a small wooden desk in the back room of his church. Neat piles of coin covered every inch of his table. He methodically pulled money from a silk bag, counted each farthing, put them into a new stack, and wrote down the amount in his ledger. Once the lot was tallied, he took two stacks from the desk, threw them into a box marked as tithing, and slid the rest into a bag he placed under the floor beneath some removable planks.

He proceeded to write out his next sermon in which he would cast loose the two stacks onto the church floor vehemently chastising his congregation for only giving this paltry amount of money for God's work to be done. He grinned at the thought of their faces when threatened with purging to sort out the demons in their midst.

He felt nothing for these peasants or their penitent confessions in fear of retribution. Their simple ways and beliefs nauseated him.

His last church delivered the money, persecuted the weak, and threw the fruitless chaff onto the flame. He separated a sick benevolent flock of sheep from a congregation of wealthy malleable patrons, who became quick to finance all things deemed worthy or sanctioned by 'his holiness'!

'A lost soul becomes indebted to the finder. You save a soul and the essence is yours to guide! It doesn't matter 'where' as long as you make sure the results are to your benefit.' He thought.

His quest brought him to this valley after many years of searching and pretending. His ruse provided him easily gained wealth, but his tolerance for these people grew thin.

He believed a treasure lay hidden within the property of Arthair Odhar that would make him a God above the Gods themselves. All the legends indicated that location, and no one was going to prevent him from finding it.

His obsession began during the time he was a prisoner at the abbey, where his father had sent him because of an indiscretion with a 'less than willing' girl. His adolescent ambitions changed when he overheard a conversation about the 'Seven Powers of Olofen' and the remarkable story of a god who endowed seven talismans with enough power, when combined, to rule the universe. These supernatural objects were alleged to exist on an archipelago along the west coast of Alba. Mackenneth believed he had found the island. The story suggested they were hidden away between a northernmost mountain range and the western shore. Though most thought the tale to be fable, Mackenneth did not. He dedicated his every waking moment to finding the secret.

In residence at the abbey, he combed the libraries daily for any particle of information relating to the legend. One book called 'The Canter of Nould' told of a Viking who upon discovering one talisman quickly lost his life. Another story from the ancient 'Tome of Myrddin' offered rumor a talisman had been successfully kept for many years until given back to the earth.

Luck revealed a damaged manuscript, which made mention of a parchment containing the poem of 'Olofen'. This scroll was rumored as buried deep within the catacombs, inside the vault of a condemned priest, who was burned for witchcraft.

Mackenneth searched those graves for more than six years until he found the crypt. The place was unmarked, and had been desecrated. The doors were barred with branches of rowan, and had been sealed by the crown. An engraving detailed the cost of removing the signet.

"By decree this seal must never be broken.
Under penalty of death!
Leave this evil to rot!"

This, he knew, was what he had searched for. With callous indifference, he broke the seal and threw off the rowan. Inside the crypt, the foul air was full of dust and decay. His burning torch hardly illuminated the darkness within. In the center of the chamber stood a stone encasement impressed with strange symbols of skull like faces screaming in torment.

He planted the torch into a cradle and placed his shoulder to the lid. With great effort he pushed the top over to one side. He picked up the torch to peer into the casket. Inside was a charred skeleton, frozen in an eternal scream. More rowan branches covered the blackened bones.

Mackenneth reached into the coffin. He pushed aside the corpse while feeling for the scroll, but he found nothing. Something within the rib cage caught his eye. A hide wrapped with twine had been stuffed inside the chest of the priest. He smashed the bones and pulled the package from the rotted debris.

He had finally found what most believed had not existed. He held an ancient scroll of human skin and written with the blood of demons. He stuffed it into his coat and made a hasty exit.

He never again ventured down into those catacombs, but rumor of ghost and ghouls roaming the courtyards of the abbey soon were the topic of every conversation. Most were afraid to leave their rooms. The abbeys grotto became a gateway for the evil dead to cross into the domain of the living. An inquiry began. The broken seal was discovered. Soldiers were requested to restore order and find the culprit.

Mackenneth didn't wait to be found out. He packed all his belongings and left during the night. He gained passage to a harbor on the western coast of an island where he believed the powers were hidden.

At this village he found associates of his father. They allowed him to begin 'Gods work'. Soon those acquaintances realized this Sagart had an unusual passion for God. He knew how to drive Satan from even the most genteel members of their congregation.

His, so-called, 'religious mission' took a toll on the small village of Muireann.

Careful to protect his father's 'patrons' by ignoring any of their indiscretions, He otherwise tortured those who looked too close at his dealings, even burning one innocent to drive fear into their hearts. He sapped their coiffures using guilt and the accusation of witchcraft.

His deliverance of God's word always finished with the imminent threat of hell's unquenchable fire. The village endured five long years before he was convinced the sea town held no secrets.

Now he set his sights on 'BlairMor'. This just happened to be the home of his nearest kin. His nephew had caused the family much shame. Perhaps the Sagart could proffer some influence over the wild impulses of a young depraved man. The timing could not have been better as their current Sagart had passed away and the village had naught to replace him. 'BlairMor might be hiding a great treasure.' Mackenneth schemed. He would leave no stone unturned.

After several days journey he arrived at the township. His sister's son showed him to the church. They had a brief conversation. Mackenneth marveled at the depravity of his kin. He instructed him to woo Odhar's daughter with promise of marriage. Once the ceremony was complete, Mackenneth could easily lay claim to certain property as endowment. The Sagart wasted no time. He elicited the young man to help find the lowlife needed to perpetuate his deeds. He spent the first seasons gathering his flock. He remained patient in anticipation of his intended cull. Now, with almost four years passed, he still didn't have Odhar under his thumb, and the girl had become pregnant before marriage. His nephew was an idiot and in spite of ruining the best laid plan, he sensed the time drawing near.

Mackenneth leaned back in his chair and pulled out the scroll from beneath his desk. He unrolled the ghastly shank of dried skin and proffered it up to the light. Written in blood, upon the decayed leathery surface, was the poem of the seven powers.

> *"Before time of earth or man, when light and dark held equal sand.*
> *Evil Gods desired 'all' to rule, with all that does glitter and make man the fool.*
> *But when the scales were tipped just so, the power of innocence began to grow.*
> *A chasm formed between the two ... yet darkness lusted with pride and grew.*
> *And every season it sought to gain, control over hearts and minds thru pain.*

*So wanton souls the devil devoured, while innocent life diminished
and cowered,*
Until hope was forged by the God Olofen,
Into seven perfect powers… for the benefit of men.
Powers obtained; not by desire or might,
But given to one afraid of the fight.

The first for the Dragon overwhelms yet controls,
A second for the sun joining bone into soul,
The third for the healing allowing aged to run,
A fourth to awaken all that were; now are none,
The fifth to cleave asunder the darkness from the light,
A sixth to protect an innocent life,
*With seven the last foretells with an eye, so all see its power of
death to defy.*
And once gathered seven, a key to the soul,
Releasing the beast that none can control.
Destroying in equal so balance is found,
Till blood of the innocent runs deep on the ground,
Renewing the seal recaptures the steed,
Containing its fury fed by mans greed.
Seven powers once gathered cannot be returned,
Their power a burden till innocence learns.
They cannot be taken, removed, or sold,
A curse to the thief it has been foretold.
But given in love all at once or just one,
The powers remain till all has been done.
Returning in secret as balance renews,
Till all secret powers are hidden from view."

Mackenneth stared at the words written in blood on human skin. He marveled at the possibilities each verse contained. He knew where he needed to search next. Only one thing stood in his way, Odhar.

Someone knocked on the outermost door of the sanctuary. Mackenneth rolled up the scroll. He placed the evil treasure back into its hiding place. He stashed away the coin and folded his writings. He cursed to himself promising to deal abusively with the interruption. He crossed the inner chamber and removed the bar from across the door.

Outside in the pouring rain was his partner in crime; Scuigin Morrissey. Mackenneth grabbed him by the arm and yanked him in. Water poured off the sordid man's clothes as a smell, very foul and unwashed, filled the chamber. In spite of the rain he appeared to be covered in filth from head to toe.

"What in hell do you think you're doing here? I told you never to be seen anywhere near this church or me. And ya smell of drink!" Mackenneth shut the door. He pushed Scuigin against the wood, pinning him to it.

"Aye, well I couldn't wait for you to send fer me so I's came ta you. An it's a goot thing ya got me watching what's going on in dis town cuz troubles a brewing!" Scuigin swayed as Mackenneth released his grip.

"What is so important you'd risk your life coming to me directly Scuigin!" Mackenneth fumed.

"Aye, can we sit somewhere near a fire, maybe share some o'dram of the good wine ye likes to drink eh." Scuigin smiled a toothless smile.

"You'll tell me here and now Scuigin before I split your skull with this bar!" Mackenneth brandished the heavy iron as if ready to strike.

"Alright, alright, no harm done. Just cold is all. It's Arthair Odhar stirring up trouble fer yer nephew. They was jis inches away from each other's throats in Barrel Bob's tonight. Odhar has blood in his eye fer him an likely he's up to no good." Scuigin grinned at the effect it had on Mackenneth.

"That inebriate nephew of mine would be better off dead. I'd be happy to be shed of him. Still, this is interesting news you bring Scuigin. Come in and secure the door. We'll talk of this near the fire, and maybe a wee taste of spirit to warm you up." Mackenneth handed the bar to Scuigin.

They crossed the church back into the small room. They seated themselves close to the fireplace. Scuigin looked around at the volumes of books on the shelves. On the walls were many tortuous contraptions, ranging from thumbscrews to a large iron boot big enough for both 'a man's' legs. A metal cage in the shape of a persons head hung folded over the mantel, secured with a lock. Scuigin shivered from the thought of its use.

Mackenneth produced a bottle from behind some old books on the shelf. He poured two cups of wine, giving one to Scuigin. The Sagart leaned back into his chair.

Scuigin gulped down his drink and moved closer to the fireplace. He reached for the bottle but Mackenneth removed the jug from his reach. The Sagart stared into the fire developing his plan.

"Odhar owns more than half the valley, and he has never given a penny to this church. Suppose I were to witness against him, even accuse him of witchcraft, I'd be hard pressed to make things look right enough to pass scrutiny. Now if he were accused of murder most foul of my own kin I'd lay claim to his land for retribution of his criminal act. Odhar's not that stupid; he would never kill him, as much as I wish such to be. Without doubt, the confrontation in the bar is almost as good. Here's what you are to do my dear fellow. Go to Cadno. Fetch him here this night. Carry him if he's past using his own legs. Let no man see you. Tell Cadno nothing more than I have a proper plan for how to deal with Odhar."

"What's yer aim sir, iffen ye's don't mind me askin?" Scuigin asked.

"I'm going to instruct Cadno to leave this town before next light. I'll offer him enough money to start up somewhere far away. You go with him until you're a good distance from this place and dispose of him tout-de-suite. His body must never be found. In his usual drunken condition he may agree, if not we'll deal with him here. Should he in any way seem unlikely to go along, you are to be quick to step in and put an abrupt termination to his misery." The Sagart commanded.

Mackenneth reached into a drawer pulling out a braided length of leather with heavy loops to each end. He gave the garrote to Scuigin.

"This will make quick work of him and keep this house free of his foul fluids. After the deed is done we must remove his clothes and soak all in his blood to be planted on the property of Odhar. Tomorrow we'll make inquiry as to the whereabouts of Cadno. After sufficient questioning of the local bar patrons, the clues will be evident whereas Odhar is to be suspect in Cadno's disappearance, upon which we'll search his property, where we shall find the bloodstained clothing. He goes to jail. Court is held, and I personally condemn him to death, to be carried out immediately. Swift irreversible justice dealt to this man who has vexed me since I came here. He should have realized my power and given me what I wanted, then all this would have been averted. " Mackenneth smiled. He rubbed his hands together as if ready to enjoy a feast. Scuigin followed every word, waiting for Mackenneth to finish when he produced his empty cup to see if any were offered; none was.

"These are dire dealings ye suggest master Mackenneth. A man be hanged or worse should such be found out amongst the town folks. Now don't get me wrong sir, I'm here to do jis what yer asking but my neck is worth more than a few shillings." Scuigin again proffered his cup. This time, wine was provided.

"Aye Scuigin, yer bound to want more when more is asked, so remember this; I'll soon own Odhar's property and your share will be the livestock he has kept from slaughter all these years. Those cows should fetch several pounds each or if butchered you'll have enough meat to last the next winter. Either way I'll put them down and feed them to the crows. You'll be a man of means Scuigin. Women are want to go fer such, plus an extra fifty shillings when all goes without a hitch. So ya in?" Mackenneth offered another pour of the bottle.

"Aye Sagart, all's good as done." Scuigin stretched his gob into a toothless grin. He laughed at the prospect of ill-gotten gains.

Cailleach cautiously approached the hut with wand in hand. The scent of a wild animal filled her nostrils. The hair on her neck stood and she sensed a very deadly creature loomed close. A 'darkness' surrounded the area preventing her from seeing the danger. She crossed the small brook holding her wand ready to strike. She wasn't afraid, but she knew she stood in deadly peril. She took four steps toward the door of the hut, before she saw the huge silver wolf.

"I advise you to put away that bone, it will have no effect on me" The wolf spoke in deep growling tones.

"That would be a bit easy for you if I did beast. Maybe it's more effective than you wish." Cailleach now started to feel fear.

"Please then, try it and see how magic and all protections cease within distance of me." He showed his teeth. His eyes lit up with fire. He moved slightly closer.

Cailleach tried to will the wand to do her bidding, nothing happened. In her mind she called Taliesin, no voice returned. Her hand began to shake. She felt sick. The wolf moved closer still.

"Now you know I speak the truth, you must to listen carefully to me. I'm the one who will strike you dead. You understand dear Cailleach that your name is in the thoughts and on the tongue of every being from God to smallest creature. You are a stupid child meddling with powers beyond your imagination, the scope of which encompasses all living, dead, and celestial beings. You have no right, and are totally unworthy of possessing them."

"Who are you?" Cailleach demanded.

"I am known by many names, none I will share. But know this, I watch your every move and though you think you're protected, you are not. I shall feast on your flesh. Now I must end this!" He bares his full brace of razor sharp teeth looking as if to strike.

"Enough Marrok!" The voice of thunder seemed to resonate from everywhere. Beyond the darkness stood Taliesin with wings fully spread. His eyes focused on the wolf.

"Ah, you do come when called. Like a dog to its master, yet you approach no closer. Too bad this girl doesn't know the rules!"

"Take one step 'Cailleach' toward me now!" Taliesin shouted.

With this Marrok attacked, but Cailleach leaped to Taliesin, barely escaping his bite. The wolf roared in anger, looking to tear into Cailleach, instead he relented once she stood beside the eagle.

"You cannot protect her from 'Me' Taliesin." Marrok screamed in fury. "I will rip her into pieces, and leave her carrion for your relatives!"

"Depart now Marrok! Your attempt is over. I shall keep you in sight. You possess the ability to dispel power within reach but you cannot stop me from sinking these talons into your evil hide. Be thankful I respect the balance of things. Take care you do not force the tipping of it." Taliesin's voice thundered.

The wolf cursed, and as lightning, bolted toward the dark wood. Cailleach sat down. Her heart was thumping like a drum. Her face was ashen with the realization she had almost died.

"You cannot remain here. You must collect your things and prepare to leave." Taliesin said sternly.

"Where do we go when winter is upon us? I'll never be able to find enough stores to get me through. I'd be better off dying here quickly, than expiring slowly of starvation!" Her voice shattered.

"No, you shall not die. Gather what you need. I will keep watch while you prepare. Now, before the darkness falls!" Taliesin folded his wings and turned toward the woods.

Cailleach was totally lost. Only an hour ago she seemed untouchable, now she was running for her life. She put the pot on the stone to cool. Her shield and utensils she stacked together, wrapping them with braided vine. Her few handmade plates were laid within the woven basket. The dried meat, bone, vegetables, herbs, she placed into the pigskin, and lay on top of the dishes.

Everything was packed onto the sled. With all secured, she made sure she had the ring and the wand close at hand. The beaker of spring water and the iron pot were carefully stored in the center. All seemed to be ready. Cailleach took a deep breath as she glanced around one last time.

"I was almost happy here." She sighed.

"Quickly now we have to go, things are gathering in the dark wood." Taliesin turned to the open valley and motioned in the direction of the steading.

"We must get to the spring before nightfall. From there we will journey to the Outland." Taliesin took to the sky and started to circle.

His voice immediately began in her head. "All is clear. Move toward the steading quickly."

Cailleach put her shoulder to the harness and slowly began the long trip to the spring. Above she saw the eagle. She gained some small comfort. The journey was mostly over open field, so once she had gathered momentum her load conveyed quickly. Her legs seemed stronger than ever. With measured breaths she kept a brisk pace. She sniffed the air but detected nothing foul.

The sun disappeared into the west. The mountain peaks swallowed the fire. Long shadows reached down into the glen. The wind grew cold. Her coat, bundled up on the sled, lay out of reach. Not wanting to stop, she pushed on.

The surroundings seemed strange, as if the appearance of the wolf had changed them. A dreadful sense of danger tapped on her nerves. Unusual sounds drifted up the valley, howling maybe, not sure. An hour went by, but she still hadn't made the distance to the apple tree. The Vikings death spot lay only a few paces to her right. Cailleach wondered could this be the same beast that killed Elrick. Not a good place to be now, she thought, so she pushed harder and doubled her pace.

The wind picked up and the sound whipping through the crags made a sinister noise. Fear coursed within her. With every step, she felt courage fall away. A flutter of wings came closer. Taliesin landed.

"Rest or you won't last. Nothing can touch you as long as I'm near. Catch your breath before we continue." The eagle folded his pinions and surveyed the path from whence they had come.

"Thank you Taliesin. I don't know what would happen if you weren't here." Cailleach sat down, drained and afraid. "We can't make the steading at this pace, not before dark."

"We'll go as far as we can, don't worry." He said looking into her eyes. For a moment she felt all her doubts disappear.

"What or who is this wolf?" She asked.

"He is an evil power in fear his days are numbered. Because of this, he is all the more dangerous. He exists in the nether world of darkness. He keeps his distance for now, but when he becomes desperate enough, he will risk everything to put an end to you, causing the balance to tip. The rules shall cease to apply as we know them." The eagle's stare seemed distant.

"He is called Marrok." His eyes regained their focus.

"In the beginning, power existed equally within opposing forces of darkness and light. Darkness, by its nature, sought to envelope everything, and struggled with the light. Life forms grew from this struggle. Their decisions and actions determined which way the scale tipped. Good chose light. Evil chose darkness. Darkness corrupted all life forms giving them immortality and magic for the price of their souls. Light developed a different magic, promising an afterlife in return for sacrifice in this world. A hierarchy formed among the evil horde. Soon the prince of darkness chose his generals. Marrok became one of those chosen. His army, massive and brutal, remained undefeated. He tipped the scale more into the darkness, until he met Olofen. Because of his blind ambition, Marrok did not imagine the power Olofen wielded. He saw only a frightened man standing between him and personal glory. When the confrontation began Marrok threw all his evil force into one massive strike, but Olofen emptied his self of all desire and absorbed the energy. Marrok was drained and defeated. Olofen cast him into the carcass of a wolf, condemning him for eternity to live powerless and wretched. His only defense is his proximity spell which removes the effect of magic within the influence of his presence. Now he has focused on you. Now you have a reason to fear. He believes the powers you already possess will free him from his curse. Within you lives hope, the hope of all mankind, and if you give up, none shall be spared. This is not an easy thing befallen you, but there are none could bear the burden 'except' you. Strength is not measured in muscle or brute force, but by the pure heart and spirit you have. Believe and keep faith in what you know to be right. A power such as your good heart is greater than all the magic evil can summon" Taliesin turned his head, glancing back to the wood.

"We must go now. Soon the sun will be gone and I will walk by your side." He spread his wings, and ascended.

She passed the apple tree with barely enough light to keep her path ahead. Her coat provided warmth from a wind unrelenting. Leaves and twigs flew past her face in a dozen whirlwinds. Not a cloud in sight, but the storm came. She looked for the eagle.

"Are you near?" she thought.

"Yes, soon I will land." Taliesin said.

Her shoulders began to ache from the strain, as a new thing happened. A kick into her rib startled her. The baby had awakened. She almost stopped, but pushed on.

"It's kicking me!" She smiled. With this her strength seemed renewed.

The sun disappeared and at the same instant, a sound of wings encompassed her. Taliesin landed beside her.

"I must change into something more sensible if I'm to walk with you."

He crossed his wings over his head. A golden light enveloped him, melting his shape into a human. In seconds his feathers vanished, as a man with golden eyes appeared. His plumage had become an armor of gold with silver layered in scales tightly fitting his shape. His blond hair fell below his shoulders in yellow ringlets. Before her stood the most beautiful man she had ever beheld. She found herself staring in amazement.

"Do I frighten you Cailleach?" Taliesin spoke with his mouth. It had a strange effect on her.

"No...no, not at all...I wasn't expecting ..." She realized her mouth hung open.

Embarrassed, she quickly composed herself and picked up her harness.

"Please let me pull the sled. You have done enough for one day. If you have the strength, I will run so we can make the steading." He smiled and her weariness fell away.

"After you sir!" She smiled back.

He leaned forward and took off into a fast gait. Cailleach indeed found the pace hard to keep up. He moved with the same grace in which he flew. She ran blind, but Taliesin seemed to find his way easily. They traveled at a fast pace and soon they approached the steading. Once within the garden, Taliesin stopped. He cocked his head, bird like, listening.

"We are safe here for now. Clear a place near the fireplace. I will gather wood."

He disappeared.

Cailleach cleared away debris and loose stone. She pulled out some scrub. The hearth was filled with dirt so she used a stick to push it out. The two remaining walls offered shelter against the wind but nothing more. They would be exposed with only Taliesin standing between her and death.

She spread out her utensils, pot, shield, beaker, and food. The light had faded and she fumbled in the obscurity. Somewhere beyond, Cailleach heard Taliesin breaking limbs of wood for the fire. She found her tinderbox with flint and laid them upon the hearth. In the far distance, flashes of lightning lit up the sky, a few seconds later thunder rolled. The rain wasn't far away. She wondered what to use for shelter but there was nothing. Steps approached out of the darkness.

"These pieces should be enough to get a fire started. Once you have a blaze I will gather more. A storm seems to be coming. We shall have no choice but to wait here." He looked concerned.

Cailleach struck the flint, creating a glow of fire in the tinder. Taliesin cupped his hands. He sheltered the flame while she fed small dry twigs. Soon they had a proper blaze. The area lit up, casting shadows upon the standing stones. Taliesin left again to get more wood.

Cailleach hung the pot over the flames. "I'll bet a long time has passed since you were there." She said softly.

She experienced some strange sense of normality in the moment. Wondering what things had been like when the family lived here. Taliesin returned. He dropped the logs just within reach and sat down beside Cailleach.

"You'll be fine Cailleach. You're made of strong stuff, stronger than you think." Taliesin the man spoke encouragingly.

He gathered her near him to share his heat. She warmed up quickly, yet the chill in her soul still lingered. He stayed close until she fell asleep.

When she awoke, she heard the heavy drum of rain upon stone, yet somehow she remained dry. Taliesin (as an eagle) stood over her with his massive wings sheltering her from the showers. She could just make him out staring into the darkness towards the apple tree. His eyes took in everything, and deep within them, she knew her own destiny could be found. She strained to get a glimpse but nothing revealed itself in the dark deluge of rain and wind. Cailleach sat up, stirred the pot, and tasted. Still good, hearty, and much needed on a night like this. She ate, and offered some to her guardian.

"Taliesin, you should eat some of this."

"Consumption is not necessary for me my dear Cailleach. I am not flesh and blood as you. But your consideration is well appreciated." He spoke into her head.

"I guess you don't sleep either."

"Suspension of consciousness is not necessary. I do, however, enjoy the pleasure of your company, and would wonder, if I would not be asking too much... can you sing?"

Cailleach made a childish face at the thought. "I only know the one song my father sang to me as a toddler, and I'm not a good singer." She sat hoping to let the idea pass.

"Excellent! What a wonderful honor for you to sing for me!" He sounded excited.

"Well...let me remember...it's been a long time! She stalled. Closing her eyes the memory of her father holding her as a small child...she took a deep breath and began to sing...

> "Wrapped in my arms you are safe from the storm,
> Each breath I take makes you feel safe and warm.
> All I have I will give unto you,
> Love and sweet kisses each day you renew.
> You came to me like bird on the wing,
> Joy and sweet love makes me cry as I sing.
> Your eyes full of life I cherish each day,
> And if you would grant me one smile I would say.
> Nothing more precious in life than your love,
> Guarded by angels and power above.
> So sleep now my dearest
> Only you I dream of.
> So sleep now my darling
> Always you I dream of."

Cailleach finished her song. She glanced up for his reaction. She thought maybe a faint smile crossed the eagles face.

"That was beautiful Cailleach. I hope you will serenade for me again sometime." His voice softly thundered.

"Yes…of course, I will sing whenever you please." Cailleach was blushing. She didn't know why.

The rest of the night they were silent. Cailleach fell back asleep. Taliesin stood staring into the darkness. The storm and rain passed later in the morning.

Cailleach awoke to birdsong. The air was heavy with fog. Taliesin was nowhere to be seen.

"Taliesin where are you?" She thought.

"I'm above you. I wanted to rise aloft the mist. I'll be with you shortly." He replied.

She stirred the fire and rubbed her hands. Amazingly the area around her remained dry, as her belongings. She grabbed her beaker and walked to the spring. Stones lay cradling the fresh water as it bubbled out into the stream. Dipping her hand in full, she drank the refreshing life giving liquid. Her body reacted as before. A soothing relaxation spread through her limbs. She filled the beaker and placed the top back on.

"The company you keep leaves me to think your choices lack wisdom." A voice boomed.

"Taliesin?" Cailleach was startled.

"Heavens no my dear, I'm much smarter and better looking than that lout!" The voice spoke again with laughter.

The sound of wings, as Taliesin landed beside her.

"Nidhoggr, I have missed our debates. Are you still bitter from the last argument I won?" Taliesin laughed.

"I would say your memory deceives you. We must now argue as to whether whose recollection is true!" The voice replied most pleased.

"Who is this Taliesin?" Cailleach asked.

"You mean Taliesin hasn't told you about me? I'm shocked! I'm mortally hurt you hold me in such low esteem dear eagle!" The voice was hiding his laughter.

"Nidhoggr is a magnificent dragon who needs constant attention. He loves to talk but mostly argue. If he doesn't get his desired deliberation, he pouts, and threatens to nibble on the roots of Yggdrasill." Taliesin's eagle face broke into a real grin.

"The roots of…what?" Cailleach asked confused.

"Yggdrasill is the tree of knowledge, without which, we are doomed to ignorance and superstition. He does this knowing we must offer debate to occupy his mouth. If he killed the tree he would be the most upset, seeing as how he loves an intelligent conversation!" The eagle said beaming.

"If I wanted intelligent conversation I wouldn't be talking to you bird-brain!" Nidhoggr couldn't contain his amusement any longer. Taliesin also lost his composure. They both seemed crippled with laughter. Even Cailleach began to chuckle because of its infectious nature.

"I must apologize for my behavior dear lady, I spoke only to jest my friend. You have found a wonderful partner to journey with. But his absence increases my desire for tree root, so since he delegates no time for me, maybe I should occupy myself otherwise." A snicker.

"Oh alright old friend let's take a moment to speak. I need to tell you of things transpired. You must help us if our journey is to be successful." The eagle pointed towards the tree near the spring.

Beside the ash tree materialized the outline of a majestic dragon. He stood taller than the tree by half. His body covered in red and gold scales. His wings carefully folded into translucent curtains of leather shimmering purple then blue. His eyes were green, within blue, within white. His smile stretched across a long extended narrow jaw sparkling with ice like teeth in rows of hundreds. He gestured in a rather comical bow towards Cailleach. A lengthy forked tail whipped around his torso hugging his huge legs. Razor sharp talons crossed his waist in an effort to properly courtesy.

"At your service dear lady." The dragon smiled. "What news do you bring me Taliesin? Something exciting I hope!"

"Do you remember 'Olofen' and the 'Poem of The Seven Powers'? Such has now come in the time of man of one who will fulfill this prophecy. Cailleach has gathered talismans already and is destined to wield more before long." Taliesin gestured toward Cailleach.

"My… oh my…news indeed! I would have thought the 'Bana-Bhuidseach' to be a warrior, perhaps a knight, but a girl. That's a twist I did not foresee. I'm sure this hasn't set well with the inhabitants of the dark wood. They must be plotting something sinister to deter your quest!" Nidhoggr stroked his chin in thought.

"What's a bana-…what you said?" Cailleach asked.

"Bana-Bhuidseach is the culmination of all magic, both good and bad in one person, pure and powerful enough to control them. Even one power of Olofen can corrupt. Several might destroy the user, but seven aligned summons another 'Demon War'. In truth, such a thing was believed too much for anyone to ever accomplish, so the prophecy became a legend that none thought would occur." The dragon said.

"You think I'm destined to become some all-powerful witch to control good and evil?" Cailleach asked.

"No-one knows, as no one has ever accomplished anything even remotely close. If you are fulfilling the law of the powers, then every action you have taken since coming here has been a test. Should you indeed acquire all seven, the world would be at your beck and call. Whether good or evil prevails, will be as you wish. But know this, evil desires more evil. To taste revenge, even revenge properly earned, is to become addicted to the dark power. Good is preserved through the constant battle with pain against desire. Evil battles not, but gives in to every debauchery. Good, fights tirelessly, forever protecting the innocent with the faithful. If you are truly the Bana-Bhuidseach, You alone will control the future." Nidhoggr looked at Cailleach. He winked.

"I can see through the facades of human nature. Your heart is true dear child. I don't know of anyone else worthy of such responsibility." The dragon reassured her. He smiled.

"We need your help Nidhoggr. The wolf has declared he will kill Cailleach before she can retrieve the powers. We are going to the Outland. Your assistance in detaining him may determine whether we succeed." Taliesin said looking back toward the valley they had just crossed.

"Outland eh, that's a long and dangerous journey. Once accomplished, you'll need safe accommodations amidst the local thieves and murderers who call it 'sanctuary'. There will be no protection there, and if the slightest news of what she carries is found, even you 'Taliesin' wouldn't be able to protect her!" Nidhoggr added.

"The purpose of going to Outland is exactly because it is such a place. The forces looking for us would assume we seek safer passage. I do know someone who may help us. I have no choice. If I stand here to fight, I may win, but I could lose, and either way, the damage could not be undone. Our worlds would collide, suspending any rules controlling the balance. You dear dragon are not hampered as am I. You can do battle with Marrok without disturbing these forces. And though you cannot kill him, the affront to his pride may convince him to alter his convictions." Taliesin proposed.

"Hmm…yes a fierce combat with flame and teeth do appeal to me…why it's been centuries since I roasted an adversary…" Nidhoggr smacked his lips as if tasting something.

"Quite like the taste of flesh as I remember…" He opened his jaws and spewed a stream of red flame into the sky. The sound was deafening. He looked down when he finished, smiling.

"I'm absolutely game for this my friend. Tell me what inflammatory speech you should want spewed at this band of brigands and I'll make sure they absorb what they can in the heat of battle." Nidhoggr laughed at his cleverness. The dragon seemed almost beside himself.

"I thought only the wolf was after me?" Cailleach asked.

"In battles most fair you would be correct my dear, but Marrok doesn't care about an honorable fight. He will bring as many as he can 'control' to do battle. Men's minds turned evil by their desires make for easy dragon fodder when he wishes to distract. I would expect some stone giants as well. Never liked the taste of them though, too much roughage." Nidhoggr rattled his head shuddering in disgust.

Cailleach and Taliesin both broke into laughter, as did Nidhoggr.

The mist cleared. Cailleach offered Nidhoggr some of her soup. He accepted a small portion, proclaiming the simple broth to be the best thing he had ever tasted, other than the delicate roots of Yggdrasill of course, while smiling at Taliesin.

Taliesin shook his head laughing. They spoke into each other's mind, planning what was to take place for the wolf and his army. Once decided, they offered the other their loyalty. Taliesin promised to come back to spend a lengthy time debating, even offering to lose should the dragon prove his case. Cailleach reached up motioning the dragon to lower his head. She kissed his cheek, and then made him promise not to get hurt. He laughed, crossed his heart with his razor talon, assuring her he would be filling his stomach with some tasty idiots before this day was done.

Taliesin changed back into a man form to help Cailleach gather her possessions.

"Wow…I wish I could do that! If for no other reason than to show Taliesin how much better looking I would be!" The dragon said.

"Yes…you sir were always my superior in debate…probably more so in man form."Taliesin offered.

"Oh quit blowing smoke up a dragons arse, I said I'd take care of things! No need trying to swell my head with compliments!" Nidhoggr replied.

They all laughed, and then exchanged goodbyes as the dragon disappeared into thin air.

"I wish I could do that!" Taliesin commented. "It would make some things much easier!"

They headed beyond the steading into a green forest, which seemed to offer hope.Taliesin pulled the sled at a good pace. Soon they were deep into a lush wood with a thick carpet of moss. Brooks, waterfalls, birds, and squirrels were flowing, living, and breathing in abundance. Cailleach enjoyed this change of scenery. She marveled at the giant trees they walked beneath.

"I've never seen such magnificent trees in all my life. They reach to the heavens. The forest has spread out so. It's like walking under huge canopies." She said admiringly.

"These are the sacred wood of the 'Cruithne'. They worship trees along with all of nature. This forest is called 'Saltus'. Our path takes us past an ancient druid grove. They don't usually allow people to walk through, but I've known them for centuries. I should have expected to encounter them before now, but I'm sure it won't be long."Taliesin had just finished speaking when several faces appeared from behind the trees.

They stood mostly naked with only animal hides covering their torsos. Parts of their skin were painted with a beautiful shade of blue, while other areas were covered in intricate tattoos depicting animals, celestial bodies, geometric designs, and shapes Cailleach had never seen. Men alongside women, walked equal in their group as all carried weapons with none subservient to another. Each person's hair appeared to be a trademark of the individual. Some were braided, others pulled to the top of their heads, one was shaved on both sides, as another had no hair at all. Cailleach guessed these styles signified status or purpose in their tribe.

A man with the tattoo of an eagle on his chest lay down his spear. He approached Taliesin offering his greeting by spreading his arms to show he was defenseless.Taliesin did the same, and then both men embraced touching each side of their faces.

This tattooed warrior spoke in a strange language Taliesin understood. As they talked, the native gestured as if brandishing a weapon and killing an aggressor. Taliesin shook his head. He motioned toward Cailleach. The warrior looked to Cailleach regarding her with strange curiosity. He nodded his head in agreement. He gestured to the surrounding forest as if to offer everything. Taliesin placed his hand on the warriors shoulder, pointed to several trees in the area, and then made a motion to each side of his head. The chief spoke softly in reply. They seemed to come to an agreement, then completed the ritual of greeting; this time adding the gesture of all the fingers of one hand on their own chin, reaching out to the other as if offering something. The natives disappeared into the wood. Taliesin walked back to Cailleach.

"Their ruler has offered safe passage through these woods. The warriors also offered to attack any who followed. I couldn't allow them to engage these evil entities. They would suffer tremendous casualties. It is not their battle, yet he would not relent unless he was allowed to create some trouble for our enemies. So I told him to place warriors in certain trees to send word when anything was sighted. They have a druid warlock who can dumbfound these woods so any direction you choose is always the wrong one. This will provide a good distraction should any follow. They could keep them here forever if they chose, or at least until we're well away." Taliesin said.

"I've never seen anything like them." Cailleach remarked.

"You're probably related to them. Their ancient ancestors left the wood thousands of years ago to take up the mantle of the invaders. These few tribes are all that remain. Those who invade their sanctity are rarely seen again." Taliesin replied.

"Where do we go from here?" She asked.

"South, until we come to the mountains, where we must decide either to go around or over. Snow is falling on the higher elevations, which will make it difficult to climb. The road around will leave us exposed and more open to attack. Once we're there, you must choose!"

"Why don't you just turn back into an eagle? You could carry me there." She proposed.

"Would seem the best plan, but your quest must be made on your own power. My intervention could change things. I cannot chance anything, which might contribute to your demise. We shall continue as we have." Taliesin gathered his harness tight and pushed on with more determination.

They traveled all day, only stopping for short rests. Cailleach was looking back the way they had come when she spotted the red-eared fawn she had met at the hut. The deer seemed to be following. Cailleach told Taliesin the story about the fawn. She was very concerned as to why the yearling followed. Taliesin looked until he saw it poke its head from behind a tree.

"Does have red ears…hmm…I think this is a good omen for you Cailleach. We shall let this fawn continue to follow. I will extend my awareness to make sure it remains safe. Intentional or not, you seem to attract an unusual variety of creatures and powers." Taliesin pushed ahead. The deer followed.

The sun was setting when Taliesin stopped under a giant fir tree. They gathered stones to surround a fire. The fawn grew brave and approached within distance; close enough to feel the heat. It sat motionless, laying down its head, staring at Cailleach.

Back at the steading the sun had set. An unusual dark cloud engulfed the surroundings.

'Namhaid' marched from the black cloud. These creatures wore the skin of those they had defeated in battle. Their heads were completely covered in blackened leather masks with only slits cut for their eyes and mouths.

They carried clubs of bone, enormous long bows that projected six-foot arrows, and whips barbed with poison thorns.

Following them emerged three stone giants standing at least twenty feet tall. Their stone skin was covered in lichens and stretched over their boneless bodies like a pasty gray canvas. Their massive shoulders supported small hairless heads with three eyes, one flat nose, and rows of razor sharp teeth. They wore no clothing. They were neither male nor female. Each carried huge stones. Their footfalls shook the earth.

Next, a dark formless shape emerged floating toward the steading. Then Marrok appeared with his head sniffing the ground, trotting behind the rest.

Beside the ash tree an invisible dragon prepared for battle. In an explosion of lightning and thunder he emerged blazing fire in all directions, while roaring so loud his voice brought down an avalanche of boulders from the mountain.

The battle had begun.

CHAPTER SEVEN / THE CARIAD

Hamish Anderson had enjoyed as much of this drunken hospitality as he could stomach. He felt strongly angered at the slander bandied about. Just as he was ready to leave, a bum walked in soaking wet and in need of some serious washing. He sat between Hamish and Cadno. Hamish moved over to give the low life extra room, he reeked.

The tramp loudly told Cadno his uncle wanted him right now. Cadno was so drunk he hardly acknowledged the man had spoken to him. The derelict grabbed him by the shoulder, hauling him out the door. Hamish hurriedly retrieved his coat and paid his bill. Barrel Bob shook his head, held his nose and threw his hands up in disgust.

Once outside, Hamish found the two men struggling towards the bridge. He followed. The rain had become torrential and keeping close enough to observe them proved difficult. Then below, some light in the chapel offered guidance. Hamish slowed, allowing the men to struggle to the vestibule. The church opened with shouts of angry voices, quickly muffled when the door slammed shut. Hamish put his ear to the wood but nothing came through. He pulled his coat closer around his neck waiting just beyond the light for the conspirators to return.

A short time passed before they reappeared. The stinky man was supporting Cadno. The Sagart bellowed for 'Scuigin' to make sure his instructions were carried out to the letter. Scuigin held Cadno with one hand, and then pulled out a garrote from his pocket smiling, waving the thing about. The Sagart shouted an obscenity at the Scuigin, threatening him to take care of everything. He shut the door. The two men struggled up to Luthias' open shed. Hamish stayed back until they entered his friend's property. He'd seen enough.

Hamish walked in just in time to catch the man called 'Scuigin' strangling Cadno. He bolted forward, slamming his fist into Scuigin's head. Both fell to the floor. Hamish removed the garrote from Cando's throat. He felt for a breath. When he assured himself Cadno lived, he sat them up, tying them hand to foot. He covered them with hay before he left to tell Luthias what happened in his shop.

Luthias had just finished eating and tucking in his children for the night when a knock disturbed the silence. He picked up the lamp and walked to the door.

"Who comes at this hour?" Luthias asked.

"It's me…Hamish!" A voice returned.

Luthias unlocked his door. "Hamish what are you doing out in this weather. I'd of thought you'd be having a few more drinks, and then off to bed!" Luthias said amazed, but smiling.

"Aye, would've been my first inclination, but the altercation between you and Cadno drew lots of attention. After you left, another man came in demanding Cadno come with him, which peaked my interest, so I followed them. They went to the church where the Sagart let them in for a while. When they returned, their intention became clear. The one called 'Scuigin' intended to murder Cadno and leave his body in your place of business, incriminating you to be his killer. I stopped him just in time. Their unconscious bodies are tied up in yer shed right now." Hamish's face went red. He held his voice down, but his anger showed.

"You witnessed him try to kill Cadno?" Luthias asked.

"Aye, this here he had around Cadno's throat when I clobbered him!" Hamish produced the garrote from his pocket.

Luthias took the leather and crushed it in his hand.

"The Sagart goes too far. But we must precede carefully Hamish. Follow me up to Arthair Odhar's house. He needs to know this. Those men are bound good enough you think?" Luthias asked.

"Aye, I've tied horses less, they're no going anywhere." Hamish replied. He smiled while tightening an invisible knot to prove his point.

"Brilliant! Well done my friend!" Luthias said. He grabbed his hat and coat, and then the two of them stepped out the door.

Arthair appeared dumbfounded by their story. He listened until they finished. The giant stood thinking for a moment.

"You mean to say the Sagart tried to kill his own nephew, and then leave the body in your shop! Why? It serves no purpose! What would Mackenneth gain by killing Cadno, or blaming Luthias? Something is amiss, as another motive speaks through this madness." He became silent for some time before his eyes lit up.

"Wasn't 'you' Luthias, he had no intention to frame you, it was me. The rain offered cover for the deed to be done so close in the village and I'll bet Mackenneth expects to create a scenario tomorrow to insight the town against me!" Arthair folded his hands and thought.

"But we possess the evidence he needs, when he shows his cards we'll show ours. For now we must take these men someplace safe until we need them. I can't hide them here. Mackenneth will surely make a spectacle of searching my property, any ideas?" Arthair asked.

"I have a covered wagon!" Hamish offered. "Built with a fake bottom in it when I need to carry certain things I don't want discovered." Hamish said sheepishly. "It's big enough to hold'em and I can locate the wagon beyond prying eyes!" He added.

"Brilliant! Let's go get the varmints and have a talk before we stash them! I'm curious to what extent they intended!" Luthias stood ready.

"To it!" Hamish added.

Arthair sized up his two friends then shook his head. The three of them could likely stand against the entire village, but he liked this idea better. They set out into the rain making their way toward the blacksmith's shed.

Arthair, Luthias, and Hamish stood framed in the opening of the shed when lightning struck, illuminating their silhouettes, huge and menacing. Scuigin had come to. He struggled with his bonds as the thunder rolled. He glanced up at the precise moment the lightning flashed. It scared him so bad he soiled his already soiled pants. He tried pushing away from the men but to no avail.

Arthair grabbed Scuigin and hoisted him up to his feet.

"Good God you stink…a trip to the Morag will cure several things. Grab Cadno, a cold dunk may refresh him as well!" Arthair shouted over the storm.

They carried the drunks down to the river, beyond hearing should they cry out. Scuigin was thrown in with only a rope tethering him to the bank. He sank like a stone and screamed against his gag thinking he was being murdered. They pulled him back. Arthair stared him in the eye.

"We're not going to kill'ya Scuigin, we got important things to do with you!" Arthair yelled.

They threw him in again, and three more times until his stench was bearable. Cadno lay snoring on the ground. After consideration, they agreed he would be easier to handle as is. Scuigin, who was now freezing, had no energy left to fight or scream.

Arthair carried one man under each arm. He hardly noticed the burden.

They took them to Luthias' barn where Hamish's wagon was kept. Luthias closed the doors to shut out the gale. Hamish untied the gag on Scuigin.

"Yer going to pay dearly for this business. All of ya!" Scuigin spat.

"Maybe, but you'll suffer first, so I'll put this plain and simple so's you can understand! Tell me what you and Mackenneth were up to and I'll let you run away unhurt, after you swear never to return or speak again of this matter. But if you refuse I'm going to crush your hands in mine until you talk. And if I'm not convinced you're telling the truth, I'll keep crushing arms, feet, and legs until I am. I think we'll start with this bag of money!" Arthair held up a leather sack. He dangled the loot in front of Scuigin's eyes.

"That's my lucre. Murder with stealing gets ya strung up! You willing to take that chance?" Scuigin grinned his toothless smile.

"Why did Mackenneth pay you to kill his nephew?" Arthair asked.

"I ain't got nothing for you ya dumb giant!" Scuigin spat in Arthair's face.

Arthair wiped off the spittle. He grabbed Scuigin's right hand in his. He began to squeeze.

Scuigin screamed and pounded his feet, but Arthair continued until a bone cracked. Scuigin begged him to stop, promising to talk. When he released him, two fingers hung sideways, dangling from his palm.

"Mackenneth said he'd blame you fer everything. I's supposed to take the body an' hide it on yer property. After accusations about yer run in with Cadno we find him and condemn you to hang. Mackenneth gets yer farm, I git yer coo's, you get the noose." Scuigin held up his mangled hand and cried.

Cadno had been awake long enough to understand what was being said. He struggled against his gag. Hamish undid it and stepped back.

"Scuigin…my uncle? They wanted to kill me?" Cadno asked.

"Nice family." Luthias quipped.

"Alright Cadno, now you know how fond your uncle is of you. I'll give you a choice. Help us bring him to justice. I'll let you leave this village with this coin never to return. Answer me no, or try to interfere and I'll kill you myself, along with this piece of garbage, and be through with the lot of ye! So what do you say, care to help us teach your kinsman a lesson?" Arthair once again held the pouch aloft, dangling it in front of Cadno.

The next day the skies had cleared. A wind swept the mist away. Father Mackenneth started early, fully expecting to find Scuigin waiting at his door, but instead he found a scribbled piece of paper saying the scheme succeeded, the body is planted, and the loot taken for payment. Mackenneth crushed the note in his hands, cursing to himself. He knew Scuigin would probably take the money, but this made his contrivance require more on his part. He needed to get someone to publicly speak about the altercation at the bar. Being a Sagart complicated such a thing to say the least. It didn't matter things were in motion. He had to find a way to complete his plan. He walked up the hill towards the village. Upon passing the blacksmith's shed, he heard someone talking loudly.

"You almost jumped in yourself Luthias! If the girl hadn't spoke out, Arthair would have killed Cadno right there and then!"

Mackenneth couldn't believe his ears. He quickly strode in to confront the men talking.

Hamish and Luthias both glanced up when Father Mackenneth walked in.

"What's this you're saying about Arthair arguing with Cadno?" Mackenneth demanded.

"They just had words that's all…" Hamish replied.

"Tis' enough Hamish, this man is Cadno's uncle and our local Sagart. He doesn't want to be burdened about drunken bar brawls or altercations!" Luthias put his finger to his lips as if to mean…say no more.

"I think you better tell me the whole story right now! Cadno was supposed to be at my church this morning at sunrise. He's nowhere to be found. You'll come with me. We'll bring this out in the open!" Mackenneth shouted.

Luthias took off his apron and hung it on a peg. He looked at Hamish as if to say…'now you've done it'.

Mackenneth escorted them to the mercat cross in the center of town. He began beckoning for the people to gather. Soon a crowd had formed, with everyone curious as to what this was all about. Mackenneth motioned for them to move closer.

"Children, mischief is afoot! Has anyone seen Cadno Mackenneth today?" The Sagart asked. People shook their heads.

"No, neither have I. His bed has not been slept in. In fact, he's been missing since last night, after he stood to face the death threats from Arthair Odhar."

"He's probably passed out with some harlot Sagart!" A voice shouted. The villagers laughed

"Enough! This is serious business. I will deal harshly with those who don't think so!" Mackenneth screamed. The crowd hushed. Mackenneth waited to hear if any doubted his resolve.

"I intend to get to the bottom of this! You sir with the foul mouth, what did you behold between my nephew and Arthair?" The Sagart pointed to the foolish man who had spoke up.

The poor fellow looked around as if hoping for help.

"Arthair Odhar claimed he kill Cadno when he got the chance!" The man shouted.

The people gasped. A swell of voices debated the accusation.

"You're a liar! Odhar said no such thing!" Luthias shouted. He became shocked and angry in spite of playing the part.

"Silence... Silence... I'll determine the truth in this! We must go up to Arthair Odhar's property. We shall find out for ourselves! Satan seeks to destroy this village. His demon comes in the name of Arthair Odhar!" Mackenneth yelled at the top of his lungs.

Mackenneth turned to boldly lead the congregation up the hill toward the farm. Other villagers watching the crowd joined the mob wondering what the fuss was about.

Hamish walked alongside Luthias. They marched solemnly along, neither one letting their real feelings show.

Betrain peered out her door. She gasped when she witnessed the crowd with Mackenneth leading the mob. She quickly put on her coat and dashed to find out what had happened. She ran up to Luthias, grabbing him by the arm.

"Where in God's name are these people going Luthias?" She demanded.

"Not God's name Betrain. Mackenneth seems hell bent on confronting Arthair about the disappearance of his nephew Cadno. Don't worry; we've got a surprise for the Sagart!" He whispered and winked an eye.

Betrain didn't reply knowing he couldn't tell her with all these people around. She held his arm, marching in step, while biting her lip. The assembly swelled to over a hundred before they reached the gate of Odhar's property, almost everyone, especially the church crowd was present. They swaggered up the hill like they already knew how things would turn out. Mackenneth even started singing his favorite hymn about trimming the vine and burning the chaff. The congregation joined in.

"Some bloody torches would make this complete don't ya think?" Hamish muttered.

"Whisht, play yer part!" Luthias punched him.

The mob surrounded the farmhouse and everything became silent. Father Mackenneth strode up to the door and pounded.

"Open up! Open up this instant! Come out Arthair! We know what you've done!" The Sagart shouted.

Mackenneth made a grand show of his accusations.

"I'm here!" A voice came from behind.

Several women screamed. A few men fell back in fear.

Arthair stepped out of the shed wearing an apron covered in gore.

"The demon appears! Drenched in Cadno's blood! Grab him! We'll deal swift justice here and now!" Mackenneth began screaming in fury.

The men all turned to each other, none stepping forward. They did not want any part of Arthair.

"Arrest him you fools! He's a murderer!" Mackenneth became livid.

"Who are you calling a murderer Mackenneth?" Arthair shouted.

Arthair flung off the apron. He ambled menacingly toward the crowd.

"Subdue him now before he spills more blood!" The Sagart pleaded.

Hamish stepped in front of Arthair.

"Words have been spoken of how you and Cadno got into a fight! He ain't been seen today, hide nor tail. We need to check yer land Odhar!" Hamish spoke convincingly.

"Aye, alright, I got nothing to conceal. But on one condition, we check Mackenneths property as well, fair dues!" Arthair stared at Mackenneth.

"Fair dues, aye, aye...fair dues!" The crowd repeated.

Mackenneth sensed the trap.

"No one will be searching my church! We'll find what we need here! I won't allow sacred ground to be touched by this filth!" Mackenneth spat at the feet of Arthair.

Fine, but if we don't discover anything here, we're coming to the church for a neb around as well!" Betrain jumped in.

With this, the crowd stood in complete agreement. Mackenneth understood he had no choice now but to try and get away. He had to make it back to the church. He knew something had reversed his plan. The crowd spread out in search of his nephew. He stood waiting until he thought no one was watching. When most had disappeared into the sheds he ran. Luthias turned in time to see Mackenneth bolt down the hill. He loudly cleared his throat.

"There he goes!" Arthair said.

Luthias pointed toward Mackenneth running through the village below. Almost at once they all started walking after the Sagart.

Mackenneth could hardly breathe when he made the door. He fumbled with his key. He struggled frantically until he got inside. He ran through the church to his room. He hurriedly removed the boards. Six full bags of money were a lot to carry so he tied them together and slung them over his shoulder. He pulled his cape over everything while making for his escape. When he stepped out, he met the crowd.

"Where were you going Mackenneth? Thought you was worried about your nephew!" Arthair asked.

"I came to get my coat. It was cold on the hill." He answered breathlessly.

"Aye, it's chilly alright. We should go in and warm up a bit." Arthair motioned for the door.

"You'll not place your filthy feet inside this house of God!" Mackenneth commanded.

"Maybe you shouldn't either Sagart!" A voice shouted from the back of the crowd.

Cadno Mackenneth came forward, walking to the front.

"I seem to be fine uncle. Nice to know my welfare means so much to you." Cadno said.

Mackenneth stood shocked. He stuttered before he could speak.

"Well of course…my lad…I'm worried …with the stories and …your mother would be upset if I didn't keep an eye on you." Mackenneth faked a smile.

"I guess everything is alright. I'm glad you're well. Everyone, it's fine, he's safe! You can go back home!" He shouted smiling and motioning for them to leave.

Betrain noticed something unusual beneath his covering. She calmly approached the Sagart.

"Father, all this excitement makes me realize my sins. I need to confess to you!" Her voice sounded sincere.

She strode right up to him before he responded. She reached up to his shoulder and yanked off his cloak, two bags slipped, falling to the steps and spilling the coin.

The mob reacted immediately at the sight of such a fortune, more than any had ever seen.

"Look at all that money! He preached we was broke! I gave half of everything I had cause he said I's going to hell if I didn't!" An angry man shouted.

"Me too! I sold my cow to pay him when he threatened to purge my family!" Another yelled.

The crowd began to boil, especially the congregation. Their anger reached its peak and they laid hands on Mackenneth. He was relieved of the coin. Several men marched him down the hill to the bridge tollbooth and locked him in.

Inside the chapel they counted the coinage. Many seemed ill at ease with money given in faith. All agreed once allotted to God, none should be returned. The congregation therefore decided to put the money into a fund to help the crippled and aged.

They searched and found his secret books thought to have been the devil script, which would have been burnt, except for Betrain, who asked to research them in case they contained some evidence against Mackenneth. The elders gave her permission to keep them until the trial.

Two men were dispatched to the eastern coast to request an officer of the 'Crown'. The town had never been so busy.

Arthair, Hamish, and Luthias returned to the covered wagon. They unshackled Scuigin.

"Listen Scuigin, If you bring yer miserable hide anywhere within a hundred miles of here, I promise I'll hunt you down, and that will be yer last day alive!" Arthair threatened.

Scuigin didn't say a word. He looked at his bandaged hand, lowered his head, and made quickly for the exit.

"Ya got anything to help me get this stench out of my wagon Luthias?" Hamish sighed.

"Yeah…Burn it!" Luthias replied.

Arthair began to laugh and the rest joined in.

The next day the gossip had spread to every home and shop in the village. Cadno seemed pleased. He made himself available to any who wanted to hear how he brought down his evil uncle. He embellished the tale until he single handedly solved the conspiracy, uncovered the money, and threw the Sagart in jail. The more whisky he drank, the better the story became.

Several nights later Cadno was again drunk at Barrel Bobs when his three captors walked in. Cadno pretended not to acknowledge them until they took seats around him.

"What may I ask are you doing here?" He smiled at Arthair.

"Your share of the reward is due of course." Luthias pitched in.

"Money for me?" Cadno repeated as he sat up.

"Aye yes, seeing as how you saved the town from that uncle of yers, its only fitting you get what we promised! Did ya forget?" Hamish laughed.

Cadno thought for a minute. He had been badly hung-over, but yes he vaguely remembered something about money…and going somewhere.

"Of course I didn't!" Cadno perked up.

"Come on then. Let's go!" Arthair replied.

Arthair stood up, motioned toward the door. Cadno stumbled, shouting out to the bar.

"Next time you meet me I'll be rich! On second thought; I'm never coming back!" He laughed as he left.

"Good riddance"! Several of the patrons shouted.

The men made their way to Luthias' shed and as soon as Cadno walked in, he was knocked out. When he came to, he was laying on his back looking up at the three that brought him. He rubbed his head, straining to sit up.

"Are you alright Cadno? I didn't mean to conk you so hard." Hamish smiled.

"What are you doing? I thought we had settled things." Cadno whined.

"Almost Cadno, there's one more thing. You must go away and never return. That was the deal and here's the money." Arthair smiled as he threw it down beside him.

"I get all this and I just leave? That's fine by me." He said as he tried to stand up.

It was then he noticed a heavy weight tethered his waist.

"What's this? What have you done?" Cadno pulled down his breeches to discover he was encased around his groin with iron and armor plate.

"That's called a 'chastity belt' Cadno. It'll keep you honest until you can find someone willing to free you from it, at least a hundred miles from here; probably Muireann on the west coast would be yer best bet." Luthias smiled.

He looked down. There was a keyhole.

"Where's the key!" Cadno cried.

"It's in the river. But I don't think you should try to find it. The water might be deep you know." Hamish grinned.

"Aye, an ya don't want that thing rusting up on ya!" Arthair added.

They broke out laughing. Cadno pulled up his trousers. He struggled to his feet. He grabbed the money and began moving toward the door. He labored with each step. His difficulty sent the men into louder fits of laughter.

Betrain passed Cadno as he waddled out of the shed. The men were in hysterics. Betrain carried several books along with a scroll. She stopped dead in front of the three men.

"Why is he walking like that?" Betrain asked.

This sent them into hysterics. Hamish was crying he laughed so hard.

"He's practicing his new walk in life!" Luthias cracked.

Hamish fell to the floor. He was crumpled, holding his stomach. Arthair could see the confusion, along with a loss of patience on Betrains face.

"What do you have there, Betrain?" He asked pointing to the books.

"Something which might explain why Mackenneth so desired your property!" She exclaimed.

This had the effect of calming both Hamish and Luthias. Arthair moved to study what Betrain held.

She opened a book, reading aloud.

"Myrddin knew about the existence of two of the seven powers found beyond the dark wood in the valley of Epona. His thoughts were that even more existed there, possibly several were waiting to be discovered above the village of BlairMor, between the northern hills and the eastern bogs." She looked up to observe if the words had any effect.

"A man named Seanáthair Odhar lives there. He showed little patience for Myrddin's questions. No search was possible." Betrain stopped reading.

Betrain closed the book.

"That's what Mackenneth was wanting. There's another manuscript, which tells of a Viking becoming victim of a talisman. He lost his life in the valley. And, here's a scroll with a poem, describing the powers themselves!" She rolled out the skin.

"Is that what I think it is?" asked Hamish.

"Aye, it's written in blood too!" She held it open.

"This looks like evil stuff Betrain. Should we even be holding it?" Luthias looked uneasy.

"Seanáthair Odhar was my great, great, great, grandfather. Many spoke that he had dealings with witches and wizards, but we always just thought it to be scary talk to keep us kids in line. There's a story my father told of what took place here centuries ago." Arthair lowered his voice as he spoke.

"There was an attack which left Seanáthair's eldest son slaughtered. Seanáthair's wife fell under a spell becoming enchanted. She talked of seeing spirits. Eventually, she disappeared into the dark wood forever. I never thought any truth in it, now I wonder."

Arthair grabbed the third book. He thumbed through its pages. He couldn't read, but the pictures painted a magical story.

Then he turned to a page where a giant horse blew flame from its nostrils, beside the stallion, a devil cowered behind a vault of polished stone.

"What does this say Betrain?" Arthair asked as he handed over the book with keen interest.

"Within the dark wood, the beast was cornered. No God or man could control the steed. Shunning all allegiances with the world of human and inhuman, the horse threatened to destroy the fabric of reality. Together, demon joined man to imprison the black horse's soul into a granite tomb. They sealed the entrance with the crown jewel of Epona and placed Díothóir in a golden cradle just within the threshold, in case the seal failed. The beast would now have to wait for the day when the power of the 'Seven' became joined to release the fury." Betrain read aloud.

Betrain closed the old parchment. She looked to the faces of Hamish, Arthair, and Luthias.

"This third binding has neither title nor author. Most of it is written in ancient Greek. Someone well versed in demonic scripture had translated the part I just read. Luthias speaks the truth, these are dark stories. I'm thinking no good can come from them. We should destroy the lot. Rid this village of evil once and for all!" She said.

She seemed ready to do so immediately.

"Wait Betrain, Cailleach is out there in those woods, or in the valley. If there's a chance these writings could help me find her, I'd just as soon keep them for now." Arthair spoke up.

He seemed lost in thought.

"I've got to go look for her..." His voice trailed as he stared into the distance.

"I've waited long enough! I need you to read over these books. Tell me everything they contain. I'll have to remember what I can." The giant man sounded like a small boy.

"You'll never retain all this Arthair. No, I'm coming with you!" Betrain said.

"But your daughter, you can't leave her alone! And besides you're a woman. I wouldn't want to think about the dangers I might come across!" Arthair knew he was walking on shaky ground.

"Arthair, I can match any man including you. My daughter can manage to cook and clean while I'm gone. Luthias will look in on her, won't you Luthias!" Betrain fumed.

Luthias grinned at the predicament Arthair had found himself in and replied.

"Oh my yes, I'll be glad to make sure she does as she should." He smiled.

"I'm going as well Arthair!" Hamish pitched in. "A fine adventure is what I've always wanted. From the looks of the cauldron we've stirred up, I know I won't be disappointed!"

Arthair didn't like the way things had played out, and he needed their help. He couldn't think of a reason to decline their offer.

"Oh, alright, but we have to be clear about one thing! What I say goes. There'll be no debate once we're off!" Arthair seemed adamant.

"Agreed!" Betrain smiled.

"Aye, we're agreed!" Hamish beamed.

"Ye make a fine trio! Keep yer wits about ya and I'm thinking yer daughter's as good as found!" Luthias said.

"I'll be looking after everything round here so don't ya worry bout a thing!" The smithy winked at Betrain.

Arthair, Betrain, and Hamish went back to Arthair's farm. They began putting together a list of supplies they needed.

"Food, extra clothing, water, what else?" Arthair asked.

"Medicine, rope, and maybe needle with thread!" Betrain answered.

"Sewing?" Hamish asked.

"Stitching skin back together!" She replied.

"Aye, sewing…what about cooking, and weapons?" Hamish changed the subject.

"I have a short sword and plenty of knives, anyone else?" Arthair said.

"There's an axe on my wagon, and some chain that is lethal when used properly!" Hamish answered.

"I've got pots, pans, and such. How are we going to carry all this?" Betrain asked.

"My horse, you'll not find a stronger beast!" Hamish added.

"Alright, go, make plans, be here in three days time, and then we're off!" Arthair finished.

That night, down at the tollbooth, a toothless man hid in the shadows watching to see if any were about. He fumbled for a key in his pocket.

"Scuigin…is that you! I can smell you a mile away?" Mackenneth spoke.

"Aye it's me. I guess ye figured what happened? They tortured me, broke two of my fingers, and took the money!" Scuigin whimpered.

"Ssss…someone might hear. Can ya get me out?" Mackenneth grabbed the bars and pulled himself close.

"Aye, I've got a key. I sleep in here and lock the door to keep people from bothering me."

"Good, open it up, we've gotta leave now before anyone comes!" Mackenneth grinned because he was glad to see even Scuigin at this point.

Scuigin turned the lock and opened the gate. "Where are we going?"

"We've got to make our way back to 'Muireann', where I've money hidden away. I know a few men who like blood on their hands when their pockets are filled. This town hasn't seen the last of me! Arthair Odhar will regret he ever crossed my path!" Mackenneth grabbed Scuigin's arm. They headed into the night.

CHAPTER EIGHT / THE DRAGON

A lightning flash announced Nidhoggr's materialization, blinding the Namhaid and causing them to fall into disorder. Some swung their clubs at the sky. Others removed their mask hoping to dishearten what had attacked. They became blinded in an instant.

Their exposed faces horrified even the most hardened warrior. Their twisted features with lips stretched wide, revealed green sharpened teeth jutting from decayed flesh. Black skin hung loose from their jaws like torn cloth, shredded and thin.

A stench of death preceded them as an announcement of their deterioration. Only wizards powerful enough controlled these walking dead. Namhaid, extracted from the deepest bowels of darkness, possessed no natural fear, making them the perfect warrior. Nothing but complete obliteration sent them back.

Nidhoggr destroyed fifteen of them in a firestorm, melting the stone walls of the steading. The rest of them took cover in the tall grass.

Arrows filled the sky as Nidhoggr ascended. His breath turned their wooden shafts into ashes before they neared his chest. He roared and banked to the left. Rock giants threw their stones into the air. Nidhoggr caught them and hurled boulders back with ferocious velocity. Two died instantly, but the third dodged its deadly path.

More arrows ascended, missing their mark. The dragon came down on the remaining Namhaid with a horrible vengeance, slicing several in half before crushing the rest.

Marrok watched in horror as his army was decimated in mere seconds. He screamed, and from the raven's mist appeared a 'Thaumaturge' with wand aloft sending red flame against the dragon.

Nidhoggr dodged the first assault. He returned fire before flying out of reach. The conjurer shot yellow blazes into the sky narrowly missing again. Nidhoggr passed through the deluge of vapors, swiping the wizard. The quick action sent him tumbling. With the wizard unable to cast his spell, Nidhoggr went for Marrok. The wolf broke into a run towards the darkness, howling.

From the cloud a new menace appeared. Something, with pale white skin and long black hair, rose into the air. The face was frozen into a horrible scream. The minute the horror materialized, a noise came from its mouth that shook every fiber of the dragon's soul.

Nidhoggr almost fell from the sky. The banshee 'Eeyul' had joined the fight. She was the queen of all banshees'. Somehow Marrok had managed to conscript her evil power for his own desire.

Dragons can't tolerate the scream. The pitch deprives them of their ability to think. Nidhoggr was of strong mind, and he was no match for 'Eeyul'.

Nidhoggr climbed higher trying to escape her voice but regardless of how high he flew the vibrations ate into his soul. As he lost all control, he became invisible, and threw himself beyond their reach. He expected they would search for him. He fell with a mighty crash. The ground rumbled for miles.

"Where did he go?" Marrok screamed.

He ran toward the sound but found nothing. The banshee stopped. She faded back into the mist. The Thaumaturge picked himself up in time to see the last rock giant running away.

"I wouldn't think he died so easily!" Marrok shouted.

The wizard held up his wand casting green clouds of mist in every direction, settling to the ground and revealing nothing.

"The banshee is gone. She has taken the Dorchadas!" The wolf screamed. The wizard turned. The cloud had vanished.

"I told you not to trust Eeyul. Her mind is filled with blackness. She serves only her twisted purpose. I had hoped you would have chosen your words well when you struck a deal with the likes of her!" The wizard shouted in anger.

"I did! I promised her the cloud of Dorchadas!" The wolf almost laughed.

"I guess she figured her work finished. We'll be totally on foot from here. You're right I said 'once the dragon had been dealt with, her contract would be fulfilled. I thought we'd have a moment to convince her to go with us. Even Eeyul knows about Olofen's powers." Marrok said dumbfounded.

"A banshee desires nothing but pain and suffering. You made a foolish choice to bring her. The Dorchadas would have transported many more powerful than her!" The wizard spouted as he cast his green mist.

"She did exactly what I wanted. She got rid of the worm. We need nothing more to deal with the young girl, much less an eagle." Marrok replied.

"An eagle? You believe he's something to be taken down with an arrow. He's Taliesin, the greatest raptor of his kind. He's invincible. He'd rip you to pieces if he chose too!" The wizard cautiously regarded his surroundings. He stored his wand back into his coat.

"The girl exposes his weakness! He won't risk disturbing the natural order because he fears anarchy. I will kill the girl because of his disdain of chaos. With the powers she has acquired, I will remove this curse and rule all existence." Marrok bragged.

"Blind ambition speaks loudly once again Marrok! Doesn't your current state serve to remind what limitations impede you?" The wizard replied.

Marrok seemed not to regard the remark. He sniffed for signs of Nidhoggr.

"I'm not convinced he's been destroyed. Nidhoggr will remain a threat as long as he exists. Cast your green mist beyond the steading! He's here somewhere." Marrok pointed to the ash tree.

"He succumbed to my spells before the banshee approached! His body vaporized the minute he hit the ground!" The wizard said.

"Enough of your bragging 'Ruairidh' keep looking until I tell you to stop. We don't need to worry about what comes from behind once we've left here!" Marrok said panting.

"The ash tree suffered no ill effects from the fire? The bark and limbs are alive and unharmed beside the molten stone. Something you know about Marrok?" Ruairidh asked.

"It seems I'm not the only one with a proximity protection. This bears further investigation. First we must get the girl, and then I'll take whatever magic this sapling contains for my own." Marrok shouted as he paced back and forth, fuming.

Nidhoggr lay almost half a mile distant, unconscious and still invisible. A voice in his mind called him from far away. He felt the cold earth beneath his shoulder and his body throbbed. One eye opened, as the morning light invaded the gloom. Pushing up upon his haunches, he struggled to recover. He shook his head, trying to rid himself of the noise.

In the distance, the wizard continued casting the green mist in an attempt to find him. The wolf paced like a caged animal. Again a voice called to Nidhoggr, but his senses detected another listening for him to answer. He held his reply until he knew it would be safe.

His body ached, and the effect of the wizard's vapors made him feel weak. Nidhoggr stood up. He attempted to take flight. His wings felt like dead weight, but with painful effort he pulled himself into the air striving for higher ground.

The dragon flew to the highest peak of the summit, making sure his thoughts would not be heard. He found Taliesin's mind. Explained to him all the details he remembered. He recognized the wizard. He knew the information should be ominous to Taliesin. Nidhoggr thought it best to stay near the steading in case others followed.

He descended into the mountain below the tree. He nibbled the root to restore his life force, being careful not to eat too much. He lay silent. He listened as Marrok and the wizard relinquished their search. They disappeared into the living forest. Nidhoggr had thought to fight again but something about this wizard gave him reason to relent. This cause would be better fought with a breathing dragon.

Ruairidh stood looking at the ash tree. He made up his mind.

"I'm going to gather some more conscripts. This magic is strong. You and I can't hope to accomplish this alone," said the wizard.

"Go ahead, do whatever you think you must do. I don't need your help dealing with this." Marrok shouted as he sniffed the ground.

"I'm not going to let them get away when I can smell her fear this strongly."

"You'll require my services before all this is over Marrok! Forces are gathering on both sides. A war beyond imagination is taking form. We are going to need more than your stubborn anger!" Ruairidh shouted as he stepped off toward the dark wood.

"I'll find you in time. Try not to make a mess of everything. Some element of surprise is always good strategy!" Ruairidh added.

"What I do need... is a counter spell... in case the Druids give me a problem," Marrok shouted.

"I will leave you my doppelganger. He doesn't talk, but his spells work, as long as you don't ask for too much." Ruairidh said as he shot a burst of energy at the ground where an exact duplicate of him appeared.

The wizard walked away. Marrok stared at the double.

"I hope you can run!" Marrok quipped.

Marrok leaped into the forest of Saltus. The doppelganger zipped into a vapor and followed.

After several miles Marrok stopped. The scent vanished, as if he had turned in a different direction. He paced the area and moved into the direction he had come. To his amazement, the scent proceeded into the opposite bearing. He cursed and took off again. Within moments he had lost the trail. Again he paced until he found the scent, in the opposite direction.

"Alright, enough." shouted the wolf.

He searched for the wizards double, and thinking of him, he appeared.

"Whatever is causing us to lose our path must be stopped! Use what you need to keep our way true!" Marrok commanded.

The double flourished its wand, and as quick, Marrok found the scent and took off again at a strong pace. 'Not bad' Marrok thought, 'and he doesn't talk back!'

Marrok sensed the presence of many hidden in the forest. His breathing labored, as if the air itself refused his lungs. He abated until the struggle eased somewhat. This forest is protecting the girl. Marrok slowed to a walk. His breathing became normal. The magic only allowed him to travel at a snail's pace if he wanted to breathe.

The wizard appeared and walked beside him.

"Can you do anything about this?" Marrok hissed at the double.

The wizard threw up his shoulders. He shook his head no.

"Cursed wood!" Marrok said in disgust.

They casually walked for the remainder of the day.

The sun began to set. Marrok sensed something stirring ahead. An arrow zipped past his nose, burying itself into the ground just inches away from his paw. He growled and crouched behind the nearest tree. A hawk flew from a perch over Marrok. People, painted and tattooed, ran from their cover screaming. They converged upon the wolf.

"Alright twin, time you proved yourself." Marrok yelled.

The wizard's double stepped out, throwing sparks into the air, and lighting up the forest. The 'Cruithne' became blinded. They faltered in their steps. Marrok jumped out. He ripped into the first one. The woman screamed. Another came to her aide.

Marrok was surrounded. A knife found purchase into his hide. He howled in pain and more approached. The wizard cast a bolt of energy into their lot causing them to fall back. Marrok seized the opportunity. He threw himself into the fray, killing one, maiming another. He managed to escape through their trap.

In spite of his restricted breathing, he kept a fearless pace until well away of all danger. When he finally stopped, his lungs screamed for lack of air. He fell down under an oak and lay panting.

"You're having a tough time aren't you?" A voice said.

"Who's there? Ruairidh, is that you?" Marrok whispered.

"No, not at all, my name is Elrick. Materializing beside him, the ghost appeared.

"I only wonder why you don't consider less violent methods in accomplishing your task." Elrick smiled.

"Aren't you the Viking I killed?" Marrok breathlessly spoke.

"Yes, you do remember ripping out my throat don't you?" Elrick picked up a stick and pointed it at the wolf.

"Of course your blind ambition to kill me kept your eyes on my neck as I cast the jewel to the ground, all in vain, how poetic," said the ghost.

"I enjoyed taking your life fool. I see you haven't found a way out of the curse!" Marrok replied as he raised himself, growling at the specter.

"Not completely, although things are better than before. You're still a bit cursed yourself it seems," replied the ghost.

Elrick smiled, placing fingers against his mouth pretending fangs. Marrok showed his for real.

"I planned to take those powers when you scared the girl into running away. Tell me, are you totally devoid of the smallest miniscule morsel of intellectual thought, otherwise known as stupidity, or is anger and terror all you're capable of?" Elrick said mockingly as he threw the stick to the ground and crossed his arms.

"Why you meddling ghost I'll..." Marrok acted as if to strike.

"You'll what…kill me?" Elrick laughed.

"Don't think because you're dead you can't be made to suffer Viking!" Marrok threatened.

"Yes, well, listen, before you miss another opportunity. I became quick friends with the girl and I will soon have her confidence. Once this is accomplished, I relieve her of the powers. She may even give them to me. I may share them if you can control yourself. The girl doesn't have to die, and you and the eagle don't have to destroy the fabric of existence. Sounds like a much more reasonable plan, don't you think?" Elrick finished. He seemed pleased with himself.

Marrok smiled at Elrick. He had no intention of sharing anything, but if this stupid ghost wanted to believe such all the better.

"What do you have in mind, Viking?" Marrok asked.

They sat discussing their plan while a silent wizard stood watching. Unbeknownst to Marrok, the real Ruairidh also heard.

Ruairidh walked back into the dark wood thinking on what they said. Marrok had struck up a deal with a dead man. This didn't surprise Ruairidh. Marrok couldn't be trusted. He remained unsure about the ghost or his intentions, maybe Marrok's gullible greed served a useful purpose. If they were planning against each other, his plans would be less scrutinized. Ruairidh headed for the eastern realm. He wanted to enlist the help of an old friend of his.

He'd wasted enough time today with Marrok. He needed to get to 'Olc Sonnach'. 'Olc Sonnach' was a secret fortress deep in the heart of the wood. It was a place to gather his forces and plan his war. Ruairidh knew Olofen's powers could not be controlled easily. If Marrok did obtain them, he would soon find their possession to be extremely consuming.

Under the Yggdrasill tree Nidhoggr nibbled. He contemplated. The wizard had a familiar name. Something tugged at his memory.

Centuries ago he remembered a young apprentice who followed 'Myrddin the Great' through this valley. Myrddin died and the tale of his death vanished with him. Some powerful relics remained unaccounted for. Could this wizard be the apprentice? Did he possess Myrddin's talismans? If so, things could go badly for everyone. Nidhoggr decided to find out with the help of a certain ghost he knew. He reached back into his cave, picked up a rib bone and started rubbing it against his teeth. He began calling a name in his mind.

Elrick eloquently laid out his plan to Marrok when he sensed something. He appeared disturbed. Marrok noticed.

"What's up with you ghost, you look like you've seen a ghost!" Marrok laughed.

"Yes quite, I've remembered a previous appointment I need to attend to, so if you don't mind," said Elrick.

He vanished. Marrok cursed. He shook his head at the silent wizard.

"I've surrounded myself with fools!" He spat.

Elrick materialized under the mountain into Nidhoggr's cave.

"What, may I ask, can I do for you Nidhoggr?" Elrick visibly disheveled.

"Just because you snatched a bone from my corpse doesn't mean you control me!" Elrick chided.

"No of course not old chum, but I did awaken you from the curse you found yourself in after stealing Epona's ring. Maybe I should let her know you are wandering about, free as a bird." Nidhoggr placed the bone between his teeth. He grinned.

"Point taken, what can I do for you most exalted dragon?" Elrick bowed.

Nidhoggr nodded his head and smiled.

"A new wizard is about. I want you to find out what's he's up to." The dragon said.

"Yes, I saw his doppelganger, not much for conversation though." Elrick replied.

"Find the real one and follow him. If my hunch is correct he's gathering forces. He's planning to use the powers of Myrddin against Taliesin and the girl. I need to know what, where, and when, as soon as you do. Please tell me you don't have a problem with my request?" Nidhoggr blew just the slightest flame out of his nose.

"Well, being the busy person I am..." Elrick replied.

Major burst of flame this time.

"It's nothing that can't wait my dear dragon. I believe he is heading for the eastern realm shouldn't be too much bother. I'll be off to get you needed info. Oh, it's a small thing, but would you mind not chewing on the bone. It does something to my nerves when you do." Elrick smiled inquisitively.

Nidhoggr sunk his teeth into the rib.

"Right, I'm off now. Have a good day!" Elrick disappeared.

Nidhoggr tossed the bone back into the cave and spat the taste out of his mouth. There were entirely too many schemes afoot in this valley. Maybe a little more tree root should ease the tension.

Marrok's wound was deeper than he thought. With all the running and fighting, he hadn't realized that he had bled so freely. He motioned for the doppelganger.

"Can you do anything for this?" He shouted.

The wizard shook his head no.

"Cursed useless moron." Marrok muttered.

He spied some broad leaves that might be made to stem the flow.

"Grab those plants and vines to bind up my arm." Marrok commanded.

He watched as the projection of Ruairidh bound his wound.

"Right, now we must hurry. Those painted natives might follow. The girl is going to escape if we don't get moving. Anything you can do as far as providing me some assistance in traveling?" Marrok asked.

The wizard nodded his head yes. He flourished his wand at the ground. A horse materialized.

"Alright, I'm a wolf you idiot. I can't sit on a horse. Do you have any other ideas?" Marrok said frustrated.

The wizard flourished again. The horse disappeared. In its place a cart appeared. Marrok was dumbfounded. The wizard motioned for him to get in, which he did. The wizard walked to the front picked up the yoke, placed it on his neck and pulled. Marrok almost laughed at the sight.

"You know, you could've kept the horse with the buggy and…oh never mind." Marrok relented.

They traveled slowly, at least they made some progress, and he actually enjoyed the view.

"Speed up you moron!" He shouted.

Ruairidh neared the granite keep of the beast. He moved well east of its walls. He had no desire to chance disturbing its inhabitant. Namhaid compared as sheep to what lay within the confines of this prison. He gave the fortification plenty of room. As he moved further east, the scrub became so thick he barely pulled through. He lifted his wand and muttered. The scrub parted before him, and as quickly as he passed, closed back up. Even at his best pace it would take several days to get to 'Olc Sonnach'.

If only Marrok hadn't given the Dorchadas to Eeyul they could have floated with the wind. Eeyul may be found at the fortress showing off her new toy and if so, Ruairidh hoped to abscond with it. His old friend Slad would certainly be of service.

Slad is the best thief who ever lived. With so many things needing to be stolen, Ruairidh could think of none better. It would make no difference as to who was holding the powers. Once Slad was given the task of taking them, they were to be considered his. Slad was a different kind of criminal. He preferred gold to power, and the wizard had a plan for this as well.

Chapter Nine / The Máthair Shúigh

Cailleach awoke with a start. The northern sky glowed with strange red fire. The horizon emitted flashes of green and yellow. The ground trembled beneath her feet. She looked for the fawn, to no avail. Taliesin stood watching the heavens. He seemed to be in conversation with someone, although not speaking, he moved his head as if agreeing. Cailleach rose up and walked to his side.

"The conflict wages on. Our friend Nidhoggr is holding on for now. Marrok has enlisted the help of many, including Namhaid and a thaumaturge by the name of Ruairidh." Taliesin spoke as if concerned.

"Namhaid?" Cailleach asked.

"Namhaid are evil warriors brought back from the dead. Their flesh rots, but their desire for blood keeps them fighting. They live, die, and arise again when summoned. Marrok once commanded a huge army of them. I wonder how many he's willing to use against us?" Taliesin remarked.

Cailleach pushed the thought away. She instead turned her mind to the dragon.

"Is Nidhoggr alright, I don't want him to get hurt!" She asked.

"Nidhoggr is the greatest 'Basilisk' ever to take wing. Should he feel the battle is lost he will fly away. He is not invincible but none are fiercer. I remain in his thoughts as he does mine. If the combat goes badly, I shall know." Taliesin replied.

He reassured Cailleach with the touch of his hand on her cheek.

"Now we need to insure Nidhoggr doesn't fight in vain. We must make haste to get to the edge of this wood."

He smothered the fire with dirt, and threw the stones away. The camp looked as if nothing had been here. Cailleach placed all the belongings back on the sled. He reached down grabbed the harness and prepared to move.

"The fawn has disappeared." Cailleach shouted for her in every direction.

"The deer was frightened by the noise but hasn't gone far. Come now, the yearling will follow." Taliesin reassured her.

Soon the small deer came into view. An expressed tenderness in the way she sighed shown Cailleach to be visibly relieved. Taliesin smiled as she spoke of how fond she had become of the creature.

Morning light arrived, bringing a sweet fresh breeze. The new day gave the trio renewed courage. They traveled in silence noticing only a few forest animals and birds.

The air got warmer as they journeyed further south. Here the grass grew greener. Wild flowers remained in bloom. She picked some as they walked making a lovely bouquet, which she laid on the sled.

The fawn moved closer seeking to nibble at the blossoms, and managing to snatch one, calmly chewing and walking unafraid beside them. By the time they reached their first stop the bouquet had been consumed.

Taliesin lowered the sled and pointed to a waterfall beyond the trees.

"There's a burn fresh and clear for you to drink. The spring water in the beaker must be saved for only the most important reasons. You go and the deer will follow. I'll try to contact Nidhoggr," said Taliesin.

Cailleach walked toward the falls with the fawn close by. In the distance, a large ring of standing stones, inside a greater circle of oak trees, caught her attention. The effect was as if both had been created with some collaboration between man and nature.

She walked beside the cascade dipping her hand to drink. The fawn also drank and for the first time, allowed Cailleach to touch her. The yearling gazed up with big brown eyes. They sat there for a few moments listening to the sounds of the falling water. It was serene. Her soul released some burdens. She had to force herself to rise. The falls had a lulling effect on the nerves, and walking back to the sled, her senses regained their sharp edge.

"You hear anything?" She asked

"The fierce battle caused Nidhoggr to give ground, but not before he annihilated the larger portion of their battalion. The wolf and the wizard retreated only to return with Eeyul. Dragons can handle most things, but a 'Bean-Sith' is not one of them. Their screaming destroys a dragon's resolve. The pitch makes them unable to think," said Taliesin.

"What?" Cailleach appeared shaken.

"A Bean-Sith, or Banshee, is an ethereal being of an ancestor returned to foretell death with their keening. Her scream is so unnerving, high pitched, and continuous, even the strongest foe retreats when confronted. Eeyul can do much more. She has been known to command the wind, disrupt rivers, rip away forest, and even crumble mountains. Her voice has not been heard for ages. Only the darkest magic summoned Eeyul." Taliesin seemed lost in thought.

"Does she come for us?" Cailleach asked.

"Not likely, her domain is the dark wood. Her desire holds her within the realm. The wolf used her power to drive off the dragon, but she does not continue. Marrok travels with a wizard. I wonder how 'Saltus' will react to such?" Taliesin asked.

"The woods are alive?" She knew the question sounded stupid.

"The forest lives with thought and memory, but also with power!" Taliesin stated.

"What about Nidhoggr, where did he go?" She asked.

"His ability to vanish allows him to move freely. Unfortunately his fondness for tree root makes me believe he hasn't strayed too far from Yggdrasill. He will contact me when his thoughts aren't being intercepted." Taliesin replied as he motioned toward the circle of stones.

"Those are amazing! Could we go closer to them? Cailleach asked.

"Of course, but remember, sacred places have spirits. Follow me." Taliesin pulled the sled to the cluster. He carefully walked through the rings.

Thirty-three blue spires stood in a perfect circle surrounded by thirteen giant oaks in impeccable symmetry.

"An oak grove is nature's creation. One sprout grows over centuries, spreads the acorns, giving birth to many beyond the shade of its boughs. The mother tree passes on, leaving a circle of life. The pedigree which spawned this ring has been gone more than a thousand years." Taliesin raised his hands in reverence.

The monoliths towered six times the length of a man. Their polished surface contained specks of blue, which sparkled when the light filtered through. Touching them, Cailleach sensed a power resonating deep within. One lay flat near the northernmost pillar with a depression carved at the head and a basin at its foot. The stone was worn from centuries of use until a perfect human shape remained indented onto the surface. A small trench had been cut spilling into a bowl. Near the center, deep scratches appeared to be stained with something brownish. She reached toward the stain, but Taliesin grabbed her hand.

"Do not touch the blood of those given in sacrifice. Their spirits sanctify this temple. Your curiosity may be misunderstood." He stepped back making a gesture with his hands and arms.

Cailleach mimicked his gestures as they retreated without turning. The fawn had not entered the circle but waited at its edge looking tense and confused.

"Your friend wishes for you to return to him. He seems ill at ease with this place," offered Taliesin.

"I'm a little uneasy myself being near something used for sacrifice." Cailleach replied as she turned to join the fawn.

"The people you said respected nature? They practice ritual murder?" Cailleach asked looking disgusted.

"You must understand, these sacrifices are not victims of blood lust. To be chosen is an expressed honor. Only the purest are considered. They are revered as heroes. Their ways are not ours. But with your sacrifice, maybe they can be convinced, others are not needed." Taliesin offered.

"Mine? I don't like the sound of what you're insinuating," She replied.

Her face showed the slightest strain of fear.

"Your forfeit involves giving yourself to this purpose. You carry a burden unasked for, yet you could easily walk away from this." He grabbed her hand.

"The world's problems are twisted into a complicated knot which defies imagination. Simple nature unlocks everything. Don't be afraid to trust your heart." Taliesin smiled.

They continued on for the rest of the day without stopping. Cailleach got weary even though she made no mention. The fawn lagged behind nibbling grass as they traveled.

Their path brought them to a swift flowing river, where salmon, in their quest upstream, breached the surface. The water carried the deep golden color of peat, releasing an earthy mist into the air. It was refreshing. The sound quickened her step.

The river's strong current chiseled out the landscape. Huge obsidian stones lay exposed from centuries of erosion, as if a wall of black glass had been carved to facilitate the flow.

They climbed higher as the river cut deeper. Powerful waterfalls cascaded hundreds of feet into a bottomless cloud. The heavy mist pooled on their skin and dripped from their faces.

Further ahead they found a stone hut similar to the one Cailleach had built, but bigger and more fortified. Taliesin called this the 'Hermitage'. He explained how the druids used this place when they traveled. Made of stacked stones against a larger outcropping, to the casual eye, the structure would have seemed nothing more than a pile of rocks.

With a fireplace, hearth, and porthole, this was the closest to home Cailleach had seen for a long time. She marveled at its interior size. She thought of her father. He would not be able to fathom the things her new world contained. The farm seemed so far away. The cows, the horses, and fields were becoming distant memories. She missed them all, and realized her past life had gone forever.

Cailleach set up her kitchen with plenty of room for her meager supplies. Soon she had a fire burning and the Hermitage quickly became warm and comfortable. The deer stood outside. The fawn seemed wary, but Cailleach coaxed her inside where she found a cozy place to lie.

Stacked flat stones had an unusual effect within this space. They tended to create faces depending on the angle you stood at. Cailleach contemplated what appeared to be the features of a bearded man staring at her from the wall. She decided such thoughts to be silly until Taliesin pointed out how the old man's spirit still looked after the hut. She took her coat and quickly hung it over the face. Taliesin found this to be funny, but tried not to laugh.

The sun disappeared behind the canopy of trees, leaving a brilliant glow, bathing everything in a crimson light. Cailleach sat in the doorway eating her soup and watching the day turn into night. She finished her meal and moved inside to fall asleep beside the fawn. Taliesin stood outside staring into the black distance when he heard the thoughts of Nidhoggr.

"The wolf and the wizard passed beyond the steading my friend. I tried to give you a good lead on them. The wizard is keeping his identity secret. His disguise is impenetrate-able. Are you safe?" Nidhoggr asked.

"Yes and the red-eared fawn is with us." Taliesin replied.

"I understand. I am relieved. Your journey needs every power. I know you think me bound to this ash, but please don't hesitate to call me if you need." Nidhoggr added.

"Our friendship is most treasured Nidhoggr. I hope we can manage without asking you to leave the tree. Take care, and practice your rebuttals." Taliesin laughed.

"If I ever needed to sharpen my razor skills, it would not be for debate!" The dragon retorted.

The forest remained still with only the faint noise of insects, accompanied by soft birdsong. The woods smelled earthy and damp. An owl hooted far away unaware of the giant eagle so near. Taliesin sat listening. He thought of the song Cailleach had sung. He heard loneliness in those words.

He woke Cailleach before the dawn.

"We need to go quickly. Our adversaries gained much ground this night. Seems the dumbfounding spell only worked a couple times before the wizard countered. My friend the hawk brought me this news. He urges us to leave now." Taliesin helped her gather her things.

"Our next destination is about twenty miles from here. We must decide which way to go. The moon is setting. The forest will be completely dark before the sun rises. The darkness provides us cover," said Taliesin, as he gripped the reins of the sled.

The little deer walked by Cailleach's side fearfully moaning now and then. She squeezed its ear reassuringly.

She knew she should have a name for the animal, and magically, one came to her; 'Fiadh'. She looked down and repeated it. The fawn rubbed against her hand at the sound. Hours passed. They traveled miles in the pitch black. Only Taliesin had sight of where they tread. Cailleach and Fiadh followed close behind.

Dawn came and Cailleach sensed strange vibrations in her arms as if her nerves were being attacked.

"Why do I feel so fearful all of the sudden?" She asked.

"The wood spirit is reacting to the presence of evil. You are experiencing his disgust. Saltus despairs of tolerating Marrok and his company. The forest dampened their magic and slowed their progress, but seems unable to halt them or turn them around. We still retain a small lead, dwindling as each moment passes. Quickly, now we must hurry!" Taliesin pressed on toward an opening ahead where the tree line ended, and morning light illuminated their path.

At the edge of the wood their trail led through a meadow of purple heather. As they stepped, a flock of grouse erupted into the sky. The field stretched a far distance, making them vulnerable. Taliesin gazed skyward as they walked. He remained skeptical the attack would only come from behind.

Finally, the open terrain ended on a slightly elevated plateau. Over the ridge, the land sloped down until leveling off onto sheets of stone. This tableland held two pools of water separated by a narrow trail. Each basin displayed stunning clear blue and seemingly bottomless lakes. A separate course lay to the side of either pond, offering three paths to choose from. Taliesin chose the center. Cailleach and Fiadh followed him beyond the water's edge and over a hill where the terrace sloped down again into a deep valley. Here, a third immense loch flowed westward as far as the eye perceived. High cliffs bordered the southern boundary of the lake. To the west a passage followed a river into the glen cradled by foothills. The track east led up over the snow-covered peaks of an ominous mountain range.

The loch appeared serene with small waves lapping the shore. Taliesin walked to its shore and threw three stones in succession, timing the first two within a breath of each other, and the last after the count of four. The lake began to churn into a maelstrom.

A slender azure tentacle broke through the liquid near the center, followed by many more reaching and flailing, throwing a fine mist into the air, which floated into a cloud of blue. The whirlpool ceased and a column of water approached the edge, towering over where they stood. Cailleach stepped back but neither Fiadh nor Taliesin seemed bothered.

The deluge receded, revealing an extraordinary creature with one huge silver eye and a golden beak like a bird. Tentacles broke the surface stretching forty feet in all directions and connected symmetrically beneath the head.

Taliesin bowed speaking a language unknown to Cailleach. They seemed to be exchanging courtesies. The creature articulated likewise to Fiadh. The fawn responded in wonder. Cailleach remained speechless.

The magical leviathan turned its eye on Cailleach. To her amazement, the kraken spoke to her in her own language.

"I am Máthair Shúigh I hope the journey has not been too unkind. I've waited all these centuries for the day I shared the presence of the 'Bana-Bhuidseach'! You permeated every dream with the burdens others could not shoulder. Danger follows and evil desires you; still, you proceed. Somehow you manage to find some good thought to keep warm. Admiration is a small word for how I feel and can only be exceeded by my dedication to this same cause. Our battle is truly won if you accept the task. Propose the challenge and I will reveal the elucidation."

Cailleach, confused and fearful turned to Taliesin for guidance.

He stepped close and whispered. "He grants you permission to ask any question, inquire anything at all, and he assuredly provides you the answer. His wisdom is sought by many, but only a few are ever granted such bequest."

"Well you might have told me before we got here! I don't know what to ask!" Cailleach complained.

"If I had done so, you would second guess everything. This way is better. The first matter which seems most important to you, you should voice!" Taliesin smiled and stepped back.

Cailleach seized the weight of her choices pressing hard in this moment. She didn't want to waste the only chance she was sure to get the correct answer to. But Taliesin must be right, the first question, which popped into her mind, is probably the best one and without any more thought she asked.

"Why me?"

Taliesin seemed taken aback with her inquiry, yet stood by his decision not to have given forewarning. He waited for the answer. Máthair Shúigh closed his eye for a few seconds. Upon opening, his voice spoke to all.

"This is perhaps the most important question a gentle hearted people ask, and definitely the one I expected to answer for the true 'Bana-Bhuidseach'. My dear, a wonderful spirit had the wisdom to know existence rested upon a nexus in the precarious weighing of the universe. The affectations of Gods and men are not unlike the manner of this world. If man desolates nature, it will eradicate him. Balance is achieved. When man's disposition becomes one sided, he eliminates himself. The same rules apply with spirits and gods. Olofen knew how inevitable evil would seek to destroy the delicate equilibrium of life in 'all' things. He created seven powers, once conjoined, to master every creature, mankind, spirit, and God. Overriding the laws of antithesis, regardless of the consequences, he set a high priority on the conditions for this to occur and he knew only the one who accomplished this would be worthy of the incredible omnipotence. Your path leads to this end, and because you do not seek power...the power seeks you."

With this, Máthair Shúigh extended an arm to Cailleach holding a slender sword. The sun touched the surface, casting a thousand colored reflections across the water. Cailleach shielded her eyes. He slowly prolonged his reach until within inches, she grasp the pommel. She pulled the weapon from its golden scabbard. The sword's weight was light and delicate, with the grip made of purest silver. The blade had been fashioned from emerald and polished to a fragile razors edge. Cailleach flourished the length of it and with each slice; a red mist appeared and faded. She marveled at the power, replaced the sword into the scabbard, and turned to offer the talisman back to Máthair Shúigh.

"I cannot take this, as I am running from everything, and no way worthy of such a cause." She held it away from her.

"Exactly because you do not seek to command, compels the measure to be offered to you. You respect life. You strive for balance. You choose only a simple part in actuality. Those who desire power should forever live without the potential to wield the endowment. Unfortunately the rules of the seven don't pertain to all existence. This is why you are asked to step forward. Grace us with that good heart. With immense respect, I ask you humbly to keep this gift. Use this wonderful spirit to heal the earth and deliver us from certain destruction." He bowed his head as he spoke.

The sense of his words guided Cailleach's hand as she clutched the sword to her chest, and she remembered what she should have asked.

"Do you know which way we go from here?"

Máthair Shúigh laughed and paused. "It is not permitted for me to speak more than one answer." His tentacle rose out of the water pointing to the eastern path.

"If asked...you didn't hear it from me." He chuckled.

Cailleach smiled and Taliesin laughed. Máthair Shúigh slid back into the depths. He disappeared, leaving the water's surface calm and undisturbed. The three companions left with lighter hearts and heavy responsibilities. Cailleach was glad the east path had been chosen. She shivered at the thought of climbing the mountain and braving the snow. A warm breeze blew from the south, making for a better day.

Taliesin decided to fly up and survey the road ahead. He transformed in a shower of gold, spread his powerful wings, and lifted effortlessly into the air. Before Cailleach had taken four breaths, the raptor soared higher than the mountains. He flew back towards Saltus. Moments later, he returned, flying further ahead and checking their trail. Fiadh gazed up as if she understood.

As quickly as he ascended, Taliesin landed beside them. The effect of his transformation created strong emotions for Cailleach. When he became the eagle, she missed the man. When he became the man she wondered how much of the eagle still existed. He folded his wings and did not change.

"Our path ahead seems quiet for now, but behind us Marrok and his wizard are gaining on us. They are less than a day from here. I think I must take a point from Máthair Shúigh to bend the rules a little. So if you two don't mind, I will carry you as far as the Làrach of Corriechatachan." Taliesin thought to her but Cailleach didn't understand.

"Làrach of Corriechatachan is the ancient ruin of the 'Lair of the wild cats'. He explained. "The fortress is remote and incredibly well hidden."

"Alright, how do we do this?" Cailleach asked.

"Bundle everything secure to the sled, you and Fiadh sit on top. You must hold her tightly and keep yourself close in. Put your coat on. The air is frigid up there. This won't take long but you may be uncomfortable for a time"

Once bound together, she crawled on top and reached for Fiadh. The young deer calmly sat on Cailleach's lap. Cailleach dug her feet into the woven straps and nodded to Taliesin.

"I think we're ready." She seemed unsure.

Taliesin spread his wings. With one effortless motion he lifted the burden, pulling them swiftly into the sky. Fiadh moaned while pressing hard into Cailleach's chest. The ground dropped away as the world revealed its secrets from above. The three pools shrank into dots. The canopy of Saltus spread out for many more miles than she imagined. The short distance they had traveled from the steading hardly represented the enormity of the ancient timberland.

The dark wood also became visible and loomed immensely larger, stretching beyond the mountains into the east, and disappearing into the horizon. Her journey through the black coppice only grazed the outer edge of what she now could see to be a huge forest. The northern hills and her home lay beyond sight, and she wondered if she would ever find her way back.

The air was getting cold. She hugged Fiadh close. Below, rivers appeared as gold ribbons. A valley spread out between two mountain ranges, neither of which she knew the names. The mountains lay covered in snow. She was thankful the trip didn't require climbing them. Small villages dotted the landscape, with chimneys puffing out wisps of smoke, reaching into the air and carrying the smell of a life she had lost.

"Are you two alright?" A voice in her head asked.

"Yes!" She thought back, "We're fine." Thinking instead of speaking made sense in this situation. "How much farther is it to the lair?"

"A few more minutes and we should be within sight of 'Corriechatachan'. Stay warm, I won't be long." He replied.

As he said, an outcrop of stone ruins appeared on the horizon rising ominously between the foot of the mountain and a sheer cliff descending thousands of feet into the valley below. A waterfall cut off the southern side completely, dropping into a cloud of mist, producing a wonderful rainbow. The stones formed into a strange construction as they flew closer. Broken walls surrounded giant marble staircases ascending to many different levels. Statues stood resembling unusual forms of man and animal, fountains flowed into elaborate pools dropping off the edge of the ruin into the depths below, and a pyramid captured the sun into a crystal peak, creating a stunning example of unsurpassed architecture. The closer they got, the more detail revealed.

Huge wooden gates stood closed to the road leading up to the fortress. Taliesin flew over them and gently landed inside an open courtyard. He touched down so lightly they never experienced a bump. Fiadh stepped off the sled. Cailleach stood up taking in the beauty of this ancient ruin.

She walked toward a statue of a feline standing over ten feet tall. She marveled at the smooth lines and lifelike curves seemingly untouched by time. Made from black and white marble with what appeared to be blue amethyst for eyes. The cat sat upon its haunches gazing over the plaza in a majestic pose, leaving no doubt as to whom this fortress had been built for.

An azure pool of water bordered the inside walls, disappearing into the mouth of a magnificent lion, flowing over the cliff's edge and into the valley.

Only one bridge offered passage to the gate. This arch was connected to a series of levers and wheels for a purpose unseen. The top of the pyramid, visible at any angle, appeared to float above the towering bulwarks and turrets. Many stairs wound around the towers behind the statue, and each stairway followed a different path. Vines had grown over most of the outside walls, but inside, things seemed untouched. Taliesin changed back into his man form. He proceeded to untie the sled's contents.

"I hope your trip was not too uncomfortable?" He smiled.

"No, I even think Fiadh enjoyed it. The view was incredible up there. I can understand how tethered you must feel walking earth bound as we do." She replied.

"Experiences bring unique gifts. Being afoot with you has been one of my most enjoyable journeys. All creatures have a tendency to become complacent in ones own protected environment. To step out of the familiar path, gives new perspective, and offers a wealth of varied experiences. You too have strayed from the safe world. I think you may find returning to your past life to be difficult." He grabbed the harness and motioned toward the steps.

"What kind of people lived here?" Cailleach asked.

"A mixture of amazons and eunuchs constructed this temple. Their combined efforts became known as the 'Interamici'. The eunuchs were 'slaves' brought from an empire of the name 'Ethiopia'. They mutinied on their ship, piloted the braque to our shores, and escaped to these mountains. Here they found a warrior tribe of amazons who gave them shelter, and because of their neutered nature, allowed them to coexist. The unlikely partners dedicated their labors to 'Bast', the goddess of felines, and with combined effort, they created a hidden wonder the world will never know of." Taliesin chose a stairway leading them under an arch around the tower.

"What happened to them?" She sensed he knew them personally.

"Because of their natures, they could not propagate their civilization. They grew old. They died, leaving only this splendid structure to testify of their existence. They were a wonderful caring people, who rallied to those needing their help. For eons, the population replenished itself with the runaways and outcast lost in the wilderness. Eventually, their numbers dwindled. Centuries ago, I held the last inhabitant in my arms as she took her final breath. She asked me to look after the temple and bring those in need to this haven. Only a selected few and I have been inside these walls. All others are kept out by reflective surfaces, which hide the true appearance. Anywhere from below, this appears to be a waterfall emptying from a sheer cliff. From heaven the courtyard is visible, but there are no places above us accessible, except by wing." He smiled.

"If someone did find their way, many fail safes protect us. The humble realize the secrets of 'Corriechatachan', and on behalf of a lost people, I welcome you both." He reached down to Fiadh, touching her ear.

They continued up the stair, which eventually emptied into a large covered hall. On the far end, a fireplace big enough for all of them to stand in appeared to be a good choice to camp. Taliesin pulled the sled over.

"We will shelter inside this hearth. There's plenty of room to build a fire. You can sleep within its walls, and set up your things. I shall gather some wood and food for you. If you wish, Fiadh may come with me to graze."

"Oh yes, fine…is it alright for me to look around?" Cailleach started to unpack.

"You may explore as you wish. But remember, more exist here than is visible. Keep track of where you are. I will be back shortly. Come Fiadh!" He turned and Fiadh scampered behind.

Cailleach spread out her utensils and looked for something to sweep the floor. In a small room behind the fireplace, she discovered a broom, some pothooks, and much to her delight, a feathered mattress. She cleaned, and then placed the bed to one side. The hooks assumed their place above the fire pit, where she hung her pot.

Once things seemed to be in order she took a walk through an archway that opened into another courtyard.

Chimes and suspended sculptures moved in the breeze. Tubes produced deep tones, glass tinkled, gongs droned by floating wooden mallets, windmills danced in circles, and flat metal silhouettes produced a symphony of music created by the wind.

She found a bench near a small fountain. She sat down closing her eyes to let the sounds carry her away. She tried to imagine this garden when the Interamici lived here.

Cailleach entertained images of men and women working together as friends and companions, without the usual attractions, which seem to create problems. She wondered how such an unlikely combination could have created a place so fantastic.

She felt something touch her foot. She opened her eyes to find a grayish kitten at her feet. She patted its head and a strong purr sounded from the tiny body. She picked it up. It had the markings of a wildcat, but before she could wonder if its mother was near, a creature standing only feet away let out a viscous scream and leaped.

Arthair and Hamish put the final burden of supplies on Hamish's Clydesdale. The steed stood taller than Arthair by two feet. He didn't seem to mind the load.

"A fine monster of a horse you got Hamish. I'm hoping he finds enough to eat." Arthair said as he tied up the last bundle.

"Aye, Stephen's a big'en alright, gentle as a lamb he is. But given a reason, he'd face down any threat. You don't need to worry about him. He'll make do." Hamish smiled and patted the Clydesdale.

"When's Betrain getting here, we should be leaving."

"She's likely telling' her daughter what to do for the thirteenth time. She's a tenacious woman to say the least. I'd lay bets she'd put the devil himself in his place soon enough!" Arthair laughed. Hamish nodded his head in agreement.

Betrain walked in carrying her books, attired like she was ready for battle. She wore boots laced up to her thighs. Her deerskin dress was tied around the waist with a braided leather strap. Her hat and coat were made of thick cowhide. The men smiled

"Goodness Betrain, you aiming to wage war? What's at your side?" Hamish pointed to something protruding from under the hem.

She pulled back the leather brandishing a short sword. "My fathers, we may have need!" She nodded her head and smiled.

"Aye, I pity the man that mistakes you for a helpless woman." Hamish said.

"So are we ready to go? I'd like to get as far as we can before sunset." Arthair asked as he put his coat on, grabbing his long knife. He smiled at Hamish as he stuffed the blade into a leather scabbard. Hamish shook his head.

Luthias walked in carrying a bundle under his arm.

"You're all ready to go. I wanted to wish you well and reassure you I'm gonna take care of things while you're gone." He approached Arthair, opening the package. A full body chain mail rolled to the floor.

"Arthair, my great grandfather made this for Eric the Red, but before Eric collected, he was killed. This marvelous weave of metal's been gathering dust all these years because no one big enough to wear the thing had reason. I want you to take this." He held the material up and still his reach left the chausses touching the ground.

Arthair touched, and then lifted the garment. The weave of fine metal was tight, strong, yet the weight seemed light.

"This is the most wonderful thing ever given to me Luthias. Are you sure about this?"

"Aye, I couldn't think of a better person or more deserving cause. You go find your daughter. Fetch her back home where she belongs." Luthias had tears in his eyes. He took Arthair's arm in his hands and nodded his head.

"The three of you need to get started. My wife made you some hardtack. These biscuits will last a long time before they go bad, so you can save them for when you run low." He handed them to Betrain. She kissed his cheek.

Hamish grabbed Stephen's reins and gently pulled. The giant horse willingly stepped forward. The lot of them walked down the street toward the bridge.

"Do ya think we should say goodbye to Mackenneth before we go?" Hamish grinned.

"Don't bother ruining the day. I'll tend to him when yer gone." Luthias spoke as he glanced towards the tollbooth. Something wasn't right, but he didn't mention it.

They crossed over the river and walked a little further before Luthias stopped.

Arthair grabbed his hand. He thanked him for everything. Hamish did likewise, promising to keep everyone safe. Betrain gave him a big hug telling him not to take any lip from her daughter.

Luthias agreed as they walked away. He stood thinking a long time and watching, until their figures disappeared over the hills. He kicked the dirt and turned around. In his pocket he had some extra hardtack. 'This'll be good enough for the likes of Mackenneth,' he thought, and headed for the tollbooth. He disliked the idea of even looking at him, 'But you can't cage a man and not feed him. You're not supposed to anyway.'

He realized his suspicions were correct. The door hung open, unlocked, and the cell empty. 'Scuigin!' The bugger let him out.' Luthias had lost sight of the trio. He knew he'd never catch up. 'Mackenneth is not coming back here. He'd be a fool to cross Arthair.'

"Good, saved us the trouble of soiling our hands." Luthias said to himself as he walked up the hill. He stopped at Barrel Bobs, strolled into the empty pub, and sat down.

"Early for you Luthias." Bob wiped the bar.

He filled a glass.

"Aye." Luthias held up his whisky.

"To my friends and their quest and may the goodness of their hearts burn a light into the darkness!"

Bob poured himself one as well. He lifted his drink.

"Amen!" He said.

The three adventurers walked in silence into the valley. The sky was clouded over, as was the usual here. A day of sunshine was rare and greatly appreciated.

Today the winter cold had set in for real. The ground was frozen. They were making good time. Stephen tried to stop and graze, but with a gentle slap on the rear Hamish kept him moving.

"What do you think Hamish? Should we cut through the forest or around?" Arthair pointed to the darkness miles away.

"The woods are thick. I'm not sure how fast we'd go; besides the hedge is near impossible to penetrate. Going round brings you to a big peat bog, which might be frozen enough to hold our weight. The place between the edge of the wood and the swamp is mostly rock. If we get to there, we can walk until we pass the tree line, and cut back into the giant's valley." Hamish waited for Betrain to react.

"Giants valley? What nonsense?" She took the bait.

"Bunch of old fables handed down by our elders Betrain. Supposedly 'Ogres' roamed this glen. My grandfather told stories about how they lived here until the Norman invaders enslaved them, made them build their fortifications. We never believed, but he did." Arthair grinned at Hamish.

"Superstitious nonsense, imaginations run amok, old men drinking too much and telling tales to scare children. So which way are we going, around or through?" Betrain asked calmly.

She knew they were 'roiling' her up and she meant to put a stop to such foolishness right off.

"I say we bypass the forest like Hamish said. I'm not superstitious but even should we manage the woods, I've heard too many strange tales for my liking to cross the hedge." Arthair replied.

"Aye, I vote for the outskirts. If the bog gets soft, we can always cut into the wood and take our chances. What about you Stephen?"

Stephen rocked his head causing them to laugh.

"Would it be alright to stop fer a moment to let Stephen chew on some of these good oats before we make him eat scrub?" Hamish asked.

"Aye lets all take a break. We need a wee bite." Arthair said as he sat down.

Betrain opened a basket of fresh scones she had made this morning. Hamish pulled down a bladder skin filled with water. They ate in silence, thinking of what lie before them.

Overhead an eagle flew. Hamish pointed.

"My god! That has got to be the biggest bird ever!"

High above, and just below the clouds, Taliesin soared.

"He's bigger'na man!"

"He seems to be searching for something. Lots of food needed to keep a creature like him alive." Arthair said with eyes squinted, watching until it disappeared over the edge of the wood.

"Hope everything's not so over-sized!"

"You're one to talk." Betrain added.

Hamish spit out his drink and Betrain almost choked.

"Alright back on yer feet. We'll no make any time snickering on our arses." Arthair grinned as he stood up.

"If we continue on like we said, we should skirt the woods later tonight."

They gathered up and moved on. Stephen took a couple extra nibbles before he joined them. By late afternoon they arrived at the brook Cailleach enjoyed as a child. Arthair pointed to a tree where he had a picnic with Cailleach, all those years ago. They approached some tad stoolies growing in the black dirt.

"If Cailleach was here she'd be gathering up those. She called them 'Golden Stewables', good enough name as any. It doesn't seem so long ago." He picked a few and stuffed them into his pocket.

The sun was sinking into the west when they got to the hedgerow. They followed the boundary until the marsh began. Hamish pulled out a staff and tested the ground. He pushed down to gauge the firmness. It seemed stout, so he walked further in. Once he was satisfied, he came back.

"Seems hard enough but we won't know the story until Stephen steps on. If he's no problem then we're good to go." Hamish took Stephen across the bog. Even with his weight, he only sunk inches. Everything appeared safe to cross, so they made their way.

They moved cautiously near the line of the wood. Stephen seemed uneasy. Hamish tried to soothe him but clearly he sensed something to close for comfort.

"What do you think spooks him?" Betrain asked.

"I'm not certain. I saw him stomp a wild boar with hardly a sweat. It's like he knows something's near that he wants no part of." Hamish patted the horse.

"I can feel it too. Something raises the hair on my neck." Arthair said as he touched the back of his head.

"Probably wolf!" Betrain added. "They hunted them one winter because of the attacks on the village. Sheep and cattle went missing. They found the remains at the edge of the wood. Sixty walked in, only four came back. They killed a hundred wolves, lost fifty three men to attack, the rest just vanished."

"I know the story, my great great grandfather survived. I was told he never acted the same from then on, always going on about ghosts and demons living too close. He died not long after, and his wife blamed the raid through the dark wood for his death." Arthair was serious this time. A chilling memory he'd somehow forgotten became clear.

"My father told of an old fortress keep imprisoning an evil beast sealed inside a granite tomb. He only spoke of this once. I never repeated anything of it until now." Arthair seemed lost in thought as he talked.

"I think we'll take your word Arthair. I'm not eager to explore those woods in this lifetime or the next." Hamish commented.

"Well, depends on us finding some trace of Cailleach in the valley. If not, then we go in, and demons be damned!" Betrain boldly replied.

"We're three and we're strong, while Cailleach is alone and pregnant for god's sake, so we've got to tread where we will, until she's safe!" She exclaimed.

"You're absolutely right Betrain. Doesn't matter where or what, we're going to find her, and the hell with anything that stands in our way!" Arthair said, quickening his pace. The rest fell silent.

The frozen bog offered no problems until almost at the southern end. Hamish ventured out and shook his head. The ice wouldn't hold Stephens weight, so they had to step in near the hedgerow on more stony ground for the final hundred yards, and with the night upon them, this could be treacherous.

Hamish pulled Stephen toward the wood, talking to him in a calm voice. Stephen did not like this at all, but obeyed Hamish as he always did in total trust. Arthair took the lead testing each step. The rock trail was slight and precarious. Betrain brought up the rear and began singing softly, trying to calm Stephen, and in fact, her voice helped them all, though none mentioned it.

They were feet away from the worst, when a wolf howled, causing Stephen to rear, and pushing Hamish onto the marsh where he fell through the ice. Arthair quickly grabbed the reins and pulled Stephen to the edge. Hamish was sunk up to his neck and still moving as Arthair tossed him a rope. He tied the end to Stephen and the Clydesdale tugged until Hamish safely lay on the ground.

"Quick now, take his clothes off! We've got to get him dry and warm before he succumbs to the cold!" Arthair looked to Betrain. She hesitated.

"There's no time for this woman, his life is at stake!"

She contained her modesty and began helping. They both showed proper humility and respect by completing the deed and keeping their gaze averted, while they covered him in blankets.

"We're at the breach of the glen. We'll get him further down and build a fire. I'll find some wood. You take Stephen and Hamish as far as you can. Strike a lamp." Arthair shouted. He knew they had to act quickly. Hamish stuttered incoherently. He held on to Stephen for support.

Arthair grabbed several logs and hurried down into the valley. Betrain lit the lamp. A fire was made. Hamish spoke in half sentences.

"Ssss ss sorry... I" He couldn't get the words out.

"Nay problem, you just hold up. Soon some warm tea a' be inside ye." Betrain reassured him.

"It seems those woods still have a wolf infestation. Perhaps a new generation needs to clean house. How's he doing?" Arthair asked.

"He's gonna be right as rain when I get some tea in him." Betrain took the kettle off the fire and poured into a cup. She blew onto its surface passing the warm drink to Hamish. He swallowed in small sips.

"Betrain, help me with this shelter." Arthair grabbed a bundle off Stephen's back along with several poles. He planted two so they intersected at the top and spread out about six feet. He did this three more times until he had a large round area staked out. They tied a cloth to one pole and rolled around until this formed a cone shape. They helped Hamish inside and brought coals into the center. The place warmed, and once Hamish finished two cups of tea, he lay down to sleep.

"Well, not the best start, but I'd say we're lucky we didn't find more trouble. You go ahead and rest Betrain. I'll stand guard until I think we're safe enough." Arthair said, as he searched the darkness for intruders.

"I've still got some scones Arthair. Those and hot tea make a warm meal on a cold night." She offered smiling.

"I guess you're right. It's been a long day." He sat down. She poured him a cup and they shared the rolls while watching the moon peak in and out of the clouds.

"What if Cailleach didn't make it Betrain? Maybe she did go into those woods? We'd never find her." Arthair lowered his head and took a deep breath.

"Are you kidding me? The girl makes up for three stout men! Don't you remember when the bear got into your pasture? Nobody would go near except Cailleach. Why she ran up and clobbered the beast good on the nose. Never seen an animal run so scared. Stupid men thought twice before testing her patience after that!" She laughed.

"Yeah yer right, she's a tomboy cause she didn't have a mum. I raised her in the fields. She could shoe a horse, milk a cow, and plow a field before breakfast."

"Now Arthair I haven't told you this but when Cadno rejected her, I had to keep her from beating him to a pulp. She was madder than a wasp. She sat in my house pulling her hair, threatening to put him face down in the river. Took me all night to calm her down and talk her out of killing him. You mark these words Arthair; she's alive and kicking. Anyone or anything gets in her way has already lost the battle!" Betrain pounded her foot with the last word.

"I guess so. She never knew to quit. I just want to know she's safe." He became silent.

They sat for a long time watching the flames burn down. Finally Betrain turned in. She hugged Arthair. He stayed vigilant for the rest of the night.

Morning light started to break and Arthair walked over to the edge of the wood to scavenge some logs for the fire. He found sled marks and footprints around a fallen tree; prints the same size as Cailleach's foot. He knew they had to be. He grabbed up some wood and hurried back to the camp. Hamish walked out of the shelter when Arthair threw down the load.

"Cailleach... Her tracks!" He said breathlessly motioning for Hamish. But before he took two steps, Betrain stepped out tucking her hair under her hat.

"Where?" She cried.

"Follow me!" Arthair ran back to the edge pointing to the footprints. Hamish studied them. He agreed. But something else had been standing here. Hamish investigated further up where the impressions weren't so trampled when he discovered some huge wolf tracks. He kept his silence. No use putting a fright in them.

"Wonderful! She's good as found!" Betrain exclaimed with a big smile.

"Aye well we best get going so we can tell her the news!" Hamish added with a strained smile.

They doused the fire and packed up. The day fared no better than the one before; except Arthair now had proof Cailleach was alive somewhere on this side of the wood. Whatever else, this alone gave him hope.

They found a stream flowing into the valley and decided to follow. A mountain range rose beyond the rolling hills, blocking the western horizon.

Betrain was the first to spy the lake. They crossed the brook and walked to the edge of the pond, but found no trace of footprints.

"Something so beautiful I've avoided for fear of the dark wood. This glen is unknown and only two days walk. Superstition has kept us out!" Arthair seemed angry.

"I travel from the coast and never tried to cross the river as it meets the mountain. I often wondered why a bridge wasn't built; what with open land visible where the streams parted from the cliffs. Would seem the only way in here is through the wood or over the bogs as we came. Beyond the crags is another valley and maybe more forest." Hamish pointed to the shape of the bluff.

"This elevation runs right down past Muireann into the sea and borders it for a hundred miles. Below that is Tèarmunn." Hamish said.

"What's Tèarmunn?" Arthair asked.

"A lagoon surrounded by rock walls. The seamen used to maroon criminals there. Eventually, they set up their own colony. The sea holds them prisoner against the sheer cliffs. Some escaped on ships foolish enough to get too close, others managed to scale the heights," replied Hamish.

"Further south is a barren plain stretching to the stone plateaus, which rise to the mountains. Druids and Picts control that land. I don't know anyone who would care to journey to such a place. Human sacrifice and dark magic prove frightening to a god fearing man."

"What do the southern villages call this?" Arthair asked.

"'Sliabh Dubh' the 'Black mountain' is the name most said. Even on the brightest day, the place is covered in shadows." Hamish replied.

"Seems to me, with such old men's tales, no wonder everyone gives wide berth to this land, but everything's lovely. Here are wild flowers, lush green grass, and a crystal clear loch with fish in abundance. If evil exist in a place so wonderful, then fear has guarded the borders for too long!" Betrain put her hands on her hips and gave them a stern face.

"Aye Betrain, we poor men don't possess the courage you do. Weren't for my daughter, I wouldn't be in this place." Arthair seemed serious even though Hamish chanced a grin.

"Well we are here, and with little time and reason to give this land any more ghost stories than it deserves. Monsters or druids make for a good fable but I only fear what I see with my own eyes." She spat on the ground for effect. This time Arthair smiled.

"Let's move on and keep our superstitions locked away until something brings them out again." Hamish added as he turned back toward the stream.

"I'll warrant there's more than meets the eye in this valley." He seemed keen to provoke Betrain.

They traveled the brook for miles. Betrain was the first to see the hut.

"What's under that elm? It seems to be man-made, maybe a shelter." She pointed at a spot several hundred yards away on the other side of the burn.

"Aye, Betrain. You've got some good eyes on you. Hawk eyes I'd say. Ya see Arthair?" Hamish also points.

"No, mine don't work so well. But let's find out if it's man made or woman made." Arthair replied. He led the group at a quick pace along the bank. Getting closer, Arthair could now make out the shape of the structure, and without word, he broke into a run.

"Arthair wait!" Hamish yelled, but to no avail. Hamish reached for something cn Stephens back and took off after Arthair. Betrain grabbed Stephen. She pulled him along as fast as he would go.

Arthair crossed the stream ignoring the cold water. The hut's door had been ripped off. Many footprints lay in the mud, belonging to men, maybe a woman, and wolves. His heart sank as he bolted into the hut. Everything was in chaos. Stones had been pulled up from the floor and tossed. A makeshift bed had been shredded. No blood though, this gave Arthair hope.

He stepped out the door, when from his left, a fierce growl sounded in his ear.

A wolf dove for Arthair's throat. He foolishly had forgotten to carry his weapon. He held up his arms in a feeble attempt at fending off the beast. But as it fell on him, Arthair heard a whine, and the creature went limp. Hamish ran to his side. He pushed the dead animal off.

"You might let a man know before ya go running like that. I was about to tell you a wolf was approaching when ya took off!" Hamish was out of breath.

"What's that you're carrying?" Arthair asked, as he stood shaking himself off.

"Oh this? It's a crossbow! This darling comes in handy for quick work. It's a good thing I'm a dead on target or would be the beast thanking me now!" He smiled and clapped Arthair on the back.

Betrain had left Stephen at the streams edge. She ran to the men.

"Dear God! You were almost killed, are you alright?" She was shaking.

"Aye, good enough, Hamish saved my life with a contraption he calls a crossbow."

Arthair knocked off the dirt and walked to the creek to wash off the blood. Betrain followed him. She inspected him over to be sure it wasn't his blood that covered him. He stepped into the water, boots and all.

Hamish rolled the body over to study. The feet were much smaller than the prints he'd seen earlier. There were also footprints of men. It appears as though beast and man had ransacked the entire camp. Hamish pulled the arrow from the corpse. He re-affixed another to the bow. It seemed a good idea to keep ready with so many possible threats. He scanned the area but found nothing else. Arthair finished washing and managed to convince Betrain he wasn't hurt.

"Did ya see all those tracks Hamish? There are more than wolves here to worry about!" Arthair pulled off his wet boots and emptied out the water.

"We've probably only a few hours before nightfall." Hamish said. He weighed his options.

"Why don't we use this hut for shelter tonight?"

"I'll fix the door." Arthair chimed in.

"We'll build a fire outside. That'll keep the wolves away." Betrain gathered her courage.

"We'll be safer here than walking into an open field at night. I'll sit in the shadows beyond the firelight in case anything else gets curious." Hamish offered.

He put his fingers to his mouth and whistled for Stephen. The horse stepped across the stream, staying well above the water.

"There's plenty of timber here to keep a blaze going tonight. Betrain if you'll straighten the inside, I'll start a fire so we can dry out." Arthair said breathlessly as he began to gather sticks and wood.

It wasn't long before he had it going. Betrain placed the stones back into the floor, and then pushed the straw down into the bed. She took some coals from outside to light the hearth inside.

Hamish removed the load Stephen had carried now for two days. The horse walked to the grassy field and rolled over on his back. The wolf attack had not frightened Stephen, yet near the dark wood, a howl made him bolt. Those woods played on your nerves unlike anything Hamish had felt. He didn't blame Stephen for being so jumpy.

"Here are some potatoes and onions to make a broth. Arthair, would you grab that pot and put a little water in it for me dear?" Betrain was taking charge of the home front.

The sun peaked beneath the clouds, painting the sky in hues of red and purple. For a while the valley was bathed in a bright colored light. The Crystal Lake appeared as a pool of blood near the foot of the mountain. The stream turned to a golden yellow. The fields of clover became almost blue. Jagged shadows of the hills were framed in a crimson fire, burning with a life of its own.

Stephen now stood beside the tree next to Hamish. Betrain stirred the soup, humming to herself as if she were in her kitchen. Arthair studied the footprints trying to make sense of it.

"I counted at least twenty different prints, maybe more. What's really unusual is the men and wolves seemed to be walking together, and over here is the largest paw I've ever seen!" Arthair pointed to a track near the stream. Hamish walked to investigate. He realized this was indeed the same.

"What manner of wolf or man walks side by side?" Betrain said calmly not looking up.

"You'd like me to say something superstitious. But this speaks for itself. A wolf print covered by a man print stepped on by a wolf. They're all too fresh to be anything else. These prints can't be easily explained!" Arthair seemed insistent.

"He's right Betrain. Humans and wild beast don't walk together, at least not to my knowledge. There's more afoot, so-to-speak, than we're privy too!" Hamish scanned the valley as the sunlight faded.

"Not saying either of you is wrong about man and wolf walking together. What and why would be the reason? I'm not ready to believe in ghost or demons as such, but evil intent does take a hand in this. I'll keep my mind open until we uncover the truth. Man or demon makes no difference in our task. Something may be lurking in these lands. I also feel as though we're being pulled in a direction. As long as a chance remains Cailleach is alive, demons and wolves be damned!" Betrain spoke bravely. She tasted the broth and nodded her head in agreement.

"Devil be a fool to cross you Betrain!" Hamish smiled. "Mind if I try a bit of soup to boost me courage?"

"You seem brave enough to me Hamish, testing your luck with Betrain like that!" Arthair remarked.

"Oye, you lads might grow up one day, but until then I'll just raise you as my own." She said and slightly smiled.

Betrain ladled some soup into a cup and passed it to Hamish, and Arthair pulled up a log for them to sit on while she poured two more cups full.

They ate in silence. Everything was packed for the morning. Betrain was given the bed. Arthair lay down by the fire outside. Hamish sat in the darkness between the hut and the tree, while Stephen grazed just beyond the stream.

All agreed to take turns at guard. Hamish took the first one. He stayed alert for the rest of the evening, not bothering to wake anyone. He'd had enough respite the day before. Besides, certain feelings of dread kept away any hope of sleep.

Red eyes glowed in the far distance, watching the camp patiently and unmoving. More appeared as the night grew late. Then the howling began, and Hamish laid his arrows in a row at his feet.

CHAPTER ELEVEN / TÈARMUNN

Mackenneth walked down the wooden planks along the seaport of Muireann. Neither he nor Scuigin wanted to be recognized. They kept their faces covered with their coats and their hats pulled down. Their presence hardly impressed the hundreds of seamen transferring cargo to and from the ships.

Bars lined the docks north to south, so that recently paid sailors found drink, and or companionship within steps of their livelihood. Many a fool was soon parted from his money on this shore.

The day's activities came to an end and the sun began to slip into the sea.

Mackenneth scanned the harbor for a ship christened 'Clampróir', its name meant 'troublemaker'. Its captain, known to be a criminal of the worst kind, called himself 'Brúid,' the beast, and most pirates gave him wide berth at sea, as he followed no code, wantonly killing any who got in his way. His crews consisted of castaways, murderers, and thieves.

Scuigin complained about his hand and begged for a drink to help the pain. Mackenneth ignored him. He had no intention of showing his face openly on chance of being recognized.

Relatives of his past burnings might be among the bar's patrons. He didn't need the attention that would bring. He reached over and squeezed the hand, felling Scuigin to his knees.

"Listen you pile of shite! I will not hesitate to put you out of your pathetic misery here and now. Get up and help me find this ship!" Mackenneth growled.

He released him. Scuigin whimpered. He followed without further question.

The light faded fast, and a shore-man walked casually along the boardwalk lighting lamps near the shore. Lanterns created a wall of darkness around the flame, and firelight danced on the black water illuminating each vessel in fiendish hues of red and yellow.

The lights of the harbor faded long before they reached the last mooring. The bare bones of a ship drifted like a corpse in the darkness, as if floating on a gray mist. Three masts supported filthy tattered sail above the blackened wood of the 'Clampróir'. Rusted chain lay in heaps next to a broken anchor.

All light got swallowed up here, leaving darkness, rot, and decay to assault the senses. All was eerily silent, but for the sound of waves lapping against an aged creaking hull.

A single wooden plank breached the gulf from the boardwalk to the ship. Mackenneth cautiously stepped on the cracking board, loudly announcing his presence. Mackenneth shrugged off his anticipations and boldly strode up as if he had all authority. Once at the top, a blade crossed his throat. Its wooden handle clutched by a man with only one bloodshot eye.

"Think maybe you've lost yer way mate! But since you're here I'll jis relieve ye of any valuables ye's carrying!" His breath stank.

Mackenneth stared into that red socket and spat. Scuigin slipped behind the guard and gutted him. The one-eyed pirate groaned and slumped to the deck.

"Guess you're worth a drink after all!" Mackenneth said, patting Scuigin on the back. Scuigin smiled his toothless grin in return.

"State's yer business before I skin the both of ye!" A voice came from the shadows.

"I don't think you want to kill the golden goose before it lays its eggs do you Brúid?" Mackenneth boasted.

"Mackenneth, is that you?" A man with a gold tooth stepped from the obscurity examining the bloody corpse lying on the gangway. His long black hair lay in twisted piles across his shoulders.

"Why'd ya kill 'ol Skedgy? He's only doing his job!" Four others stepped into the light. Mackenneth extended his hand, as did the man.

"Scuigin, this is Brúid! He's not as cordial as I am so I suggest you steer clear at every convenience. Sorry about the 'Skedgy' but he seemed anxious to cut my throat. Hope you're not too put out." Mackenneth offered.

"Aye, he be more trouble than he was worth. Good with a blade though. You're right he would've sliced your head off. So what brings the illustrious Sagart to my ship?" Brúid asked with drawn blades.

"I've some work that needs your expertise Brúid. I want you to gather as many as a hundred men. Have them assembled as soon as you can. Bring rations for a week's journey inland."

Brúid sized up Mackenneth and smiled.

"Ashore? We're seamen or haven't ye heard? Besides where am I gonna get so many? We number all of twenty, minus one, thanks to you!" He leered at Scuigin.

The four pirates grabbed the body and tossed it into the water without a second thought.

"Due south of here is a place called Tèarmunn. I think you know where I'm talking about. There should be more than enough men desiring passage off that desolation." Mackenneth said.

"Aye, but who's gonna control'em once they get to safe ground? They'll cut n' run! Besides, getting in and out of that harbor is why they're still prisoners. No one escapes the jaws. " Brúid sheathed his swords. He walked over to the bulwarks. The pirate seemed unlikely to accept terms.

Mackenneth stepped close to Brúid and spoke softly.

"What I seek is going to give you riches beyond the dreams of Solomon. Desperate men are always willing to gamble for the chance of a lifetime. I know the black heart that beats within that soulless chest, Brúid. Use your cunning to make this happen." He stepped back.

Something clicked in Brúid's eyes. He smiled as if remembering some past adventure.

"Well Mackenneth, perhaps you wouldn't mind coming with me to convince these fine gentlemen! You having such a sharp tongue for eloquent speeches, I'm sure your presence is required. We'll sail in the morning!" Brúid commanded before Mackenneth complained.

"And we'll be a skeleton crew if we're to bring back so many, yer Scuigin will have to stay here!"

Brúid's men went to work preparing the ship. Mackenneth took Scuigin below decks. He found the old drunk some rum as payment in kind for his bloody deed.

"Keep yourself hid and out of trouble. I've got things to do before I leave. Drink a sot's lot tonight if you must, but tomorrow when I'm gone you're to hang back unseen, with eyes wide and ears open." Mackenneth threatened with a slash across his throat.

He opened a closet, found a long knife, stuffed it into his coat, walked up the steps, crossed the deck, and left the ship. The old mission was his next destination.

The parish built on the north side hill faced the harbor. A graveyard stood between the church and the sea. Many generations lay buried here. Something people found comforting in knowing their lifeless bodies would forever rest beside the ocean. Mackenneth also took comfort in the knowledge his money properly resided with one of the residents.

Grabbing a shovel he located beside the gate, he walked among the stones until he stumbled upon the unmarked grave. A beggar thought to have died of the plague was rotting below the loam, guarding Mackenneths money. Of course the man succumbed to a poison provided to mimic the Black Death, making all things easier to privately bury him and never worry about someone digging him up.

He shoveled down two feet when he hit something. He knelt down and dredged with his hands until he found the shroud beneath the surface. There was no coffin here, only bones and a lead case full of gold. Scraping away more dirt he finally hit the metal. He produced a key, unlocked the box long enough to grab a fistful of doubloons, shut it, relocked the cache, and covered everything up as before.

In his hand he held enough to wet the taste of desperate men, knowing one glint of the yellow metal would start a fire in their souls. He now wanted a bath, a change of clothes, some food, and when all accomplished, one good night's sleep in a respectable bed.

Mackenneth knew one particular pub with everything he needed called the 'Wounded Pride'. The Sagart remembered a back doorway to come and go unnoticed.

When he neared the town, he crossed to the alley and meandered his way through the filth; cramped with rotting fish, buckets of feculence, the occasional bum, and though this did not provide the most palatable entrance, a more discrete approach did not exist.

The fourth door down was slightly open and giving access to the kitchen. It appeared to be his best way in. He approached when a cook burst through and tossed a bucket of dirty dishwater full in Mackenneths face. The servant immediately recognized the Sagart.

"Oh good God, I'm so dreadfully sorry! Sagart sir, I didn't know! Please let me help you!" The disheveled man babbled.

"Aye, well I guess you start by getting me some clean clothes and arranging a room with a bath!" Mackenneth knew this to be good fortune and cost him nothing.

"And a generous helping of your steak pie with apple crumble to calm my nerves! I expect to be treated with better manners, and I don't want anyone knowing about this. Embarrassing enough without insult to honor in drunken bar gossip! What accommodation do you have ready?" He shouted.

"Second floor room three, you can take the back stair." The boy said shaking.

"I'll have water drawn and fresh clothes delivered right away. Please sir, don't hold this against me, I promise to make it up! Your food will be brought up as soon as you're ready!"

The cook, horrifically afraid of what Mackenneth might do, screamed into the kitchen, shouting orders and demanding all other activity to cease.

"I expect the food within the hour and my bath right now!" He shouted.

The Sagart was totally pleased with how this had played out. He took the stairway to find his suite.

With the apartment spacious, and the berth clean, he approvingly walked over to the window to check his view of the harbor. Throngs of drunken people filled the streets, laughing and shouting among the bars.

He closed the shutter and sat down in the one chair that occupied the room.

Only minutes passed before several women with pails of steaming water knocked on the door. They filled a wooden tub. New clothes were placed on the bed, along with fresh towels and soap. This allowed Mackenneth a long awaited opportunity to indulge himself.

Mackenneth locked the entry, pulled off the soaked clothing, and threw them into a heap to be discarded. He kept his knife close at hand.

He eased into the tub. His body had not been washed in over a week. The hot water burned into his chafed legs. The discomfort became bearable, transforming into wonderful. His muscles relaxed. He scrubbed himself from head to foot. He finished his bath and stepped out.

Another knock came. Mackenneth covered himself with the towel and unlocked the door. The bar maid brought in his food. She looked at the soggy old man and winked. Mackenneth cleared his throat.

"Thank you my dear, please put everything on the table." He gestured as such.

She provided him with plates of food and one bottle of red claret. Mackenneth dismissed her and proceeded to eat every bite.

When he finished the wine, he lay down laughing to himself before falling into a deep sleep.

Next morning at first light he was awakened by yet another girl carrying a platter of eggs, bread, and gammon, all steaming on a plate, with hot tea and scones. He dismissed her, and made short work of the banquet.

His clothes fit but their suitability for seafaring seemed doubtful. Nonetheless he put them on and left the building with only a warning that he wouldn't be as forgiving next time.

Mackenneth found better attire in a leather shop next door. So with new boots and a seaworthy coat for the harshest weather, he made his way back to the 'Clampróir'.

Pirates continued loading the ship as Mackenneth walked on board. Brúid busied himself with some barrels when the Sagart strolled up.

"Well ain't you all nice n' fresh like a bouquet of posies!" Brúid chuckled, nudging his first mate.

"I'm glad you approve." Mackenneth pulled two pieces of gold from his pocket. He handed them over. "Now, has Scuigin been about this morning?"

"Haven't seen hide, hair, nor smell for that matter!" Brúid laughed again.

The Sagart surveyed the area.

"Are we ready?"

"Aye, we'll be leaving shortly. Your accommodations are over yonder. I gave ye my cabin for the trip. Hope everything's to yer liking!" Brúid smiled and motioned.

"I've given thought to getting through to the harbor. If we anchor beyond reach of the tide, we could send in the rowers connected to a towline. Once we get some men, we just pull them back and continue until we have what you want. We make them think we're returning another time, but we don't. That'll keep'em from causing us a problem when we're set to leave." The pirate laughed.

The plan seemed a good one. Mackenneth agreed.

The captain resumed his work. Mackenneth busied himself with exploring the vessel until everything was aboard, and the sails ready. Four small boats towed the ship out into deeper water, where they threw off their tethers. The black galleon turned into the breeze. The crew pulled the towropes in, stowed them for the task ahead, and dropped their sail. The vessel groaned and creaked under the strain.

The ship moved like a skeleton coming to life.

With only a small crew, all the men stayed busy making adjustments. Brúid steered away from the rocky coast until a thin line of land appeared on the horizon. The breeze grew stronger and the sails made a sharp noise with their flapping.

"We'll be two days journey afore we sight the jaws. Better have your silver tongue ready when we cross into their harbor. You'll get one chance before they either decide to accept terms or kill us all. I likes them odds!" He laughed.

"I never met a dishonest man that didn't want to be rich! They'll join us!" Mackenneth shouted above the wind.

The gusts came from the southwest, opposite of what they needed, so they tacked out into the sea toward the horizon. Mackenneth noticed the direction. He did not understand.

"We need to go south down this coast and yet you head in west?" Mackenneth asked.

"Aye Sagart, we have to sail southwest using what breeze we can. When we reach the right point and angle, we change and head due east, bringing us to our destination. The wind doesn't care where we want to go, unless your man upstairs actually listens to you." Brúid laughed.

Mackenneth observed the sailors as they hoisted smaller sail on cue from Brúid. The coast faded from view, with red tainted skies staining the horizon. Mackenneth knew this to be a sign of bad weather, but the option of delay didn't cross his mind. The risks must be taken. He went below to check the condition of the ship's hull.

He stepped through the main hatch onto the wooden steps and carefully descended. The smell of decaying shellfish took his breath away. Mackenneth pulled his scarf over his nose as he continued down. Taking a lantern from the post, he lit the thing to illuminate his steps into the pitch-black darkness. The bowels of the 'Clampróir' allowed no light from the outside to penetrate.

He could see most everything had been cleared to make room for the crew they intended to take on. Lashed tightly to the hull were barrels of food stores containing mostly dried pork and salt fish. Newer casks holding a supply of fresh water had been carefully sealed against infiltration from the sea. Things seemed to be in order, so the Sagart turned to leave.

Then his nose caught the unmistakable stench of the most undesirable human waste known to man; 'Scuigin'! He lay passed out between two barrels, one of them being an open barrel of rum.

"Move you miserable piece of shite!" Mackenneth kicked him until he aroused.

"Get up so I can throw you over to feed the sharks!" Scuigin pulled himself into a sitting position looking confused and lost.

"I thought you wuz going ashore?" Scuigin asked.

"That was yesterday you fool! You're supposed to be watching things in Muireann! Get up! Get up on deck! Lend a hand! You're not going to lay down here while good men work! Move!" The Sagart screamed.

Scuigin stumbled up and out. He immediately ran to the rail to heave the contents of his stomach into the sea. Mackenneth followed him up the steps. He caught Brúid eyeing Scuigin.

"Thought he's supposed to be gone." Brúid quipped.

"Well he's not! Make him work! Don't let him rest! He can sleep on the deck tonight!" Mackenneth bellowed furiously. Brúid laughed and motioned for one of his men to take charge of Scuigin.

The first day they seemed to make good time, and, as Brúid said, they steered the ship back toward the coast, increasing their speed more than double. The sky began to cloud. All light slowly died away. Eventually the sun disappeared, and the gathering clouds transformed the sea into a black churning cauldron.

"A storm's coming Sagart, you better find a place to ride her out. I expect bad seas before morning. If ye can't swim, stay in yer quarters."

In spite of the imminent storm, his men continued their work keeping the rig running full and hard. Mackenneth went to his cabin. He tried to rest but the constant motion prevented any hope of sleep. Finally late in the early morning he got up to check on their progress. Sailors remained busy pulling and shortening the sail as needed. Mackenneth grabbed hold next to Brúid. He braced his knees hard to the cleat.

"This probably ain't the time to come strolling aboard deck Mr. Mackenneth! That storm is close! When she hits, its every man for himself!" Brúid yelled.

"I've had enough of that casket you call a cabin! I need to breathe some fresh air!" Mackenneth wailed against the wind.

"Enjoy the breeze while you can Sagart, cause things are getting ready to change for the worse real soon!" Brúid shouted back. A lightning bolt shot across the sky revealing the storm fast approaching.

"Why don't ya tell me yer plans fer dis crew Mackenneth? I've known ye's long enough to smell the darkness beneath all this talk of gold! I've already sold my soul to Satan! Are ye planning on bargaining for something more than ill got gains?" Brúid laughed as he turned the ship into the wind.

"When I possess what I want Brúid, your dreams of riches are to be fulfilled beyond imaginations! Albeit as I have found the thing I'm looking for, the world will bow down to me, including the devil! I'll give you back that soul and more!" Mackenneths voice was barely audible above the storm.

Brúid's face faded of all color. He was no longer laughing. The Sagart's words left him wondering if the man had lost his mind, or intent on playing games with forces beyond comprehension. Brúid had only a second to reflect, when a bolt of fire rang down from the sky.

"Ya see that! That's one big monster of a storm coming straight for us. You need to get back to the cabin now before you don't have the choice!" Brúid shouted.

The rocky sea calmed. The wind died. The waves fell motionless. In the distance were flashes of lightning, followed by rolling thunder. The sailors stopped their labors. A green glow enveloped the upper-most portion of the main mast. It was St. Elmo's fire, and the pirates being the superstitious lot, all fell away from their appointed tasks, stumbling backward as the emerald light moved down into the ship. Their mouths hung open, and before Brúid could shout for them to get back to their duties, a sound from the blackness began to roar.

Another bolt of lightning illuminated the horizon. The stunned men watched as a giant wall of water approached.

Mackenneth stood staring. He swallowed hard. He had never seen a wave this size. This had to be driven by an unseen force. The sailors rushed back to their post. They pulled more sail to turn the bow directly into the onslaught. Mackenneth bolted for safety.

"Secure the hatches! Furl the sails! Brace for impact 'Mr. Morgan' we're in fer trouble! Tie yourselves fast mates, this ain't gonna be fun!" Brúid tied himself to the wheel. He prepared for the collision.

A sailor secured Scuigin to the main mast for his own safety, and to keep him out of everyone's way.

Mackenneth got to his quarters and quickly fastened the door. He braced himself. He did not know what to expect, and from the expressions on the crews' faces, he didn't think they did either. On the shelf, a bound leather book with the words 'Holy Bible' gilded on its surface caught his attention. If he got out of this, he might spend a little more time in study, he thought.

Then a noise like a bomb exploding rocked the galleon. Mackenneth closed his eyes, and sunk his nails into the wood. The ocean pressed in through every crack with tremendous pressure. The cold salty water soaked him to his bones. The ship pitched, and rolled with the sound of cracking beams. Something slammed into the hull throwing Mackenneth to the floor. He lost all sense of consciousness.

When he came to his senses, his head ached, and feeling the back of his skull, discovered a deep gash with dried blood.

Light filtered in through staved planks pulverized by the storm. He lay in brackish water; his whole body ached as if he had been beaten.

With feeble effort, Mackenneth pulled himself up. He tried to steady his body against the cabin wall. The door remained stuck between twisted frames and resisted his efforts to open, so he kicked hard, but nothing moved. With his shoulder, he slammed several times until the wood gave free. His eyes took a moment to adjust to the light as blurred images slowly focused, he saw the carnage.

A piece of one mast, where Scuigin had been tied, solely remained of the three. Two dinghies strapped hard, seemed untouched. The others were gone.

The entire forecastle was destroyed, as if the hand of some gigantic beast had swiped the ship. Mackenneth walked to the hold and saw the hatch fastened by a large wooden peg. He found a mallet and pounded the spoke free.

"Hello! Ahoy! Is anyone alive down there?"

Silence was his answer.

Mackenneth stepped down into more than a foot of water, with loose barrels floating on its surface, but not a soul. He climbed back to the deck cupping his hands.

"Ahoy! Ahoy!" No answer.

Near the bow, a tumbled coil of rope hung over the side. He leaned over to find the only other person still with the ship. A sailor remained hanging by his neck in a tangle of torn sail and rigging. The lifeless body rocked in cadence with the rising of the waves.

Mackenneth realized the horrible truth of the situation. He was the sole living person aboard, and fear swelled in his chest.

He searched the horizon for hope, and within sight, towering cliffs rose above the crashing waves. His mind raced as he looked to the wheel, which remained intact, minus its captain.

Mackenneth pulled his weight against the helm, slowly turning the wreck. Devoid of sail, the tide determined his fate, and it was pushing him towards the rocks.

Mackenneth struggled in keeping the bow on a straight course, but as the ship got closer, the details of the cliffs grew strangely apparent. Two vertical towers of stone extended from the shore, meeting almost in the middle, with only a narrow gap to separate them. Beyond those, mountains rose directly from the ocean, without shoreline, or hope of purchase on which to land.

The tide had a strong grip on the battered ship, and Mackenneth knew his best attempt to shoot unscathed through the narrow cavity seemed unlikely. He prayed for a safe harbor inside, and watched the approaching rocks, marveling at how their formation resembled a gaping mouth; an open jaw of death.

The ship pushed to the edge of the sheer cliffs. The rock face jutted out into the deep water like the lower mandible of a gigantic skull, with a jagged smile pulling the sea through the gap of its missing tooth.

Entrance into the mouth depended on his approach being in concordance with the suction and spewing of the jaw. If the boat turned sideways it would lose the bow and stern; quickly sinking to the bottomless grave beneath.

The 'Clampróir' with no sails, depended on the haphazard navigation of a skeg, more likely to spin the ship in circles.

Mackenneth held the wheel tight, keeping the rudder against the incoming tide. This entrance would be a miracle at best, as the bowsprit swayed left, then right. The gap, only yards away inhaled the galleon towards life or death, and all Mackenneth could do is wait for the toss of the coin.

The sea hauled him close, and the Clampróir turned sideways. His fate appeared final, and within feet of crashing, a wave gushed out, straightened the ship, and dragged the wreck intact through the hole. For the first time in his life, Mackenneth thanked God. But God had little to do with a man's fate upon this shore, for once inside the gigantic walls; the eyes of the devil were revealed.

In the center of a black sand beach, at the bottom of the sheer rising cliffs, a cavity opened into the depths of the earth. Hundreds of feet above, balanced in evil symmetry, two ocular holes burned red with flame. The ship came to rest against the sand, sucking tight into its grip. Mackenneth didn't know yet, he had found Tèarmunn.

The Sagart walked back to the cabin where the leather bound Bible still lay perfectly in place on upon shelf. He picked it up scheming of some way he might use the volume here in this desolation. With little else but his long knife and the clothes on his back, Mackenneth stepped off the ship and staggered toward the cavernous opening in the rock.

Inside these walls, the ocean became a distant rolling noise. Then the aroma of smoke, tainted with the smell of burnt meat, awakened Mackenneths dormant fear. He remembered what human flesh smelled like when put to the fire and he now understood his good fortune had changed drastically.

The opening grew in size as he approached, being many times larger on the inside than the entrance revealed. Dark caverns stretched out in all directions, pitch black in descending and ascending steps. To his left, something smoldered, but without entering the cave he couldn't make it out. The fear became overwhelming, and the ship outside beckoned him to return for his life's sake, so he turned to retreat.

"Would you not like to visit our home before you run off as if uninvited?" A huge naked man adorned with bone necklaces and long blades draped across his chest, smiled with rotted teeth. The black giant blocked his way.

"Your friends have already joined us. Please go in." He did not request as he pulled his knives from their sheaths. Mackenneth thought to defy the man, but knew it would be useless.

Inside, his eyes took moments before he realized, in the limited light, his worst fears to be reality. Bodies had been tied to wooden crosses and laid over open fire pits. These sailors weren't only murdered; they were to be consumed. Mackenneth wasn't squeamish, but cannibalism made the bile rise into his mouth. He remained silent, showing no emotion. His captor stood in amazement because of his lack of distress.

"Do you understand what you witness? Your friends died screaming in horrible anguish? Are you not afraid?" He asked.

"You have done God's work here and saved me the trouble." Mackenneth looked the savage in the eye smiling.

"What is your name sir? I am in your debt!" The Sagart sang his words.

The native seemed confused. He answered.

"Miol, I am servant of the great chief. I look at a crazy man. How do they call you?"

"Father Mackenneth, Sagart, Holy Sword of God's will on this good earth. These men you have killed were to be brought to justice for their crimes. Your methods remedied their pathetic existence. I commend you for not letting them get away. Once I return to Muireann, you shall be handsomely rewarded." Mackenneth schemed as he talked.

"No escape from here, only these paths through the darkness. You are prisoner until you die, which will be decided soon!" Miol threatened with his knife for Mackenneth to take the path that led down. Further in, torches burned, consuming human fat. The reek almost choked the Sagart.

A carved stone stairway descended for hundreds of feet before leveling out into an alcove where silent warriors remained motionless. They stood like statues, and if their chests hadn't shown movement when breathing, Mackenneth would have thought them to be.

Their entire naked bodies covered in white chalk gave them the appearance of skeletons. Miol took no notice of them as he walked past. The black giant pushed Mackenneth into the next chamber, where a second group of men stood with crossed swords guarding the entrance to some secret room. The giant spoke to them in an unknown language and they stepped aside. He grabbed the Sagart by the arm.

Inside the chamber, well lit with amazingly fresh air, walls were adorned with coral; creating a textured canvas of color against a huge shell, emptying an endless flow of water into an alabaster pond. But what Mackenneth mistook for white sand, was in fact thousands of pearls, many inches thick, covering the bottom and glistening in the abundant light.

Strange fish swam in the pool. Pale, without eyes, with needle-like teeth protruding from their mouth; they glided aimlessly, as they too had no souls. Beyond the fountain was a throne of ivory whalebone. On this chair sat an ancient black man with pure translucent eyes.

As they approached, he turned his head in their direction. Blue flame flared behind each white pupil, giving Mackenneth pause to retain hope of living. Miol spoke again in the unknown language, until the ancient man raised his hand to silence him.

"You claim to be sent from God, but as you can see, God has forgotten us. Does he now remember his lost children after so many years?" The leader gazed toward Mackenneth.

"It would be God's will indeed for me to have found you by bringing his written word to lift these spirits to heaven and save your immortal souls!" Mackenneth produced his Bible. The weak leathery figure on the throne smiled, but had no teeth.

"This world took vengeance against us and condemned each one to this place, yet you would seek to save us. And once saved, do we grow wings and fly beyond this prison into the welcoming arms of your civilization? No, I think we die here. We forever perish into the sand, as will you. Escape from this wretched hell exists only in dreams. Generations have passed believing in abdication, and that hope becomes relentless torture." The old man paused to cough and spit. He cleared his throat.

"To contemplate salvation is to achieve madness. We have accepted our fate, as now you must. Do not fear death. We embrace the reaper. We offer ourselves to him willingly. Your destiny will not be to die by our hands, but to live long and contemplate why God brought you here to suffer until the end." The ancient man turned his head away and closed his eyes.

Miol grabbed Mackenneth by his arm and led him out. Mackenneth walked dumbfounded. For the first time in his life, he was helpless and doomed.

Miol allowed Mackenneth to return to the floundered ship. A group of subordinates busily unloaded the usable stores. A single barrel of pork lay on the beach. The Sagart took several slabs and climbed back to his cabin. He threw the leather bound book into the room, cursing his luck.

On deck he found an untouched cask of fresh water, which he opened and sat down to consider his position. Dried pork and water made his first meal in captivity strangely acceptable. He gazed out beyond the mandibles toothless smile, where a free world existed less than a hundred yards away.

He watched as pieces of wood went crashing into the rocks and being reduced to splinters.

He did not accept his fate here. He would find a way out sooner or later. He pulled a thick piece of pork from the barrel and threw it into the ocean in disgust. The meat sunk about four feet, and then was sucked in the direction of the gap.

"It may be sooner!" He said to himself and laughed.

CHAPTER TWELVE / 'OLC SONNACH

Ruairidh crossed into the desolate valley where stony ground vented sulfurous vapors into a windless sky. Orange liquid oozed from burnt stone, flowed into a pool of green metal, and mixed with the dark remnants of a long forgotten demon war.

Jagged lumps of slippery stone provided an extremely precarious walk of faith for the 'mage' who had seen his glorious empire become this wasteland, and yet he maneuvered his large frame over scattering rocks with scarcely a thought of it.

The wizard unaided by map or compass crossed the terrain without hindrance. Ahead, a large outcropping of boulders had settled onto heaps of scree. Ruairidh made his way up to them, all the while searching for a hidden entrance into the fortress below.

Steps away from reaching the summit, he found an effusion of blue liquid oozing from beneath two massive stones locked against each other, allowing a slight opening near their base.

Ruairidh stepped over the stream and squeezed into a dark crevice large enough for his frame. He pulled his body through the tight slit until past the stones.

No sunlight managed to invade the chasm, so his sense of touch became the only means to move ahead. A flame from his wand could easily illuminate the way, but with all the volatile gases concentrated around him, he thought it better to explore unaided.

With his hands, he groped in the darkness to find a chain fastened against the stone. This was the 'latch' he sought. He wrapped his hand around the chain and pulled but nothing happened. He used both hands and pulled with his entire weight. The thing remained unmoved. In a last desperate effort, he hung on the chain and threw his legs against the wall until something clicked and gave way.

His weight hit the floor as an ancient mechanism came to life and parted the stone parapet that had once defended this city. Ruairidh looked at the blood flowing from his hands. The smell of the past brought him to his senses. He got on his feet and willed himself to step through. The soil of a thousand years lay before him unsullied by wind or flesh. He placed his foot down into the dust and left his print deep within the grain of centuries.

The passage lay devoid of sentry or guard as most dead ends were treated as such. He turned to the south and walked downward, ever descending into the depths of oblivion. Here the earth gaped open, remained sorely wounded, and die festering. His memory of this place began to return.

He pulled his wand as he entered a junction where many caves converged into a singular circular cavern. To the far side a great archway stood supported in glistening chiseled stone, adorned with skulls upon crossed bones, and protected by an army of sadistic nihilist.

The wizard knew them. He knew the shape of their brow and the weave of their hair. He suffered their lungs to fill with air and their hearts to pump blood. His eyes raged silently vowing never to forget their insurrection.

Ruairidh stashed his wand and walked across the cavern floor to the entrance. When he passed under the arch he found a gate guarded by twelve soldiers. His approach brought their weapons to bear.

"State your intent, show your hands, and stop where you're at!" A large warrior shouted. Ruairidh raised his arms. He stopped half the distance to the gate while appraising the security.

"I said state your business!" The guard demanded.

"I'm Ruairidh and if you detain me one moment more, I will remove the wind from your lungs! Step aside!" Ruairidh shouted.

Their faces lost all expression and fear of his name caused them to part without hesitation. They opened the barrier gate.

Somewhere above, Ruairidh sensed a threatening gesture. With the flick of his wrist, a bolt of energy found its way into the mouth of an archer who was foolish enough to target him with his arrow.

The soldier fell from his perch. He writhed violently on the ground. He turned blue, and died twitching in agony. Ruairidh turned to face the guards.

"If any of you so much as breathe my name in your sleep, the punishment which befell this man will pale in comparison to what I'll do to you and your families." Ruairidh's eyes glowed for an instant. The effect was complete. The guards swallowed hard and stood motionless until the wizard was well away.

The road to the fortress was wide and grew even wider as he neared the city. The cavern dome rose to great heights, disappearing into the darkness far above the illumination of torchlight.

Bodies of hundreds, lining both sides of the way, had suffered being nailed and chained in every conceivable form of torment. He saw skeletal bodies in various forms of decomposition, but most were still alive, suffering starvation and dehydration. Ruairidh had no stomach for torture. He believed sudden death was humane and just. He never excused himself for his deeds. He understood full well his desires motivated his actions. He did not expect mercy when his time came. He welcomed a quick death.

Something to his right caught his attention. In the darkness he made out a small cage being much too small for a man. He turned and crossed the wide road to get a better look.

A dying child was locked in a metal trap. He approached to assess its condition. A boy hardly ten years old raised his sunken eyes. He looked at the wizard but could not speak.

Ruairidh, as hard and merciless as he was, had one small tender spot in what was left of his black heart. He did not tolerate cruelty to children. Something in his past came to memory. His anger boiled deep inside him.

He pointed at the lock on the cage causing the iron to melt away. He gathered the child into his arms. The boy whimpered silently as Ruairidh sat down and pulled the child onto his lap.

The wizard reached into his cloak producing a small vile of silver liquid. He removed the cork and poured a few small drops onto the parched tongue of the urchin. Within moments the boy opened his eyes. He began breathing with new energy. He acted to speak but Ruairidh placed his finger against his lips. He held the boy, watching his eyes grow bright. At last the child sat up and reached around the wizard's neck, hugging him tightly.

"Thank you sir," was said before he closed his eyes to die in Ruairidh's arms.

The wizard eyes filled with tears. He hugged the child knowing what he had done; allowing the boy to die without pain or suffering.

The potion produced health with euphoria before extinguishing the fragile life force. This was all the wizard could do for a child so horribly suffering an irreversible death.

He pointed his wand at the stone wall and burned a small sepulcher into its depth. Here he lay the boy and sealed the tomb.

He scorched an inscription above which read, 'Revenge is earned by those who harm a child!' He left.

Ahead in the distance, high walls surrounded a contingent of moving shadows in multi colored flashes of light, with waves of noise like voices, people trading, people fighting, and people dying.

Ruairidh moved toward those noises and once inside, he walked among traders, cutthroats, and thieves.

Tables loaded with fine silk and woven rugs, weapons and armor, poisons and potions, all filled the market space, but the busiest booth in the bazaar was the parts man.

The parts man sold heads, hands, legs, and every piece in between. He had a bowl filled with eyeballs, one with teeth, and one for gonads. The trader recognized Ruairidh and waved for him to approach. He was smiling in the knowledge his best customer had arrived. The wizard strolled to the table and picked up the lower mandible of a donkey. He checked its balance in his hand.

"You're still the man for quality merchandise Abdul. How have you been my friend?" Ruairidh asked.

Abdul opened his arms to embrace the wizard. He motioned for them to retire into the back room of his booth.

"Times are good my friend. Lately, there's a great need for dark magic. I can't keep monkey brains in stock, and if you want lizards tongue, well, forget it. There must be something important happening for so many to travel so far." Abdul sat to light his pipe.

"Yes, I think you're right, something is stirring. People are feeling death near their door. And yet I'm sure it's only a ripple in something much greater.

You have found a value in this fear, and whether the threat is real or not; coin tossed is coin lost, eh?" The wizard relaxed in the company of his old friend.

"It seems the 'Crown' has been very busy. I saw hundreds of dead and dying lining the road." Ruairidh's tone changed.

"Yes, they show no mercy to the unfortunate when taxes are due. Man, woman, child; they don't care. Their coiffures are overflowing, yet they provide nothing for the poor or sick. A starving woman had her hands removed because she took some rotten apples from the garbage. It's enough to make an honest thief mad!" Abdul spat at the ground in anger.

"But my need today is to find a real thief, and you normally discern his way. This business deal needs the touch of an expert in acquiring certain objects of…"

"You're looking for 'Slad'!" Abdul interrupted.

"Yes I am. I hope you can help me find him." The wizard smiled.

"Not a problem. He comes here to move his, shall we say, acquired merchandise. Some of my best parts I get from him, no questions asked. Always of the best quality, always fresh, not your usual grave robbing. He's due here tomorrow to bring me some virgin oil from an undisclosed eastern source. If you're here before noon you'll be sure to find him." Abdul offered Ruairidh a pipe.

"No, none for me please, but I do need a place to stay for the night. Is the room still available over the sacred pool? It had a lovely view of the lava flow as I remember."

"Aye, that flow is silent at the moment, but the room is still there. You're most welcome to the accommodation and supper will be brought at your bequest. Why don't you take a walk and discover the diversity of correction our glorious 'Crown' now enforces. Public mutilation has become a favorite punishment of late. I witnessed the removal of a witches tongue two days hence. She shouted openly at the 'Crown', cursing their treatment of orphans," he grinned.

"I paid top price for the tongue and sold the flesh at double profit before day's end. I could use a few more of those." Abdul could see Ruairidh did not share his amusement.

"Of course there's the 'Wizards Gauntlet' where ultimate survival is awarded a special bit of magic called the 'Dorchadas', a transportation device of some sort." Abdul said.

Ruairidh's eyes lit up, "Dorchadas, where did they get it?"

"Eeyul sold the cloud to the 'Crown' for a hefty amount. I personally think they bought the thing to get rid of her. Her presence always makes everyone feel uncomfortable. Even when she says nothing, she gives off some real bad feelings. On the day she came to the bazaar, she frightened the customers away, and if we don't make money, the 'Crown' doesn't make money. Not too hard to figure out." He relit his pipe.

"Interesting, this gauntlet, I may investigate the possibilities. Whereabouts may thus be found?" Ruairidh inquired.

"It is beyond the lake near the lost cave. You'll see fire flowers streaming through the air above and colored smoke rising from a lighted stage below. You can't miss the spectacle."

Ruairidh thanked Abdul, bought the jawbone as a token of appreciation, and headed down into the city.

His needs seemed easily accommodated, leaving him feeling wary of such easily gotten gains. Slad was available. The Dorchadas was waiting to be taken for the price of running a gauntlet. All seemed too easy. Ruairidh didn't trust this run of luck. He stopped at a booth near the edge of the bazaar, where he bought a scarf, tied the silk to the jaw, and slung the odd looking contraption over his shoulder.

Beyond the bazaar, the city spread out into different levels and heights. The walls were so distant, shadows died before they reached them. The upper levels were mostly brothels and dens of iniquity.

The lower levels were chambers for the darkest black magic. Namhaid were conjured from the bowels of these regions. Few of even the bravest dared to venture beyond those extents where the depths remained rife with sleeping behemoths and conqueror worms.

The middle areas provided dwellings for travelers and facilities for entertainment. As long as the money flowed, the inhabitants of this level had only to worry about their share of tax owed for money traded

The highest dwelling was for 'The Crown'; an establishment of wizards and thieves who controlled all the evil power within these deep walls. So to insure that no 'one' person or organization gained ultimate power, an equal company of 'selected' officials were intended to keep a balance among the tempest of the evil intent and those wanting to exist in peace.

Ruairidh hated the Crown. Common knowledge was of his accusation of the former 'High Justice Medraut' for killing his father. Medraut never faced those accusations, and the Crown denied any collusion with the deposed leader. A blood price had never been paid, nor offered. The offense of returning is great and the affront his presence instigates will be indigestible for the sensitive palates of the Crown.

The wizard stood remembering and oblivious, when a Namhaid knocked him back. Marching from the depths, hundreds of them succumbed to the spell of a warrior wizard recognized by Ruairidh as 'Demorele'.

Years ago they fought as allies against the Viking hordes from the north. He admired the Vikings for their lust of blood and death. He did not admire 'Demorele' because of his inability to fight strategically. Demorele threw his soldiers into battle like a blacksmith throws coal into a fire, hoping a hot battle will melt the enemies' resolve. He won a few battles but usually had nothing to wage war with afterward.

Ruairidh wondered where he was taking so many Namhaid now. Abdul was right about something developing. He needed to find out what was at hand. But first he needed to see this gauntlet and develop a plan to defeat it.

'The Wizards Gauntlet'

The stage covers a narrow distance of over 200 feet. Four levels must be accomplished in order to qualify for the final test. No one yet has proceeded beyond level two.

Level one tests the ability to dispel vapor magic.

Any wizard worth his salt should not experience trouble dispersing any mist, regardless of content. However the vapors change with each test and are applied differently as well. The vapor chamber is a hall roughly 20 feet in length and 8 feet width. Small crevices in the walls, floor, and ceiling are used to emit the mist. In most cases, a metallic additive shields against normal dispelling tactics.

The first challenger was a wizard in training who suffered terrible burns when he used a simple conjuration to repel vapor. His teacher analyzed the residue left on the apprentice's arm, and asserted himself into the challenge, succeeding to create a safe bubble around him, only to find a new additive in the mist had solidified on its surface. He safely escaped with the determined efforts of several axe men moments before the air within his solidification ran out.

Level two tests the ability to discern.

Within a mirrored maze, the wizard must recognize truth from deception.

The first wizard found himself between a Namhaid and a troll. His bad decision was he chose to challenge the Namhaid, which having turned out to be the illusion, giving the troll the opportunity to bash his arm with a club. Had he chose the troll and the Namhaid turned out to be real; his head would have been separated from his shoulders. His fear determined his decision, not his intellect. If he had perceived a ring on the Namhaid's finger, the truth would have been obvious, because Namhaid do not wear metal close to their skin.

Level three is a test of solution.

In only seconds a wizard must solve a puzzle by correctly combining three objects in order to produce a defensive weapon, which, if properly assembled, will disable whatever threat appears.

The only wizard to make level three walked into a room where a table supported a finger bone, a ring, and a glove. He quickly shoved the bone into the ring finger socket of the glove and slid the ring over the glove with the bone inside. Seconds later a Dobhar-Chu appeared. The wizard pointed the fingered glove and when nothing happened, the creature ran him through with its single long horn protruding from its head. The wizard did not die, and given time to analyze his actions, recognized the finger bone was not a ring finger. Instead an index finger placed wrongly into the glove rendered him vulnerable. But even when he realized his mistake, he could have repelled the creature with a simple enchantment. The rules of the solution chamber do not exclude using your own magic. However, a foolproof weapon, if properly assembled, provides a key to the next level.

Level four is a locked room with a single word written above the door; 'Abandon'. Since no one has entered, no knowledge of what is inside exists.

Ruairidh stood contemplating the long stage while a man beside him took note of his interest.

"So far none are dead, but it's only a matter of time. Are you thinking of trying?" The man asked.

"I have no knowledge of you sir! My intentions are not your concern!" Ruairidh dismissed.

"No problem. I thought you might want to increase your chances, seeing as how I designed the thing." The man started to walk away when Ruairidh grabbed his arm.

"My apologies to you sir, please disregard my rudeness. I'm Ruairidh, apprentice of Myrddin." He properly bowed and flourished.

"Ruairidh? Your name awakens many childhood nightmares, would appear you're more than a myth or legend. Your participation in this will be interesting to say the least. My name is Tógálaí; would you care for a drink?"

"Absolutely, and would be my pleasure to pay." They walked to the nearest pub, sat down, and ordered two draughts of rum.

"Tógálaí, are you a wizard? You wear no cloth." Ruairidh went directly for information.

"No, I'm a shipwright from Muireann. I was captured ten years ago off the eastern coast. We were on our way home, having delivered a three masted galleon to the Spanish King, when his pirates caught up with us, took our treasure, clapped us in chains, and sold us as slaves. My father and brothers were sent back to Spain, while I was sold to one of your 'Crown'. My design of this gauntlet gives me freedom to walk openly among you. More I guess, I shouldn't hope for." He drank his rum and seemed resigned to his fate.

"What if I told you I could get you out of here? Would such be worth information about your design?" Ruairidh smiled.

"Aye, it would. Understand this before you commit, I designed, built, and created the manipulations, but the dark areas of magic installed were done so by the 'Crown'. I'm privy to what they do, but not to how they work." Tógálaí took another drink.

"This should be sufficient. Give me your knowledge and I will take you out of here. A deal between us sir?" Ruairidh extended his hand. Tógálaí took the hand in his and shook.

"The first level sprays a vapor of any combination of five fluids. They are aigéad, mearcair, potais loiscneach, airgead, and arsanaic. The combinations are uncontrolled and will change in every instance. The second level is under the control of a wizard, chosen randomly, only moments before the challenge begins. He is shown the manner of the real threat and told to develop a flawed fake, which can be spotted with the discerning eye. The third level is taken from the last five chapters of the 'Tome of Myrddin' in which he describes in detail the perfect weapon in any confrontation. Your susceptibility in such a confrontation would be minimal to say the least," he smiled.

"The fourth level is the room which induces you to abandon your instincts entirely and choose the opposite of what you discern to be correct. It is more a test of faith than skill. When you reach this level the perimeters of the test will be brought in a sealed box to the 'Crown' on the morning of the challenge. One wizard will be chosen having knowledge of the participant's limitations. Those limitations will be used to defeat the player. Finally, if you accomplish the first four, you will be brought before the 'Crown' and asked to solve a riddle developed especially for you. This riddle will be designed so in solving, you must reveal your deepest secret. The 'Crown' believes this alone will prevent anyone from winning, and the game will go on forever. What do you think?" Tógálaí finished his rum and relaxed into his chair.

"It is all very devious. Your device is extremely clever indeed. I think I shall enjoy this distraction. How about having another drink on me, tomorrow should be very interesting for everyone." They relaxed and talked like old friends.

A hooded figure had been silently listening to their every word. He carefully removed himself and went directly to the chamber of the 'Crown'. A lone guard unlocked the secret entrance allowing the man to enter. Once inside he crossed a lavish marbled floor and pushed an unseen hinge on the wall's wood paneling. A door opened and closed when he entered. Another panel opened and he stepped into the 'Chamber of Law' where seven men and two women sat in conference. They were all adorned in regal golden robes. Upon his entrance they stopped talking. They allowed him to approach. The man walked before them and bowed.

"News?" The oldest looking man with a floor length beard asked.

"Yes, as you predicted, the slave found a wizard to help him escape in return for his information." The spy related.

"The wizards name is Ruairidh."

Audible gasps among the members were hardly restrained.

A woman stood up.

"Shouldn't we prohibit him from participating, after all his power is certain to overcome any obstacle we develop? What sense of fair play resides in this, he'll easily win. We might as well give him the Dorchadas and save the trouble." She seemed exasperated. A few agreed readily.

The eldest wizard shook his head and stood.

"A golden opportunity exists to gather Ruairidh into our fold once and for all. We anticipated the builder would make this move. We allowed his freedom for one reason, to entrap those seeking to cheat. Since Ruairidh decided to participate, we'll change the rules. His cleaver inside information will serve to easily defeat him when he trusts his information. As he steps up to take the challenge, we will only allow him to do so if he accepts his failure automatically secures his loyalty to the 'Crown'. If he accepts, his public humiliation will serve to discredit him and serve our cause. I don't think a spider has woven a stronger web. I motion we allow him to enter 'The Wizards Gauntlet' under those circumstances. All agreed say yes!" The crowd gave their approval; save one. The woman sat down and turned her back. The motion was passed. The spy was dismissed.

Ruairidh awoke the next morning eager to make his way to the bazaar. Slad was already waiting in the back room of Abdul's booth.

Slad was a small slender man with extremely delicate hands, except for his moustache; one would have mistaken him for a woman.

The wizard and the thief embraced. They exchanged greetings.

"I thought you to be rid of this place Ruairidh. What adventure brings you back here?" Slad smiled exposing two rows of gold teeth.

"A proposition for you Slad, you know of the seven powers of Olofen?"

"Yes." Slad replied. "My mother told me the story, among other tales of pixies and fairies; put me to sleep as I recall."

"This is no fairy tale my friend. The powers exist. They are being gathered. Do you not feel the disturbance? People are agitated with not a clue as to why. Our world is about to dramatically change and unless we get involved, I fear we may be washed into a sea that has no shore." The wizard's face told Slad how serious he was.

"Alright, tell me what you want from me. Keep in mind I don't work for causes. I only work for gold, and if what you say is true, much will be needed to convince me." This time Ruairidh saw the serious expression on Slad's face.

"Today, after the noon observance, I am going to challenge the 'Wizards Gauntlet'. When all become aware of who I am, the entire body of the

'Crown' will come. I'm also sure they will impose some special restriction on me in exchange for my participation. When their eyes are all on me, you will access the Crowns coiffures. You will find more gold than you should hope to carry. But understand this; one opportunity is all you'll have. In exchange for this, I shall require your company in the retrieval of the powers of Olofen. Once accomplished, you keep all the gold and your part is over." Ruairidh extended his hand. Slad accepted it with a bright golden smile.

They sat working out the details of their plot until after the noon observance. Slad left. Ruairidh gathered a few items from Abdul and proceeded toward the gauntlet.

Ruairidh approached the stage noticing a larger crowd than before. Someone was already challenging the gauntlet, and judging from the cheers, was winning.

Ruairidh ran to the front of the crowd where a young wizard walked from the third level with a key in his hand. The crowd cheered again as the young man opened the fourth level. When he walked in, the door closed behind him. Instantly the crowd became silent. Nothing could be seen at this level, so everyone listened, intent on his progress. Within seconds a blood-curdling scream came from the chamber, with pleas for mercy before the sound was cut short.

Minutes seemed like hours until a wizard appeared. He opened the door. He looked in, and motioned for the slaves to enter. The wizard stood shaking his head as four slaves carried out four separate remains of the young wizard. The gauntlet had claimed its first victim. The crowd started to disperse until Ruairidh stepped forward shouting to the wizard on stage.

"I challenge the gauntlet! I desire to defeat the thing here and now!" Ruairidh's fist rose into the air. Some in the crowd realized who had spoken.

"Who raises this challenge?" The wizard on stage looked toward Ruairidh.

"Ruairidh is my name." He replied.

The crowd erupted into a mix of gasps and cheers. Everyone feared the name. They also knew his power. If anyone could defeat this gauntlet, undoubtedly Ruairidh would. They quickly re-assembled as more came pushing for a better view.

"You must wait here Ruairidh. The 'Crown' must be informed." The wizard left.

The crowd increased. Abdul appeared. The bazaar had totally emptied upon the news of Ruairidh's challenge.

Soon the nine members of the 'Crown' gathered before Ruairidh. The one with the long beard stepped forward to greet him.

"Ruairidh you honor us with your presence and your challenge. However, you must understand our misgivings about your participation. Your power is unequaled. In a contest such as this, we must adjust the rules to suit your advantage. Therefore, all fail safes, and all restrictions, will be removed from the first three levels. Also, your endeavor will require a price of admission. In return for this chance, you must give us your oath in the event you should not succeed, you will become a loyal member of the 'Crown'; subservient to its majority, subservient to its will. How say you sir?"

Ruairidh studied the man for a moment, and simply nodded his head. The crowd burst into cheers as many more flooded in. A document was produced stating the terms of the challenge. Ruairidh signed his name in a broad flourish. The crowd began chanting his name. Abdul joined in.

After the 'Crown' was properly seated, a gentleman wearing a black hooded robe opened the door of the first chamber. He motioned for Ruairidh to enter. Once inside, the hooded figure locked the door, while the onlookers gapped through slatted walls.

Ruairidh reached into his pocket and threw a purple dust into the air as all the crevices erupted with multi colored mist. The purple dust floated around Ruairidh, clearing all the mist in seconds. He had anticipated they would use all the fluids at once, so he had created the dust to neutralize every possible poison, and the creation worked extremely well. The crowd went wild. The members of the 'Crown' seemed unfazed, except for one woman who had a 'told you so' look on her face.

The next level had no walls, but multi-mirrored surfaces reflected many images of Ruairidh to the onlookers. They grew silent in anticipation for the threats to appear, when two opposing mirrored panels slid back, revealing on one side a Namhaid wearing a ring, and on the other side, another Namhaid wearing the same ring. The dilemma became immediately apparent to Ruairidh. Both Namhaid were real, and the rings were not. With one motion he aimed his wand at the Namhaid furthest away, while removing the scarf attached to the jawbone and flinging the weapon into the neck of the one almost upon him. The effect was amazing, witnessing one vaporized and the other beheaded simultaneously. The crowd became insane. They cheered in delirious approval. The 'Crown' remained silent, but now more of the assembled 'Crown' showed concern.

The third level door was opened. Ruairidh recognized the items on the table, a bone from the forearm of a fallen warrior, a vile of serpent's blood, and a blindfold. This meant only one thing; Medusa. He pulled on the blindfold and drank the blood, but when he picked up the bone wand he knew the thing to be worthless. The panel pulled back. The crowd screamed and turned their heads. Ruairidh felt the serpent's blood draw his hand toward the head full of snakes. He aimed the fake wand causing a blue fire to erupt from its tip, consuming the Medusa. He heard the crowd cheer and pulled off his blindfold. Now all of the 'Crown's' members looked confused. The eldest wizard seemed to recognize something new in all this but held his peace as Ruairidh approached the fourth challenge. A key materialized and Ruairidh grasp it. He handed the key over to the hooded attendant.

The hooded man opened the door and once Ruairidh was inside, he bolted the door. The crowd listened intently for any indication of what was happening. Ruairidh stood silent in the dark when before him appeared a choice of two rooms; one was a pool of water, the other was a pit of molten lava. He chose neither and waited.

The floor beneath him dissolved, so he levitated above a chasm of razor sharp crystals. The ceiling began to descend upon him, forcing him to choose. He realized now the rules had been reversed. 'Abandon' now meant 'stay', so he ignored the ceiling that passed through him.

When the apparition reached the floor, a door on the opposite side opened. He stepped through the door to a thunderous applause. The 'Crown' stood, but they did not share the crowds' enthusiasm. The eldest wizard gathered his golden robes and walked onto the stage beside Ruairidh.

"You are to be congratulated on your success Ruairidh. Now we have a simple riddle for you to answer and your challenge is over. I shall put to you a question. Being faced with betrayal in the third challenge and discovering the bone to be a fake, how did you manage the bones blue fire when your life and pride were at stake?"

The elder stepped back assured he had thwarted the wizard. Ruairidh realized the scope of the question, and for the first time pondered whether or not the Dorchadas was truly worth all this.

He looked to his friend Abdul, and to many other faces he recognized among the crowd. Finally he lowered his head. With his reply, he knew not only would history forever be altered, but the lives of thousands as well.

Slad was busy filling his extra large pockets with everything gold within reach. The locks used to secure the vault were a joke to him. Once he had knocked out the only two guards left in the building, he had made quick work of all seven seals.

His knowledge of the inner workings of a lock made him a man who couldn't be imprisoned. Now he was filling his sacks with enough gold to live like a king.

He heard the final cry of the crowd, and if he had counted correctly, the gauntlet was almost done. He finished filling the sacks. He tested their weight and indeed, it was all he could carry.

For a man so small, he was incredibly strong, and as he moved toward the door, he saw a blue diamond, bigger than his fist, lying on a silver pillow. He wrapped the jewel in his tunic, and though it was not gold, he couldn't resist.

He walked out of the trove. He descended the stairs and headed for the southern gate, as according to Ruairidh's plan. They would enter the Dorchadas and leave 'Olc Sonnach' for the last time, unobserved and unstoppable. He accidentally dropped a small gold bracelet onto the stair below, and for the first time in his life, he decided to leave it.

Ruairidh stood before the massive crowd looking into the eyes of his friends and his foes. He carefully studied the faces of the members of the 'Crown'. He wanted to remember each one so he could one day return and exact his full revenge on them all. Their faces looked empty. All seemed genuinely confused except for the elder who asked the question. Some whispered among them, looking lost as to what was next.

Ruairidh realized the elder had not asked the question agreed upon, but for some reason substituted his own. The elder was a wise man, because his question was the only one to have given Ruairidh reason to reflect.

"Do you provide an answer Ruairidh, or do you admit defeat?" The elder wizard smiled. His loathsome demeanor erased all doubt as Ruairidh realized his hate and desire to destroy them all, regardless of his quest.

Ruairidh stepped forward and spoke. "I did not need your bone wand, fake or real, you repugnant worm, because I have my own buried deep within my arm. My name is not Ruairidh. Ruairidh was the name of my young son apprentice. He died at the hands of your filthy 'High Justice' Medraut! My true name is Myrddin, and I will possess the Dorchadas!"

Chapter Thirteen / Mísheanmhar

The ribbon of red and gold crossed the evening sky because Nidhoggr flew so fast his invisibility could not keep pace with his wings. Only once before had he ever left the Yggdrasill tree unguarded. Only once before did the needs of others outweigh the need to protect that singular guardian of balance. Before, as now, he flew to the Làrach of Corriechatachan, rushing to aid a dying friend. His heart pumped his green blood into those gigantic wings at a massive pace and soon he was over the walls of the fortress and landing before the altar of Bast.

His mind called out "Taliesin! Where are you? Is she alright?"

"We're here under the Peristylium, Nidhoggr. She's dying. Fiadh has not moved since we found her." Taliesin shouted.

"What happened?" Nidhoggr asked softly.

"A trap had been set. Her presence unleashed a pit of vipers in the wind garden. The cat killed them all, but not before she was bitten. Fiadh and I were gathering food. When we came back, the kitten and its mother sat brooding over Cailleach's body. We've done everything we can. She hardly breathes!" Taliesin replied.

"Vipers, in this sanctuary of felines and how does any snake survive long enough for a trap to spring?" Nidhoggr surveyed the temple. He sensed no threat.

"A catch under the bench releases a door." Taliesin said, as he pointed to the seat.

"Our advance was anticipated. I'm not talking about Marrok or his wizard. Someone else knew we would come here. She's near death Nidhoggr! Her throat is swollen and she has stopped breathing!" He fell beside her body and lay his ear to her mouth.

"Reach into her mind Taliesin, reassure her. Tell her to hold on. We need more time." Nidhoggr extended his razor sharp claw and breathed white flame across its edge.

Taliesin pushed his thoughts deep into Cailleach's conscience. She was farther away than he had thought. He was struggling to reach her. Vague shadows crossed as he searched for Cailleach. He barely found her when an ethereal pulse materialized from within. Something powerfully evil was stalking her and trying to draw her away from life.

Cailleach became conscious in a world where the ground mirrored the sky. Purples, blues, and greens converged into a horizon of gold. The place she appeared undulated as if responding to her presence. She floated in a yellow mist as strange metallic shapes drifted by. She remained still but her thoughts acted like a beacon, drawing 'things' to her.

"Is someone here? Where am I? Who are you?" She thought. Silence followed her pleas until 'a thing' moved closer. A red vapor swirled, whispering a tortured name, 'Medraut'. Something horrible slithered nearer.

"Cailleach, are you with me Cailleach? Come back to me! You're going the wrong way!"

"Taliesin, tell me what to do?" Cailleach turned towards Taliesin's voice.

The vile presence of evil reached out to corrupt her. She bolted to Taliesin.

Almost instantly, a golden glow pushed away the mist, revealing Taliesin 'the eagle' spreading his wings to gather Cailleach close to him.

She ran to his embrace and buried her face into his chest. Taliesin recognized the monster that nearly captured her. He swallowed hard at a sight he never thought to behold. He led her to a safe place and held her hand while he reached back to Nidhoggr.

Nidhoggr placed his talon on Cailleach's throat to cut a small hole. Her chest immediately expanded. Her body responded to the precious air her lungs were breathing. His heated claw kept the wound from bleeding. Everything depended on Taliesin to bring her back.

"I found her. She's safe for the moment." Taliesin 'the man' opened his eyes. She was returning to her healthy natural color. He looked to the dragon. Nidhoggr knew things were serious.

"Taliesin, What have you seen?" Nidhoggr dipped his claw into a pool, cooling the talon in a cloud of steam.

"A presence within her mind was something I never knew to be possible. " He stared past the dragon as if he was watching the apparition slither towards him.

"What?" Nidhoggr asked.

"The leviathan was there, and the only power known to create a titan inside the firmament of divine energy is the most diabolical sorcerer who ever lived."

"Medraut!" The dragon finished what Taliesin was thinking.

"We now have reason to fear. She and her child are not safe, no matter our intention. We must appeal to Epona. Such magic is beyond me. Flesh, blood, stone, scale and fur I can sink my teeth into or incinerate, but necromancers don't burn or die. " Nidhoggr became agitated and looked skyward as if he expected something might attack.

"Cailleach is the only one who can find Epona now. We, at best, can guard her until she wakes. Aid or battle is for her to determine. The power of her decision is why we are here. Olofen knew this day would come. Only the purest soul will be able to deliver us from Armageddon. You and I must make sure she gets the chance," said Taliesin.

They lifted the body and carried her inside the temple. Nidhoggr lit the torches as

Taliesin placed her form on the polished stone altar. He covered her with the thick red velvet cloth adorning the chantry.

Her hair had lost some of its deep color. Her black locks turned brown in the torchlight. A change was taking place.

The turquoise temple was bathed in crimson flame as Nidhoggr finished. Fiadh lay down at the foot of the altar breathing in heavy sighs.

Taliesin became the eagle. He raised his golden wings over his head stretching his beak to the heavens. Nidhoggr did likewise. Together they reached out to Epona for help.

Outside a strange wind kicked-up leaves from the courtyard. Overhead, the cliffs released a deluge of water onto the fortress below. Strong downward gusts brought a barrage of loose sticks and stones seemingly aimed at the temple. Black clouds came from the west, blotting out the sun.

Soon the rain fell in sideways sheets obscuring the plaza entirely and bolts of lightning brought pounding thunder, shaking the foundations of the castle.

Nidhoggr and Taliesin seemed lost in thought. They gave no indication to the immensity of the tempest. Fiadh sighed. She trembled at every sound. The torches danced in their sockets with each vibration.

Then a distant noise brought them both back. They opened their eyes, and again the feeble intonation occurred. The faint tinkling of a bell somehow carried over the monstrous discord of the storm.

"It's coming from outside the wall!" Taliesin said as he strode toward the sound.

Nidhoggr followed him into the gale.

They crossed the courtyard and stood at the edge of the pool. Taliesin reached for a slender totem. He pulled it to an angle. This set off a movement of gears and cogs, pushing a stone bridge over the water, and linking to the gate.

The bell rang again as Taliesin crossed over. He threw the bolt to pull the massive door open.

A fragile old man wearing a conical hat stood in the pouring rain. His eyes were slanted. His skin was a brownish yellow. His wispy gray moustache blended into a beard dripping steadily onto his sandals.

He grinned up at the eagle and dragon as if they were exactly who he expected. He smiled showing only three upper teeth in an otherwise toothless mouth. He lifted his hand to shake a small bell, which tinkled softly yet somehow pierced the din of the raging storm.

Nidhoggr vanished. Not knowing what to make of this strange intruder, he decided it would be better if he had an advantage. Taliesin stood transfixed by the ancient fellow. He finally sent his thoughts to him.

"Who are you and what is your purpose?" The eagle asked.

The old man stepped into the fortress and marveled at the structures.

"I'm Jakobar. I'm here to help the girl?" He turned looking the eagle squarely in his eyes.

"Take me to Cailleach." He gracefully motioned to proceed.

Taliesin closed the gate and bolted it. He silently led him to the temple, where

Cailleach lay unconscious. Jakobar walked up to the altar. He spoke in his own tongue; words with rhyme, yet sounding mysteriously powerful and calm. He reached out over her body and threw a silver dust, which floated into a sparkling blue cloud over the altar.

He danced in a extremely low stance while stretching his arms over the girl in an almost catlike posture. Nidhoggr watched unseen. He searched his mind for the name Jakobar.

Jakobar sank to the floor. He crossed his thin legs. His hands extended out, then upward, holding his ring fingers to his thumbs. He became silent.

For the rest of the night, he remained motionless. In the early hours of morning, when the storm subsided, and first light peeked from beneath the clouds, he opened his eyes and stood.

"Many things we must do now. Cailleach understands we're here and what happened to her. Coinneach is extremely anxious. He fears for their safety." Jakobar walked toward the courtyard.

"Who's Coinneach?" Taliesin asked.

"Her son, he's such an incredible child. He's eager to make the acquaintance of you and your invisible friend." The old man kept walking as he spoke.

Nidhoggr materialized.

"He wants to meet us? How did you meet him?" The dragon asked.

"Oh I didn't. He met me! I was reaching for Cailleach when he popped into my view. He's been using some of his own magic to keep her safe. Quiet the wizard he is already!"

Jakobar sat down on the same bench Cailleach had used. When he did, a hinge fell open releasing a trap door beneath. Jakobar got down on his knees. He reached into the opening. He pulled his hand out holding a small greenish brown plant with yellow leaves.

"This is why the snakes remained undiscovered. This herb puts them into a trance which is only broken when fresh air stirs them. It also masks their smell. Even if the cats had been looking for them, it's unlikely they would have found them." Jakobar tapped his chin seemingly lost in thought.

"But enough of this, I need bark from the east side of a tree recently struck by lightning. Scrape the husk at least three inches deep. You're to be gathering an ample amount to make several poultices, plus a bit for tea. Come on now let's move, time is against us!" Jakobar ordered.

Both Taliesin and Nidhoggr did immediately as they were told, flying out of the fortress in separate directions. They kept in thought with each other as they searched. Thanks to the recent storm, a freshly struck willow was smoldering nearby.

Nidhoggr summoned Taliesin. Together they stripped the tree. Nidhoggr used his long teeth to sink deep into the wood. When they flew back into the courtyard they found Jakobar arranging things on a table just outside the temple. He showed no notice of their return.

"This should be more than enough, well done!" He commented without looking up.

"I could use one of your feathers 'sir eagle'." He gazed up as Taliesin plucked one from his lower wing.

"Thank you, I hope you don't mind me taking over here, but time is fleeting. And you 'sir dragon', a scale would be most appreciated." Nidhoggr did not hesitate to remove a large bluish green scale from his waist. Jakobar accepted, and bowed reverently in doing so.

"Now my friends I ask for your patience with diligent indulgence by allowing me to work alone as I strive to save this poor girl and her son." He smiled, and turned his back, saying nothing more.

Nidhoggr and Taliesin left the altar room. Outside the temple they stood staring out beyond the fortress. Each of them was afraid to voice their thoughts in fear of bringing bad luck to more bad luck. Hours went by. The day turned to night.

Inside, Jakobar was communicating with Cailleach while applying her medicine.

"Cailleach, some concerned friends are determined to have you in better health. You must fight hard. Listen to my words! The gift Taliesin gave you the first day, the 'Gait of Power', you must use it. Run toward my voice!" He reached out until he felt her moving.

"Wonderful, now, pick up your knees, and lower your head. Run with longs strides...yes, yes...your strength is returning!"

"I'm here Cailleach...reach out to me!" Jakobar shouted.

Cailleach saw the form of a man looking black of skin, with the gentlest smile she had ever seen. She ran full speed until she approached within feet of this apparition. She stood breathless, yet renewed in strength.

"Who are you? Where am I?" She stared deep into his face.

"I am the one who started this quest you have found yourself on. I am the one who encouraged you to continue in spite of the dangers. I am the one who separated the forces because one became obsessed with power. I am the one who relented when another chose to overcome. Many names dear child, but for now, you may call me Jakobar. Later you will know my real name, when it is time to bring on the tempest."

Cailleach became silent. She waited. She was afraid this being might not be as gentle and kind as he appeared. His smile grew as he could read her anxiety.

"I'm not the enemy Cailleach. While we are alone, I need to teach you a means in which to channel your powers. These methods must be known only to you, so best we do them in this spiritual domain I have created."

With a flourish of his slender hands the mist around them changed into a bamboo garden with small ponds of brightly colored fish. Delicate carvings of eagles and dragons stood behind thin curtains of crystal water, cascading over jade and ivory fountains. Cailleach could hear insects, birds, and distant animals' noises she didn't recognize. Her bare feet rested in soft sand, which appeared to have been raked carefully in one direction, giving her the inclination not to move for fear of disturbing its perfect form. She felt strangely calm in this garden.

"No other being can see us, hear our thoughts, or witness our actions here." His face changed. He now resembled the old yellow man in the conical hat.

Cailleach blinked. She kept her silence until she touched her flat belly. "My baby...what has happened?"

"Your child is still in your physical body, but in your spiritual body, it is separate. Would you care to meet your son?"

"My son! Yes of course...please!" Cailleach now believed she was dreaming.

Jakobar pointed to his left. A young spirit appeared not fully formed yet the eyes and mouth had shape. He walked towards Cailleach.

"He has not entered the physical world, but he consciously participates in your daily life. Cailleach, this is your son." Jakobar motioned toward the spirit.

The child diminished until only a 'sparkle' hovered above her face and softly nudged her cheek. She could feel a world of emotion in that slight touch. She stared transfixed until the light faded.

She started to speak but the small man turned. He directed her attention away from her questions.

"We must quickly prepare you for the maelstroms on the horizon." He walked to her side, taking her right hand in his.

"These middle and ring fingers are how we connect to the power which exist all around us." He held his own hand up and focused on some unseen point.

"If used with good intent, you can communicate with any creature by doing just so. Used in concentrated focus, one can defend against even the most powerful spell." He lowered his arm and helped Cailleach hold hers in the same manner.

"When needed, you can tap into power with one hand while channeling out to the other, like this." Jakobar reached out to a large tree with his right arm extended until a green pulse of liquid light began to flow into his body. He then reached out with his left hand and expelled the energy toward a bare rock, covering it in moss and small delicate flowers. Cailleach smiled. She marveled at such wonderful magic.

"You may reverse this process, but for now, I think I'll leave the flowers." He smiled showing his three teeth.

"It is also possible to absorb with both hands or expel with both hands. I would suggest you don't. Absorbing with both hands can destroy the source of the power you channel, while expelling with both hands depletes your own personal power, even to the point of your own destruction." He quickly turned to walk in another direction.

"You may reach out long distances to mentally touch or communicate with others." He extended his arms outward with the palms up, and then touched his thumbs to those same fingers.

"Just close your eyes. Release your thoughts until the internal conversation has ceased. Go ahead, reach out, can you find someone?" Jakobar insisted.

Cailleach closed her eyes. She realized there was indeed a constant conversation going on in her head. It took a long time, but when all was silent, she attempted to find her father. Moments later, she opened her eyes. She nervously turned to Jakobar.

"My father! He is in danger! We've got to help him!" She grabbed Jakobar by his small shoulders.

"Do not worry child, he is with good company. Few could stand against them. If you distract him; you will put him in greater jeopardy. For now believe powers keep him and his friends under protection. But the truth above all is none of you are safe until 'you' dear girl complete the gathering of the seven." Jakobar again turned. He walked several paces before he reversed back, and produced two objects.

"Your friends have given you special gifts, and I now give to you. You must never acknowledge they gave them, nor even mention their existence. Their power exists totally in the fact they were given freely, without question, for the sole purpose of helping their friend. Do not diminish their gift by divulging their actuality or source." With this he produced a giant gold feather and an equally large green scale.

"This scale must be absorbed into the body over your navel. It will provide protection against an assault of black energy. This feather will give you the ability to move freely into and out of the firmament. It also provides the ability to suspend you if needed for short periods of time." As he said this, the scale and feather floated to her. The scale faded into her abdomen. The feather disappeared into her shoulder. The yellow skinned man once more turned away. He walked several paces before turning to face Cailleach.

"One more thing, my presence here at this time and place must not be known. I will abolish the memory from your friends, but I cannot remove it from you if you're to use the knowledge I've given. So for your sake, the sake of your friends, and your son, do not remind them or speak of me in any way. Use your powers only when needed. Remember your greatest strength is in the fact that others have always underestimated you, and, oh yes, something else, the bone wand must also be absorbed in order to complete your transformation."

Cailleach no longer stood still. She walked toward Jakobar. "I can't...I won't...it's a horrible thing. The power is uncontrollable!" She seemed unwavering.

"Such potential can be truly horrible, and a dreaded responsibility, but you have already conquered it, by choosing not to use it. You must take the bone into your arm so no other can remove it from you. You have the power to control it. Use the capability to protect all you hold dear. Don't risk losing everything from the fear of it." Jakobar looked ready to go when he spoke again.

"The sword that Máthair Shúigh gave you can be used in many ways, but the ultimate purpose is to separate darkness from light if they ever chose to occupy the same space. Balance is essential to existence. The sword is the key to the door, which separates them. I will meet you again my dear. Keep faith and strong heart, don't give in to fear, be mindful all kind words are not to be trusted, but trust your instincts and protect the powers you've been given."

With this he changed back into the tall black man with the incredible smile.

"I'll be watching you Cailleach...I'll be watching..."

He disappeared and so did the garden.

She felt a strange heaviness on her chest as darkness consumed everything around her.

Nidhoggr stood outside the temple doors staring beyond the fortress walls.

Taliesin had returned to Cailleach's side to monitor her condition.

A voice came into Nidhoggr's mind.

"Hello dragon, why the long face?" The question was followed by restrained laughter.

"Elrick I'm not in the mood for your stupid jokes. I hope you brought some information for me or my patience with you is at an end!" Nidhoggr sneered as he looked into a cloud of dust materializing beside him.

"All right...all right...jeez you'd think a man dead and cursed for so long would be allowed some morsel of tolerance. It's only humor my good dragon, and wouldn't hurt your scaly hide to lighten up just once in a..."

"Tell me!!" Nidhoggr threatened.

"Right, Marrok is almost to the lake as he suffered greatly from the attack in Saltus. He's being conveyed by a doppelganger of the wizards, a funny sight to see but, oh yes, you don't see humor...never mind...and there's the presence of three villagers in the valley of Epona, attacked by a wolf and are in danger of engaging the whole pack if they stay, also a huge horse is with them, and no ...not the one you're thinking. Also, another interesting piece of information I know you'd love to hear." Elrick stood grinning from ear to ear waiting for a response.

The dragon stared unmoving.

"What?" He growled.

"Guess." Elrick put his hands together in anticipation.

"Ghost, I will eat your bones and deposit them into the deepest darkest grave of a Namhaid if you don't speak now!" Fire flew from both nostrils.

"You know, you just spoil every possible..."

"Tell me!!!" Fire erupted from Nidhoggr's mouth searing the cloud of dust where Elrick was standing.

"Ruairidh returned to 'Olc Sonnach' and obtained the Dorchadas. He and others are preparing to attack as soon as they locate Cailleach, but the best bit of news I've saved for last..." He waited...waited... (Silence)

"Oh what's the use...Ruairidh is not Ruairidh at all, but in truth he's 'Myrddin'. It seems that Medraut, who mistakenly thought he murdered Myrddin as ordered by the 'Crown', killed Ruairidh. So Ruairidh, who was actually Myrddin, who was in fact Ruairidh's father, plotted his revenge by assuming his son's identity, allowing all to think Myrddin was dead and Ruairidh was his surviving lowly apprentice...Am I boring you dragon lips?" Elrick seemed to have lost his fear.

"I'm listening with ignited breath." He growled.

"It is rumored that Medraut somehow crossed over into the firmament of divine energy but no one is saying how or why. Evidently he still walks in the flesh when he wants to, so the 'Crown' uses this rumor to hold absolute control over every creature, magical or otherwise. I believe our worlds are going to collide soon. If you, or the eagle, or the girl have a plan, now would be the time to share." Elrick finished.

"I'm not so stupid as to give you any information Viking. I know the loyalties you pretend for such selfish desires as you are chained to with little regard for anyone else." Nidhoggr turned away.

"That's not true Nidhoggr, I do care. You and the eagle and that sweet girl may well be the only real friends I have. Your disdain and total lack of friend-ship in these matters hurts. It hurts me to my bones!" Elrick shouted.

Then it happened. First, just a cough, next a snicker, then a chuckle until it became a full all-out earth-shaking laugh which totally disabled Nidhoggr, dropping him to the ground until he was laying with his feet up in the air and barely able to breathe.

"What was funny? Now you laugh? I was serious! Dragon, you really should learn some manners!" Elrick vanished in a huff.

Taliesin came swiftly outside looking for the source of the disturbance. He found Nidhoggr upside down gasping for air.

"Are you alright Nidhoggr? Taliesin changed into human form and ran to the dragon's side.

"Yes I'm fine…it's just that Viking ghost, he's so funny sometimes."

Taliesin appeared completely confused.

"Forget about him." The dragon up-righted himself and stood to shake the dust off.

"He did have some important news. Your fears were well founded. Medraut is moving into the divine realm." Nidhoggr grimaced in pain when he brushed his side. A scale was missing.

"Hmm…must have lost it when I fell over." He looked around for it; but to no avail.

Taliesin stroked his chin in thought.

"Does this mean Medraut is dead?" The eagle asked.

"Not according to what I've heard. He still appears in the flesh when he desires. Incredibly dark magic exists within this creature. He's found something or managed to tap into depths beyond anything known before." Nidhoggr touched his wound and flinched.

"If Medraut is able to walk into the realm at will, then his body must be left somewhere behind and that is his weakness. We find his abandoned flesh while he crosses into the realm, and we can stop him." Taliesin said.

"I saw his form in the other world. It wasn't curiosity that brought it so close. It wanted control of her life force. If I hadn't intervened, Cailleach would not have survived. Worse still, he is aware of us. We now have more enemies to add to our list." Taliesin lamented.

"I'm afraid there's more news. Ruairidh is not the apprentice we thought; in fact he's not even Ruairidh. Medraut killed Ruairidh. Ruairidh was the son of Myrddin. Myrddin assumed his son's identity to seek vengeance. His desire for the seven powers is all about destroying Medraut." Nidhoggr spoke plainly.

"Which means Marrok comes for us, Myrddin intends to take the talismans by any force necessary, and Medraut stalks our very dreams to do likewise. At least we've got a good lead and a secure stronghold for now." Taliesin could see the dread in his friend's eyes.

"What?"

"I'm afraid we shall have company sooner than you may wish. Myrddin obtained the Dorchadas. He will no doubt be heading in our direction as soon as he gathers his forces."

Taliesin rubbed his chin again.

"Well I didn't think this was going to be quite so complicated, even though I knew what was at stake. I just hope Cailleach awakens soon. If not I'll risk carrying her and Fiadh to safer haven. Would you consider joining us Nidhoggr?" Taliesin placed his hand on the dragon's talon.

"I was afraid you might ask. My allegiances are to Yggdrasill, but should your quest fail there will be nothing left to guard. I knew this when I came here, so I sealed the cave and placed certain proximity charms around the tree to alert me if any should come too close. I have been your friend Taliesin for longer than these mountains have stood here. I would not let you risk everything without me. I'm at your service, and I pledge my life in protection of that young girl. I do not fear death. I welcome the chance to fight at your side." Nidhoggr bowed gracefully.

Taliesin smiled and did likewise.

"I knew you'd come. Now, we must try to awaken Cailleach or prepare her for flight as is. If you bear Fiadh and the belongings, I can carry Cailleach. We shall go straight to the Outlands; there is no other choice. I may easily fit in, but I'm afraid you will need to stay invisible for the duration, or at least as long as you're in the city." They both nodded.

Taliesin turned back into his eagle form, and then proceeded to walk back into the temple. Nidhoggr pointed to a place on Taliesin's shoulder.

"You lost a feather."

He looked at the spot Nidhoggr pointed to.

"So I did. You lost a scale. I lost a feather. We seem to be falling apart old man." They both smiled.

Taliesin looked at Nidhoggr and pointed to his mouth. "You've got some bark between your teeth."

"Really, where'd that come from?" Nidhoggr asked as they entered the temple.

CHAPTER FOURTEEN / THE SPÀIRN

For several hours Hamish listened to the noises. He sensed; something, or things, getting closer. He kept his nerve and alerted no one. Arthair had fallen asleep and softly snored. Whatever roamed beyond the firelight became aware Hamish watched.

Later in the early morning, clouds parted, allowing the full moon access into the valley. The open glen lit up in a bath of pale light and Hamish realized how dire their circumstances had become. At least thirty wolves encroached.

He searched for the alpha male among their ranks and determined that one large wolf near the front kept them all in check, with a crimson fur and yellow eyes; he stood out from the grays.

The wolves noticed Hamish taking aim and with one accord fell into a quick trot towards the camp. Hamish tossed a rock at Arthair; up righting him. He immediately sensed the danger and moved over to Hamish's side.

Arthair pulled his blade out of its sheath. He crawled to the door of the hut and opened it to alert Betrain, who was already strapping on her sword. She also sported four small knives; one on each hip and one strapped to each leg. Her hair, tied up and stuffed under a tight red scarf gave her the appearance of a dangerous woman Arthair hardly recognized. She pulled a bottle out of her sack when Arthair heard the crossbow sing out.

Somewhere several hundred feet away, a wolf cried out in pain and the pack abandoned him.

"I missed the leader, got the one next to him instead." Hamish had already reloaded. He stood up to get better aim by purchasing on a tree branch. The wolves had scattered but quickly gathered again, this time forming a single line and heading straight for the hut.

"Betrain you better lock yourself in, I don't think we're gonna be able to hold'em!" Arthair shouted.

Seconds later, the beasts, within twenty paces, converged. Hamish managed to hit another one and proceeded to reload as the pack surrounded them, pressing near, slowing their pace, and exposing their full brace of razor sharp teeth. Blood and saliva poured from their jaws in anticipation of the kill. Hamish fumbled for his arrow when the entire pack leaped. Arthair stood brandishing his sword.

Betrain burst out the door screaming so loud Hamish almost dropped his weapon. The wolves immediately halted inches from the fire. This gave Betrain the second she needed, and with one motion she tossed the contents of the bottle into the flame.

An explosion ripped through the demons, killing almost half, while setting most ablaze. Hamish and Arthair were thrown back. A wolf attacked Betrain. She lunged toward the beast shoving her short sword into its gaping jaws. Arthair waded into the fray making quick work of the few animals still lingering. Stephen kicked the dead carcasses of two wolves into the blaze before he turned to stomp another foolish enough to attack. Hamish fired several more shots at the retreating wounded that managed to survive. They stood quietly for the next while until their eyes and ears told them the pack had gone. Arthair broke the silence.

"My God woman yer one hell of a fighter is all I can say. That was the gutsiest move I've ever seen!" He regarded the lady who had saved his life with newfound respect.

"Aye Betrain, you scared the shite out of me and the lot of them as well! If I hadn't witnessed with my own eyes, I'd never believe it happened by neither man nor woman!" Hamish shook, almost laughing.

Betrain stood frozen and crazed clutching her blades tight, with eyes wide and breathing in quick short breaths. Arthair walked over to her. He massaged her wrist until she dropped the knives and broke down sobbing into his arms.

"Everything's alright Betrain, the worst is over. They're gone." Arthair motioned for Hamish to investigate the surroundings. Stephen stood grunting and pawing the flattened corpse of his last victim. Arthair held Betrains face in his hands and stared deep into her eyes.

"You're one hell of a woman!" Then he kissed her, and she kissed him back.

Hamish dragged the dead bodies to the edge of the lake. Using some of Betrains liquid, he set them on fire. The crimson wolf wasn't among them.

In the distance, he heard the remaining pack, howling in anguish, as the flames grew higher. He stood with Stephan, watching the flesh burn and the smoke rise.

He had never come so close to dying, and something inside him awakened. He thought himself a brave man before this night, instead his terror reached a level beyond anything he ever experienced, and the experience changed him.

The smoke rose into the cliffs, catching the wind above the mountaintop. The fire burned away, leaving only charred bones smoldering in a black pile of ash. The morning light peaked over the forest as Hamish lay down beside his horse. He fell into the deepest sleep of his life.

Sometime around mid-morning Arthair roused Hamish. He brought him some breakfast. He also had sugar for Stephan.

"Wake up boys we need to move out as soon as you two can manage." Arthair, now clean and washed, appearing more rested.

"How's Betrain?" Hamish asked as he ate the porridge Arthair had brought.

"She's slept, eaten, and I think, come to grips with everything. She's better. I don't believe she had any idea what she was capable of. No one does until it comes down to the moment. I'll tell you this, next fight I'm in, put her in my corner, and pity the poor fool who thinks she's an easy target!" Arthair proudly bragged.

"Aye, that's one feisty woman Arthair. I've lost all doubt as to whether we're up to this. The three of us..." Stephan grunted. "Aye ...four of us make a formidable lot. So what's the plan? Which way do we precede?" Hamish quickly finished his food.

"There's some tracks going southwest, with drag marks like a sled, probably to carry whatever she managed to collect out here. She left home with barely the clothes on her back, so now she needs a cart to manage her burden. The girl has a determination like her mother." Arthair appeared sad and sullen. Hamish sensed it. He quickly changed the subject.

"What about Stephan, he showed himself last night and not a scratch on him." Stephan shook his head in agreement and pawing the ground in pride.

"So we'll be on Arthair. We've got your daughter showing us how things are done out here. Let's make her proud eh?" Hamish stood and slapped Arthair on the back. The three of them walked to the camp.

Betrain had everything packed. She even managed to straighten the hut. She smiled as they approached, and though somewhat strained beneath her reserved manner, she seemed as solid as a rock.

"Good morning Hamish, I hope you got enough rest."

"Aye, I slept like a baby, and now I'm ready to take on whatever needs be. I think Stephan is too. Let's get him loaded so we can move out." Hamish began to burden his horse.

"Betrain, what concoction of liquid did you use last night. I recognize the smell." Hamish asked.

"Aye, would to a man. It was fathers own special brand of pure whisky. He made a strong deadly brew, and died before he was 30 years old. I loved him with all my heart but neither mother nor I had the strength to pull him away from the bottle. Now what I'm left of him is the barrels he made. I suppose I can finally say some good came out of it, but I'd trade all back for the life he wasted. Got more when needs be, an' don't think for one minute yer gonna be drinking any. This stuff can put any man in the dirt before his time, besides; I need you both sober and strong if we're ta finding Cailleach!" Betrain quickly dropped the subject as finished. The men did likewise. Betrain picked up one of the books she brought and started to scan the pages.

"Been reading about this valley. The Viking lost his life after he stole a ring from a sacred temple. Somewhere between the hills is an apple orchard. The tale is, a wolf killed him in this glen and a curse got laid upon him because of his theft. No one would touch his bones for fear of bringing the bane on themselves." Betrain paused for comment, but the men remained silent.

"What of it Arthair, are these books fairy tales?" She wanted an answer.

"After last night Betrain, nothing will seem beyond reason. Those wolves acted unlike wild animals. They came at us like warriors in battle. They thought with one mind controlled. If you think the slightest possibility these stories are true, then so do I!"

"Aye, me too Betrain, I'm not one to believe in fantasy, but Arthair is right. That wasn't a normal pack of wolves. Something's afoot in this valley beyond our sensibilities. I'll wager we've just scratched the surface of things to come." Hamish put the bridle on Stephan.

Arthair went to the brook to get water when he found a marker with strange symbols.

"Over here…it's a kind of grave." He fell to his knees to examine the stone.

"Something is written, not like normal writing, Betrain, what do you think?"

She walked over and knelt beside Arthair.

"Viking script, maybe runes, nothing I can decipher."

Arthair started digging with his hands. He soon uncovered a bone.

"Could she?" He couldn't finish.

"Not at all, this bone is ancient, almost dust." Hamish squatted down.

"These have been placed here recently. Someone reburied them." Hamish said.

They all sat up as if they had the same idea at once.

"You don't think she moved the Vikings bones?" Betrain asked what the others silently thought.

"Well, if anyone had the guts, she held too much regard for human life to leave something sacred undone. I just hope she didn't bring anything upon herself," Arthair said.

They agreed and added their own reverence.

Arthair carefully placed the bone back saying a short prayer in doing so. All three spoke 'Amen' as they turned to walk away.

They loaded Stephan, fastened the door of the hut, and set out. The day faired crisp with a chill, yet bright and beautiful. A few breezes from the northeast sliced like a knife through their clothes, and even this seemed refreshingly welcome after the night before.

The trees, splendent in full color, had the three travelers agreeing that none of them had ever seen a more beautiful day in their lives. Stephan also trotted happier as he lifted his huge hooves. He wanted to prance with every step. About mid-afternoon they approached an ancient orchard with one remaining tree at the edge of the open field. They made their way towards it.

"Before you woke me last night Hamish, I dreamed of Cailleach. She appeared different, with lighter hair, and determined with strength, the like I've never seen. Her features had softened. She didn't speak, yet I sensed her concern for me. Her presence was so real." Arthair spoke softly.

"A good sign I'd say Arthair. Yer gut is telling ya, she's still reaching out. Who knows? Maybe she is. You two must have a strong connection. Each step we take and every trace we come across convinces me she's alive. We'll soon find her or her us?" Hamish smiled.

They came to the tree. Stephan stretched up and pulled himself an apple. Hamish did the same.

"Hmm, for such an ugly apple, the taste is the sweetest I've ever had." Hamish reached for another one, as did the rest.

"Oh my, they're so delicious!" Betrain exclaimed. "Gather some. I'll make a crumble tonight."

Arthair sat down. He glanced back towards the valley.

"What kind of man was this Viking? Where did he come from? Did he have a family? Why here? He tossed his life away. He died alone in this place. What's worth that?" Arthair asked.

"Most men don't think like you Arthair. You put value on family and home, not gold or jewel. Some desire power above all things only to become servants to their lusts. Perhaps the Viking died when he lost sight of his own reality. In his mind, a better world existed beyond his grasp. People in our village suffer because they fret over every aspect of their day. Believing only their death and crossing into heaven will give them peace. Why would anyone want to throw away their lives, condemning themselves to be miserable, convinced they were unworthy to enjoy life? I've known self-pity, but I'll tell you this, after last night's brush with death, I don't intend to waste another moment being sorry for myself. Every breath I take now is a gift which I shall use to find your daughter and make a better life for everyone I care about." Betrain said.

She winked at Arthair. Hamish couldn't help but notice. Betrain pulled down another apple. She bit into it with relish.

"Have you read the beginning of 'The Canter of Nould' Betrain?" Hamish asked.

"Not yet, I will when we camp, and I have given some thought to the name of the book. If you literally translate the title, 'The Gait of Nould', Nould being a bible word meaning 'would not', the words are senseless." Betrain responded.

"I think someone is declaring Elrick to be a person that didn't conform to expected behavior. A Viking is fierce and romantic. They seduce women. They take what they want. They live by the sea. This Viking traveled alone, and moved further inland. Maybe he was a 'poof'!" Hamish laughed.

"Now that's a stretch! The man dies a horrible death in the middle of nowhere. He suffers the indignity of not receiving a proper burial and you call him a 'poof' because he doesn't conform to your idea of what a Viking should be. Come on Hamish; let's know a little more before we label the man." Betrain chided.

"I'm just responding to the title. Either way I was just stirring yer kettle ta tell if ya still had some meat in the stew." Hamish laughed and so did Arthair.

"You boys aren't growing up anytime soon. You'd think near death experiences would've grayed a hair or two, but not you chuid. I don't know whether to scold ye or just take ma hand off yer face." Betrain stood as if to do so, causing the men to fall back. This made her laugh.

"Com'on an get up, we got more to do than neb about here." She was enjoying herself.

They gathered the apples and soon they were off again.

The scrub at the foot of the crags encroached onto their right side. The beginnings of a forest began to their left. By end of day they approached the remains of a steading which appeared to have been struck by lightning. They slowed while cautiously moving closer. Stephan seemed ill at ease with the place. Arthair walked up and placed his hand on the glassy surface of stone

"What do ya make of this? I've never seen lightning do this. The ground is burnt beyond the grass. It looks like fused metal from Alistair's furnace." Arthair scratched his head.

"And this you have to see to believe!" Betrain shouted. She stood at the foot of a tree untouched by the force, which blackened everything within twenty feet of it.

"It's absolutely pristine! How is that possible?" Arthair and Hamish walked to her side. Hamish reached to touch, but Betrain grabbed his hand.

"I wouldn't Hamish. Whatever protects this tree may not understand your intentions." Betrain said.

Hamish agreed.

"So, we have more mysteries. We'll need to camp before too long, but I don't fancy being near this place. Something bad has happened here, and judging from the shape of things, not many days ago. We'll keep moving and find accommodations elsewhere." Arthair said.

Arthair walked past the tree giving it wide berth. Betrain and Hamish did likewise. They all proceeded without word. The wood converged to the crags and stopped. They unloaded Stephan and pitched their camp near the edge. A stream flowed under the scrub making itself known only by the sound. Another noise emanated from the forest, unlike any bird or animal they had heard before.

It sounded like "chi...cho...chi...aalwa..aalwa.." Then was answered by "whoo-ta...whoo-ta...nee."

"What do ye make of that Arthair? Are those birds are talking to each other?" Hamish stood listening.

"Aye, you're right Hamish. I'm no expert, but that doesn't sound like an animal. More like human voice's I'd say." Arthair put his hand to his sword.

"We have to make our camp here. Tomorrow we'll decide if we want to venture into these woods. I don't think we have a choice. This is where the tracks lead." Arthair said.

"It can't be worse than a pack of wolves. I'm ready for the next battle. What say you men?" Betrain flourished her own sword.

"Aye, me too, but I think it can wait till morning, besides, we'll have a better go of it out here if anything attacks." Hamish tried to calm the bravado.

"Agreed." said Arthair.

"Agreed." said Betrain and they sheathed their weapons.

The shelter was raised and a fire tendered, as Betrain pulled dried beef and potatoes from a sack. She sliced a few wild onions into water, emptied the skin, and handed it to Hamish.

"Would ya mind dear n' fetch me some more water for the broth. Somewhere over there a burn runs by the sound of it." She smiled as Hamish grabbed the empty skin.

"If ya run into something just call out. We all need to stay within reach of each other." Arthair warned.

"Don't worry, I'll scream like baby if I come across anything." Hamish grinned.

"You do and you'll be acting yer age." Betrain chided. They all laughed as Hamish threw his hands up and nodded. He walked to the edge of the scrub and looked for an entrance.

The scrub ran into the forest and back around the crags. He noticed a rabbit dart through a small opening only as it disappeared. He went over and lay down to view how far the burrow went. He could make out a clearing to the creeks edge. He decided this was his best bet.

Hamish pulled out his knife hacking away enough bracken to pull himself in. The hole widened after he was a few feet inside. The brambles were thick, thorny, and perfect for small creatures to hide. Not so good for full-grown men crawling on their bellies. He tore his shirt and pants as he pulled himself to the place where the ground dropped away. He craned his head over the edge to spy the burn at least eight feet below him. This meant he would have to devise a method of getting down and climbing back up. The banks seemed solid with plenty of stone to grasp and he decided to drop down, besides he was within earshot of his mates. Hamish knew any teasing from them, should he not make it back up, would be worth the gamble.

He gripped a strong root below the bank to pull himself out so he could drop his legs into the gorge. He hung for a moment and plummeted down to the sandy ground. It was a perfect landing with one flaw. When he looked up he knew he had misjudged the depth. The root he had swung from was out of reach from even the highest purchase he could manage.

"Oh well, another laugh at his expense might be in order." He said to himself.

He filled the skin, and then quenched his own thirst. The water was really sweet and revived him almost as soon as he drank. He sat watching the scratches on his arms and legs close. They were healing before his eyes. Renewed strength coursed through his veins. He opened his shirt only to view an old knife wound to his shoulder had changed. Still there, but looking slightly healed.

His first thought, 'Man, I should've brought more skins!'

He drank his sufficiency until he could hold no more. He stared up to the root thinking he might easily jump the height when his attention caught a flash of blue and the heel of a man who had been watching from further down the bank.

Hamish strapped on the skin and ran down the burn towards the place where the person had stood. He searched for a foothold. A yew tree grew from the edge, but he would have to jump nearly double his own height to reach it. With three great strides he lurched with all his might. With nothing to spare, he touched the tree grabbing hold.

His amazement caused him to hang a moment before he swung his legs up in one mighty motion onto the forest floor. He looked around before he stood. He found himself inside the woods where no scrub continued.

The woodland seemed empty, but his senses told him different. He listened intently thinking he heard another heartbeat close by. Something urged him to stay put, yet his newfound energy encouraged him to go on. He did.

The sound got louder as he walked fearless towards it. He felt the vibrations on his skin; a rabbit ran under his feet into the scrub. Hamish stood motionless listening, but nothing else came to his ears.

The wood darkened and soon he would not be able to maneuver. He cautiously made his way back towards camp by following the line of scrub. Somehow it seemed much further than he had thought. He walked for at least twenty minutes before he realized he was going the wrong direction.

Hamish looked to find the scrub now on his right instead of his left. He almost became dizzy at the thought. He turned around and headed in the opposite way, but after only a short distance, he knew he was again misled. This time he ignored what his mind was telling him and continued.

The terrain kept changing as if something was causing his perception to flip flop directions every few minutes. He closed his eyes keeping one foot in front of the other until a fresh breeze hit his face. Without concern he ran out stepping into another moonlit sky. He felt as if he had been released from a prison. He also knew it would take more courage for him to go back in again.

The spot where he exited the forest was not the place of his entrance. Although the moon made the valley visible, he didn't see the camp or the crags. His trip had led him further east than he had thought. He walked west along the edge keeping his knife in hand, in case he had need.

After what seemed like an hour he caught wind of the broth that Betrain was making. The moon moved behind a large group of clouds. Soon the darkness began to swallow everything. Hamish could see nothing and kept walking towards the aroma. Finally he saw the faintest glimmer of a campfire. He broke into a trot.

He couldn't wait to offer them the water knowing how they would marvel, the closer he got, the slower he ran, until he walked very slowly. Something was amiss. He found Stephen feeding on the fresh grass, but Arthair and Betrain were not to be seen.

Then Hamish became embarrassed. Maybe they were in the tent. He decided to walk up to the camp making his presence known by coughing and clearing his throat. Stephan looked up and replied with his own guttural noise.

"Aye there Stephan, you're looking none the worse for your part in that battle eh?" Hamish glanced toward the shelter.

"You'll want to try some of this special water I've brought back I'm sure." He said loudly.

"I said I've got this water what heals all yer ailments!" He shouted. He waited and nothing.

"Oh alright already you guys come out here, I'm not kidding about the water!" There wasn't a sound.

Hamish became concerned enough to brave opening the tent and he did so finding no one. He looked to Stephan and ran to grab his crossbow.

"Arthair...Betrain...Where are you!" He screamed so loudly it echoed of the cliffs.

He ripped old cloth from a bag and wrapped it on a limb. He dipped it into the fire, creating a torch. Hamish searched around the camp until he found some tracks leading into the forest. The small track of Betrain, the giant footprint of Arthair with several barefoot imprints of different size disappeared into the wood.

It didn't make sense. Why would they walk off leaving everything, including Stephan? There was no sign of a struggle. Betrain and Arthair would not leave willingly, not without providing him something to go on. Hamish walked over to Stephan and marveled at how calm he acted. Stephan always let his feelings show, and now he seemed content.

There was nothing left to do but wait it out. See what the morning would bring. Hamish ate some stew. He sat down upright against his pack so he faced the forest. He didn't plan to sleep this night as long as his friends were missing. He wanted to go find them but it made more sense to stay and wait. The fire slowly went out.

The nocturnal creatures came to life. Overhead Hamish saw an owl flying in search of prey. Tree frogs and other beasties croaked and chirped in a symphony of sound. Distant wolves howled their disapproval to the dark world and beyond. Hamish felt closed in by all the unseen threats. He didn't drink any more water because his sensitivity was too acute already. Stephan walked over and nudged Hamish, almost giving him a heart attack. He clutched his chest and lost his breath.

"Oh goodness Stephan you really gave me a fright. I nearly jumped out of my skin! Come and lay down here, I'll be better knowing you're close by."

Stephan folded his knees then dropped down beside Hamish. He pushed Hamish with a loving nudge and placed his head down beside him. Hamish was tired. He failed to stay awake.

Morning was announced by a blackbird finding the cooled stew to be delicious, and gripping the edge of the pot while dipping its beak into the broth. The raven would have stayed there happily eating had it not chose the wooden spoon for a better purchase. The weight upended the utensil and plopped over into the ashes, causing the bird to go flying noisily over Hamish's head. He awoke with a start realizing he had slept in spite of his intentions.

Stephan was once again grazing on the fresh grass beside him. Hamish stretched and rubbed his eyes, hoping for some trace of his friends. Nothing had changed. Dread fell on his mind. They weren't coming back. He would have to go find them in the woods. Betrain was right, he truly felt like a lost child. All his fearlessness of the day before had completely gone. He got up and began to take down the shelter when he found two words scratched into the dirt inside. 'Wood men' had been hastily scratched into the loose soil and covered by the edge of a blanket.

"Wood men?" Hamish pondered the meaning. "Does that mean they were men of the wood, or men made of wood?"

He decided it made no difference. He would follow and hope the trail remained fresh.

Once he had everything packed and stored on Stephan's back, he grabbed the reins to lead him into the forest. Overhead the early morning sunlight faded suddenly, causing Hamish to look up. Above him a huge black cloud moved in a windless sky. But unlike a cloud, the shape hardly changed. Its direction seemed determined. Hamish looked at Stephan and patted his neck.

"Well, I guess we asked for adventure ol' friend. It looks like we got it." He turned toward the wood, and then he and Stephan walked into the thick of it.

CHAPTER FIFTEEN / THE MÚSCAILT

Taliesin and Nidhoggr entered the temple to find Cailleach sitting upright on the altar. She held her wand.

"Cailleach, we thought we'd lost you?" Taliesin changed into his man form while running to her side.

"My inability to accept fate has endangered everyone. I'm joining this fight." She concentrated on the wand.

"What are you trying to do Cailleach?" Nidhoggr asked.

"I must absorb this, with no idea how to, except by using it." She flourished and squeezed, but nothing happened.

"I'm afraid you're going to get the opportunity soon, as our enemies are gathering. We must leave immediately." Taliesin placed his hand over the bone.

"If you want to absorb the wand, go outside and I'll show you how. This cannot be reversed. Once bonded, you will never be free. You must be mindful of the power at all times. A harsh thought or pointed finger could destroy." Taliesin warned.

Cailleach nodded her head as she dropped off the altar. The three of them walked out into the courtyard with Fiadh following. Once they were clear of any obstruction Taliesin pointed up.

"Aim the wand at the sun. As you feel its power engage, focus all your worst emotions into one thought. When the blue flame erupts, the bone will begin to bond with you. This will take several minutes. The pain will be intense at first, but soon your body will become numb. Once completely bonded, you must clear your mind to stop. If you don't, the sun will return the flame and consume you. This is not an easy thing you do." Taliesin tried not to show his fear.

"Step aside." Cailleach commanded.

She raised the wand and closed her eyes for several minutes. With tears flowing down her cheeks she opened her eyes. She shouted "Shaaaa Taaache!!!"

The blue flame erupted like a bolt of lightning headed straight for the sun. Fiadh stood close to Taliesin. Nidhoggr was awestruck by the sheer violence of the power. Taliesin carefully studied for any indication that she might hold too long.

The wand started to move into her palm. Cailleach began to scream but she held fast. Blood trickled down her arm and pooled at her feet. The heat, sound, and smell of the flame became intense. The sky changed from blue to yellow. The ground started to rumble causing rocks to skid down the mountain. One of the statues in the courtyard came crashing down. Only the tip remained visible. Taliesin had to make sure she let go at the proper time. Nidhoggr spread his wings to protect them from the falling stone. The bone disappeared completely. Taliesin shouted for Cailleach to stop. She seemed transfixed. He screamed again, but she continued. Her whole body became covered in blue veins as if vines had grown over every inch of her skin. Her mouth stretched into a wide grimace. She had lost control and the power was returning. The time to release had passed.

Fiadh leaped into Cailleach knocking her away before the flame struck the polished marble where she had stood, burning a hole into the earth, extending to unseen depths. Taliesin ran to their side. He gathered the fawn into his arms, its leg badly burned.

Cailleach lay motionless with eyes wide open. The blue veins pulsated over her body. She couldn't speak. Nidhoggr leaned down. He gently stroked her forehead. Her face showed no emotion. They all huddled together for several hours until the paralysis subsided. Cailleach began to move and struggled to sit up.

"My arm is completely numb." She noticed Fiadh hurt and reached for her. "Is she alright?" Cailleach cried.

"She's going to be fine. We'll carry her for a while." Taliesin placed the fawn gently beside Cailleach. Using her good hand, Cailleach stroked the fawn's fur and spoke softly.

"I'll gather your things. As soon as you're strong enough, we need to travel. Nidhoggr had graciously agreed to come with us on our journey." Taliesin smiled.

Nidhoggr looked down at Cailleach.

"I'm immensely impressed with you dear girl, completing a feat unlike anything I've seen in all my years. What a great honor it will be to accompany you to wherever this journey requires. And you, fearless Fiadh, astounded me with your bravery. Within your small chest beats the heart of a lion." Nidhoggr chuckled to himself.

"When you two are ready, it would be my pleasure to carry you to our next destination."

Cailleach agreed. She smiled for the first time.

Taliesin returned to the courtyard. He packed their belongings and carried the beaker of life water.

He gave Fiadh a small drink and the leg healed.

Nidhoggr crouched down to allow Cailleach and Fiadh to climb onto his back. Taliesin affixed a leather strap around Nidhoggr's waist so they safely held tight during the flight. He covered them with the thick velvet cloth and cushions from the temple. Once they sat secure, he changed into the eagle.

Taliesin grabbed the bundle, and then he and Nidhoggr spread their wings, lifting everything into the sky.

Cailleach wrapped herself and Fiadh comfortably in the altar coverings. The air became biting cold but the scenery was incredible. Fiadh pushed her head under Cailleach's arm and quickly fell asleep.

Cailleach marveled at the power of Nidhoggr. His great muscles flexed with every beat of his wings. Taliesin, above them, seemed to be scanning the area. Cailleach wondered what distance he gathered in a glance.

The day, slowly fading, sustained a brilliant sunset from this height. The air grew slightly warmer as they traveled further south. A full moon rose from the southeast. Cailleach felt her child kick. Somehow she knew he enjoyed everything through her.

She turned back towards the fortress, remiss at the chance to explore the wondrous castle in the sky. The world was so urgent now. She actually longed for the slow mundane life she left behind. She closed her eyes and fell asleep.

When Cailleach awoke, she lay on the ground next to a small fire. Fiadh chewed on some grass beside Taliesin, as he stood in his human form.

"You slept for a good while. I'm sure you needed the rest. We decided it would be better if you were on firm ground before the two of you slipped off. Nidhoggr is scouting around for food to eat. I unpacked your pot and found some fresh herbs, and something you call turnips. I hope they will suffice." Taliesin smiled as he carried forked branches over to the fire, pushed them into the ground on either end of the flames, and laid a straight branch across the two.

"Now, you can hang your pot from there. I'll fetch some water for the stew." He walked into the dark.

Cailleach smiled at Fiadh and decided to try something. She extended her hand. She pointed her index and ring finger trying to communicate with the fawn. Nothing happened. She tried again. She did not receive or send the simplest thought. The small deer had risked its life to save her.

'What is the truth about this creature?' she wondered. Fiadh reacted as if sensing her thoughts.

Taliesin brought the water. Cailleach made a lovely stew. She mistakenly offered Taliesin some broth but he smiled and declined. She remembered and blushed.

"Truly your cooking would be the most pleasurable appetence one could desire. Sadly it is my loss." He smiled again.

Cailleach finished her food and placed the pot on the ground to cool. The fire began to die, so Taliesin left to gather more wood. Fiadh sat near the edge of a thick covering of brambles, when a noise stirred in the dark. A deep growl brought Cailleach's eyes to bear on the deer.

Fiadh turned, as behind her stood a creature more beast than human. With the eyes of a man, the jaw of a wolf, covered completely in matted black hair, feet spreading out twice the size of a man's, and hands ending in razor like claws where fingers should be. The monster lurched towards the deer. Cailleach pointed her hand shouting, "Shaaaa Taaache!" The beast vanished in blue flame.

Taliesin burst through the brush. Nidhoggr materialized just over their heads.

"What happened?" Taliesin shouted.

"A beast, half man…half wolf maybe…the thing tried to get Fiadh." She cradled the fawn in her arms.

Nidhoggr landed beside Taliesin. "I noticed the blue fire from up there. You said part man and part wolf? I'm afraid we've been discovered. If I'm right this was some of Medraut's magic."

"If Medraut suspects we're here he'll send more. I'm sorry Cailleach but rest must wait. Quickly gather everything. We leave." Taliesin put out the fire. He stored their belongings.

"Cailleach, you ride with me. Nidhoggr will carry the bundle with Fiadh. We're going to fly extremely fast, so you must brace yourself."

"Who is Medraut?" Cailleach asked.

"He is a sorcerer of the highest order. A human, but his power rivals the Gods themselves. He devastates armies and levels kingdoms. We are no match for him here. We must get to the Outland." Taliesin gazed to the sky as if anticipating something.

Nidhoggr wrapped the fawn in several coverings as Taliesin tied the bundle on the dragons back. Once everyone was ready Taliesin changed into the eagle. He hugged Cailleach around her waist. Nidhoggr procured Fiadh in his talons. They lifted off. Taliesin followed.

Almost as soon as they cleared the trees, hundreds of monsters converged on the site. Something flew past. The creatures caught sight of them and hurled some form of magic towards them. Nidhoggr turned and circled back. He dove toward the crowd releasing a giant plume of flame engulfing the entire horde. He quickly re-joined Taliesin and Cailleach. The landscape burned. The flames remained visible for many miles until they vanished in the smoke.

The terrain, which flowed beneath them, became more mountainous. The land thinned out with only spots of coverage, with campfires everywhere. They flew over a decimated village, houses in flames, and the lifeless bodies of the inhabitants.

They traveled throughout the night. Only when the sun began to rise did they settle between two mountains. The road barely allowed for Nidhoggr to spread his wings. This land, lifeless, dead trees, no water, scorched earth, and the smell of sulfur brought Cailleach to a dark place in her spirit. She had never seen these things before.

Nidhoggr released the fawn. Taliesin removed the bundle from his back.

"I must leave you now. The road ahead restricts my ability to defend you if any should attack. I shall keep watch overhead and invisible." The dragon smiled. "I have no doubt about your abilities to take care of yourself."

"Why here? Cailleach asked.

"This is the way to Outland. We cannot travel by air, as our arrival would be easily anticipated. The trail before us is called 'Greim-bàis'. Never safe, but it does offer the advantage of secrecy. Only wizards, demons, and spirits enter the city this way. Humans and beasts are mortally afraid. If anything, the narrow trail will limit the number of our aggressors." Taliesin answered

Nidhoggr stretched his great wings.

"I shall alert Taliesin of imminent danger, and though I might not land, I can still fire from above should an enemy try to ambush you. I leave you now with one warning. The dead on this trail do not rest. Their spirits are envious of life. They endeavor to disrupt your thoughts and cause you trouble. Keep your wits. Don't give them credence. They can do nothing if you offer nothing." With this Nidhoggr lifted into the sky. He became invisible.

"What did he mean?" Cailleach asked.

"Ghost will scare you, trick you, because of all the magic used here, those unlucky enough to die within the boundaries of this pass, are never at ease. Spirits attempt to gain their freedom by attaching themselves to you, hoping you will carry them beyond the bond of their prison. I know you possess a kind willing heart, but do not be tricked into believing you can help any of them. These spirits are black and evil. This place keeps them here for a reason." Taliesin warned.

Taliesin changed into the man and grabbed the reigns of the sled. He motioned for them to proceed. The three began to walk towards 'Greim-bàis'.

They stood at the entrance. Two opposing walls of stone encompassed a path hardly big enough for a wagon to clear. Rowan trees grew to either side of the trail. Beyond the gap, only shadows remained. Sunlight cleared the mountain ridge, but little fell upon the path.

As soon as they crossed the threshold, the air became cold and damp. The smell of mold and decay assaulted her senses. Other than the rowan trees at the entrance, no vegetation whatsoever survived.

The day seemed to last for only a short time. The towering walls restricted the sun, and within a few hours the sparse light dwindled. They walked in silence keeping their thoughts to themselves, as if something explored a sense of them. Cailleach sensed her mind being probed. She resisted by using the trick Jakobar had taught her. 'Stop the internal conversation.' He had said. For now the resistance seemed to be working.

The face of the wall to her left became as if washed in blood. As the sun went down, the crimson shadow of its flame flowed up caressing the highest peaks, and then it was gone. The path faded into pitch black.

Taliesin's thoughts came to her mind. "I can maneuver the darkness as easily as you walk in the light. You two should get on the sled. We must continue through the night. Whatever happens, don't respond to anything you hear."

Cailleach held fast to Fiadh. She had no notion of their progress. Several times in the distance some vague flashes of light erupted, but so far nothing had threatened. She closed her eyes. She was barely asleep when something whispered. She sat up almost losing her grip on Fiadh. Fiadh let go of a whimper and the ghosts appeared.

Blocking the passage, more than a hundred specters with empty skulls and mangled forms no longer resembling anything human reached out. The one in the center held a staff. From the rod, a green light emanated, bathing Cailleach in an eerie glow.

"If you know what I carry, you know my power. This rod is known as Traxis and its power is immeasurable. I can keep you here forever with a word, but a word from you will free us all." The ghoul threatened with his staff.

"You must give us passage if you want to leave." The staff holder demanded.

Taliesin remained silent. He continued toward them.

"None survive who refuse our toll." The ghoul touted.

Taliesin did not waver.

"The pet of Epona carries no weight in this realm eagle. Give up this burden or we'll clip your wings forever." The staff holder stepped closer.

A large ghost reached out to Cailleach. "Daughter…do not abandon me to this place."

Cailleach shook in terror. 'The apparition sounded like her father?'

A presence in her mind slithered closer.

"I gave you life…don't abandon me…I'm begging you to help me." A female beseeched her.

The voices tore Cailleach apart. They reached into her thoughts, and something familiar in each one touched her heart. She was losing control.

A small child-like specter reached towards Cailleach crying for mercy.
"Please help me dear mother." It pleaded in tears unseen.

Cailleach forgot her silence.

"I'm so sorry...there's nothing I can do..." She replied.

"No Cailleach! Don't engage them!" Taliesin shouted, but too late.

A swarm of light engulfed Cailleach. Their cold touch seeped into her body. Something swallowed her consciousness, and in only seconds she lost all connection with the living world.

She fell into a dream within a dream. Hundreds upon thousands of souls reached out to her. They first tried to completely possess her, but something held them away. An understanding between her soul and theirs took place without any conscious effort from Cailleach. She observed as the dead lowered their gaze from her. The staff holder walked to the front and spoke softly.

"We did not know who you were. We mean you no harm. This curse upon us has driven us to appeal to all who pass through. Forgive us, we now understand. You are the one who can rescue us. You must complete your task. You must bear this child. We anticipate your completion. My name is Kraven and my transgression created this prison we exist in. I now know there is hope. We await your call." He lowered the staff and the green light paled.

Kraven turned and faded into the expiring midst of countless spirits. Within a moment they all dissolved. Cailleach opened her eyes to find Fiadh beside Taliesin, hovering over her.

"Are you alright? I was afraid we had lost you." Taliesin leaned close. She barely made out his form as the morning light broke through the dark.

"So many asked for my forgiveness, saying they would wait for me to call them. What does this mean?" Cailleach looked around, but nothing remained.

"I'm not sure. No one ever escapes them. Your purpose here is beyond any single reason. Would seem many worlds are converging with you and your child. All the more imperative we get to our destination before something does intercept us."

Taliesin turned and stared into the distance before he spoke again. "If they are for you, then nothing will be allowed to follow. We must make haste. The days are not long enough."

High above something glistened for a moment. Cailleach noticed, as did Taliesin. They doubled their pace. Cailleach now suffered the stress of her added weight, she neither complained nor slowed. Things moved quickly, and she had no other choice but to suffer these hardships.

Fiadh remained faithful as always, with a simple need to be near. This gave Cailleach confidence and courage. The frail little deer inspired resolve and strengthened her determination. Cailleach sensed a purpose for this wonderful creature in her life, and something more.

Taliesin pulled them at a strong pace. The daylight manifested, and diminished as the day before. The blood sky painted the mountain peaks. The jagged cliffs resembled the bloody edge of a serrated blade. All light disappeared and it quickly became black.

Taliesin stopped. He instructed the two to climb on the sled. Something changed his demeanor. He looked to the sky. He seemed to be listening. Several moments passed as he stood still and silent.

"Nidhoggr has company. A clan of dragons is approaching. He doesn't recognize the riders, but if I'm right they're from an ancient sect that cares for neither honor nor justice; 'Gall-òglaich'."

"Who are they?" Cailleach asked.

"They are killers for hire. They give no loyalty. They disdain morality. To join them one must murder their closest kin in ceremonial blood lust. The dragons they ride feast on carrion. Such is their taste for all the dead and decayed." Taliesin understood his words frightened Cailleach.

"Not to worry…Nidhoggr can destroy the entire clan in a breath. The riders would never survive."

"The night will protect us. Dragons do not possess sight as I do. In this blackness their vision is compromised. Nidhoggr keeps track of us by his telepathy. He is unique of his kind in this way." Taliesin began to pull at a quicker pace.

The darkness closed around them. Nothing save the highest peak, where some sliver of moonlight illuminated it, was visible. The spirits remained silent but Cailleach sensed them to be near. She felt Fiadh's heart beat against her chest as they huddled together. Then the faint sound of water trickling over rocks could be heard. A stream nearby made Cailleach realize her thirst.

"I'm thirsty." She reluctantly asked.

"I'll get you something." Taliesin stopped the sled. He grabbed the pot from the bundle.

Cailleach heard him moving beyond to her right side. He was close enough. She wasn't afraid of the spirits anymore, but even so, the pitch-black trail offered no comfort. She glanced up thinking a flash appeared from above. The sky was empty. Then it happened again. Something green flared, and disappeared.

"Nidhoggr is growing tired. His invisibility is fading. I'm telling him to rest on the mountaintop for a while. We should be safe in the dark for now. I would prefer to continue, but we need Nidhoggr to keep a lookout from above. Here's a cave from where a brook flows. We can take shelter till morning." Taliesin carried a pot full of water Cailleach heard sloshing.

"We're blind in this darkness. How do we get there?" She thought to Taliesin.

"I'll go inside and start a small fire. I'll come get you. I won't be long." He sat the pot down and walked away. Fiadh smelled the water, and dipped her nose into it. Cailleach waited, and then cupped her hand blindly into the liquid. They drank enough to quench their thirst.

In the distance, the smallest flare of a flame became visible, deep within a shrouded hole. Had she not stood directly in sight, she knew she would not be able to see it. Anything above would see nothing. The figure of Taliesin moved away from the flame walking back.

"You and Fiadh go inside. The path is clear to the cave. Walk carefully and you should not stumble. I'll bring the sled. At least we'll be warm tonight." Taliesin gathered their belongings.

Once in, Cailleach spread their coverings on the floor. The cave went further back beyond the light. Drops of water echoed from deep within. Fiadh lay beside her. She seemed uneasy.

"What's the matter Fiadh? Are you still frightened? We'll be safe here." She whispered. Fiadh placed its head down with red ears fully alert.

Taliesin stood at the entrance facing the trail. He too seemed to be sensing something.

"What?" Cailleach thought to him.

"Nidhoggr is strangely quiet. Even when he sleeps I can hear his dreams. Please stay here; this will only take a moment. I will know your thoughts should you need me." Taliesin nodded to Cailleach as if to get her permission.

"Yes…yes…please go…we'll be fine." Cailleach insisted. She put her arm around Fiadh and gave her approval.

Taliesin changed into the eagle with the usual gold shimmer. He spread his wings. As he left the ground a giant plume of green fire enveloped the place where he had stood. The earth shook. Rocks began to fall. Before Cailleach could react, a mountain of stone covered the entrance. The interior of the cave held, but several stones had fallen near Fiadh. Cailleach shielded the deer with her body. The thick dust created a red haze around the fire. Fiadh began moving toward the back of the cavern.

"Wait, I'll make an opening." Cailleach raised her hand and shouted, "Shaaaa Taaache!"

Blue flame shot from her palm and burned through the stone. The entrance became clear for a moment. Something illuminated and menacing, stood glaring from the outside. A tattooed man with long black hair looked at Cailleach and smiled before the mountain came crashing down again. Her blood ran cold. She knew this was her nightmare. Cailleach grabbed her sword, the ring, and the life water.

"Taliesin...speak to me!" Her thoughts unanswered. "Taliesin...where are you!" Still, there was no response.

Fiadh nudged her toward the blackness of the cave. The roof began to crumble. Cailleach had no choice but to follow into the unknown. They slipped through a tight crack before the entire room filled with rock. The ground shook. Cailleach fell forward into blackness. The floor angled downward sharply. She lost her footing and slid towards the bottom. After scraping across stone and scree, Cailleach stopped abruptly against a boulder. She coughed and called out to Fiadh. Moments later the deer's nose touched her face.

"Oh dear Fiadh...what would I do if you were lost to me?" Cailleach spoke through tears.

She reached out and cuddled Fiadh to her chest. The deer trembled. Cailleach felt its body and found a horrible gash pouring blood from its side. Cailleach didn't hesitate. She ripped her dress and bound the wound as best she could. Fiadh shook, with her breathing becoming shallow. Cailleach took the life water and poured it into the fawn's mouth. Fiadh struggled, but Cailleach held firm until the vessel emptied. Cailleach clutched Fiadh until her body quit shaking. Her hands felt for the injury until she knew the water had taken effect. The blood had stopped. The wound healed. The deer stood up and licked her face. Her cheeks were wet with tears, and Fiadh tenderly licked them all away.

Her eyes adjusted to the darkness, and she saw some light further down, where something faintly glowed. Cailleach gained her footing and the two began the descent. Each step was problematic, as she could see nothing in front of her. She only knew Fiadh to be close, because of her touch. The path was sound and finally, she stood without leaning. Beyond was a bend where the light emanated, silhouetting the edge of the rock in its glow. She carefully found her way to the bend. Once around, she stood in awe.

A great hall reached above to towering heights unseen. Torches hung on the walls yet their wicks had never been lit. No visible source of the light was apparent even though everything shown clear and well illuminated. Inscriptions and runes marked many different passageways branching off of the main chamber. A small creek flowed beside the far wall into the darkness beyond.

On a peg of wood, dangling above the water, a leather sling with an odd indented ball tied to its end; white as bone with a brownish stain like dried blood. The sinister object caused Cailleach to step away.

In the center of the hall, a round polished stone, looking similar to the one she had found before. She knew she had to try, so she placed the ring on her finger and waited for the goddess to appear. Nothing happened. She closed her eyes thinking to reach out to Epona. Her thoughts unanswered.

"Why have you come here?" A voice from one of the chambers asked, sounding like a woman, but with the strength of a man.

"I had no choice. The cave we sheltered in collapsed. We barely escaped." Cailleach strained to see who had called out to her.

"We all have choices. Our choices define us." A woman stepped into the hall supported with a tall staff.

She dressed as a warrior. Leather and chain mail clung tightly to this ancient woman. Her face bore the scars of a thousand battles around eyes, steel blue and piercing. Her body appeared muscled and taut, but age had taken its toll. She carried a short sword and a sling like the one hanging on the wall.

"I choose to fight for the good. My choices have put a lot of people in mortal danger. I'm told I possess the power to overcome everything, but my resolve fails me." Cailleach voiced her own fears. She did not know why.

"You have the will, but your mind needs to find the space between the beats of the heart. Defeating an enemy requires fear to surrender to patience. Fear immobilizes us. Patience tells us when to act. You are with child. Has your husband been killed?" The warrior woman asked.

Cailleach placed her hand on her stomach and sighed.

"I have no husband and this child will know no father to claim him. Because of this, I started this journey. I'm running away." Cailleach replied.

"Few men rise above the purpose of procreation. I do not pity your lack of him. This path would test even the most hardened man, yet you carry this mantel while bearing a child. The ring and the sword in your possession do not belong to you, but the fact you possess those means you are considered the Bana-Bhuidseach. Whether true or not, is something time will determine. If the Máthair Shúigh has given you his sword, he believes you to be so. I am 'Scáthach'. You are in need of instruction. But first we must get you and your friend some food and rest, and clothes. Your dress is threadbare. I have suitable clothing for you, and when you have given birth, something more befitting a warrior. Follow me." The woman moved toward the chamber.

"Please, my friends outside. They are in danger, we have to help them." Cailleach pleaded.

"We cannot help them, nor can you speak to them. These walls are protected by eons of magic that prevent thoughts from penetrating. For this reason, I reside here, to be safe from the prying thoughts of the like who seek you now. You must remain for a while my dear. Your friends will no doubt be worried for you as well. But right now silence is our greatest defense." She turned and proceeded. "In 'time' is where you will find the weakness of your opponent." Cailleach followed in silence.

Chapter Sixteen / The Ceannard Diabhal

After a week of contemplation, Mackenneth decided he needed help if his plan was to succeed. Miol no longer took any interest in his fate. Mackenneth dreaded walking into that horrible underworld again, but he had to appeal to someone who might not believe the same as their chief. Mackenneth knew he may be risking his life by doing so, and he'd as soon be dead as rot here in this hellhole.

He grabbed his long knife making the resolution he would cut his own throat before he died on their burning pit. He stepped off the wreck of the 'Clampróir' and glanced up at the elevated holes above him.

Black eyes with red flames flickered, glowering into oblivion.

At night, the lagoon appeared as though Satan himself was staring down upon the troubled waters of Tèarmunn. The devilish glow changed the water in effect to blood lapping the shore.

Mackenneth now stood at the entrance of the caves. He clasped his knife as he stepped into the fetid inferno.

Once inside, he waited until his eyes adjusted to the darkness. Unseen flames illuminated the maze of narrow corridors. He moved slowly listening intently to every sound. Nothing stirred.

His hands were wet and shaking; no matter how hard he tried he couldn't stop them.

The walls were slick with a thick brown slime, leaving only a narrow path on the floor. He covered his mouth to prevent coughing from the putrid smells of rot, decay, and smoke. Several corridors branched off in other directions but he stayed true to his chosen course.

Finally his path came to an end, facing a wall offering only left or right to continue. The right passage descended slippery steps, as the left ascended and was much dryer, thereby determining his next course of action.

Mackenneth struggled against the assurgent path. He had to pause on occasion to catch his breath. This stair appeared endless, offering no reprieve or option.

After ages of trudging upward, a bluish light glowed in the distance. The climb ended on a smooth stone angling in a moderate grade. He remained motionless for a moment and listened intently for the slightest noise, nothing.

The air seemed less abusive to him as he ascended. As the path arched to the right, he found himself walking into a gigantic open chamber filled with blue light.

In the center, an altar abided before a throne. Unlike any chair of royalty he had witnessed before, this one was magnificently huge.

High above, rays of sunlight filtered in through a hole at least three hundred feet from where he stood. Birds flew in circles below. Mackenneth marveled at how these brutal savages created all this.

No one appeared to be about, so Mackenneth cautiously maneuvered his way down to the shrine. His steps echoed off the bare walls as he descended. His apprehensions increased, as the room seemed to grow around him. Then he approached the massive table made of pure gold. A thick swath of blue silk covered the altar whereupon six different idols; a goat, a wolf, a raven, a bull, a deformed man, and a horse stood side by side, nearly as large as the creatures they depicted. The Sagart reached impulsively to touch the horse when a deep voice interrupted his intent.

"It would be unwise to do so Sagart. My toys are likely to be more real than you believe."

Mackenneths stomach clenched into a knot and he shrank to the floor hoping to crawl away and hide.

"I expected less fear from the bold Sagart. Perhaps I was wrong in allowing you to come here." The voice grew in strength and rattled Mackenneth to his bones.

"Yes, the place for you is properly on your knees in my temple, worshipping me as you always have in ignorance." The voice chuckled.

"Who are you?" The Sagart managed to speak.

"Surely you know me by now. I've watched with elation as you persecuted innocent Christians for selfish personal gain. I've never seen one so engaged as you though, the way you relished their pleas and ignored their pitiful cries for mercy. You enjoyed watching them burn alive, and made sure they didn't die too soon. You prolonged and cherished their agony. Ah! You're a demon after my own heart Mackenneth." The voice spoke his name.

On the throne, burning flames appeared and grew into the shape of a giant. When the blaze diminished Mackenneth regaled the demon seated upon the massive chair. His arms were the size of tree trunks. His frame was solid bone with thorns protruding from every inch. He had no skin or hair and his eyes were deep hollow sockets where purple light flashed when he spoke. His teeth were pointed, hanging from his mouth like the fangs of a wolf. The giant smiled. He motioned for Mackenneth to approach with elongated fingers ending in razor sharp points.

"You need not fear me Sagart. You are much too valuable to me alive. I exist in a divine realm, which shackles me. But you are free to roam about this sentient world of flesh and bone. Because of your like-mindedness, despicable character, and most of all, freedom, I shall use you to exercise my will."

"Who are you my lord?" The Sagart asked feebly.

Come now Mackenneth, I would have thought you recognized my greatness. Oh yes, I forgot, you actually don't believe in god, so therefore you wouldn't deem me to be…Ah… you may call me 'Diabhal.' I shouldn't wonder you ever thought to meet me, but viola! I am here!" He laughed as he clapped his hands filling the room with light.

The Sagart turned around. The silhouettes of the idols moved about the distant walls.

"What can I do for your greatness?" Mackenneth cowered.

"I would have you find a girl. The same one you ignored in your quest for power. The offspring of the farmer you foolishly chose to confront."

"Arthair's daughter? Her? She was nothing more than a hag. Her departure was hardly noticed by most and considered a good sign by many. My nephew shamed himself. He disgraced his family by his familiarity with her. What is she to you in your magnificence lord?" Mackenneth bowed.

"She has the ability to chain me beyond your world for eternity. She is the Bana-Bhuidseach, if she is not stopped, she will have power over you, me, and every divine realm in existence." Diabhal's eyes flashed fire. He stood.

"I do not send you to fight her or her familiar Gods empty handed. A talisman, hidden at the foot of the North Mountain beyond the village of BlairMor, remains in secret. Search for the cave of Seanáthair Odhar, marked by three rowan trees, grown intertwined, covering the entrance. Inside you will find three chambers. You must take the lowest chamber, which leads to a stream illuminated with its own phosphorescence.

At its deepest, before the water dives under the mountain, is a green translucent gem lying on the bottom. This stone, when exposed to the direct light of the sun, renders all magic, divine or mortal, useless. Use this talisman to destroy the Bana-Bhuidseach. Kill her and put an end of any chance for the completion of the gathering. Do this, and I will reward you beyond the aspirations of Avarice." 'Diabhal' smiled.

"I can accomplish this, your greatness." Mackenneth became overjoyed at the thought.

The great 'Diabhal' gazed down at Mackenneth. "One more thing Sagart; a condemned spirit guards the stone and it requires a secret phrase to gain clear passage from the cave. The one who lifts the gem from the water must give the proper locution or provide compensation. The price is death, thereby exchanging places with the spirit, forever to be condemned to guard the stone for eternity. But not to worry…the passwords are ……"

"Wake up master Sagart…wake up Father…it's me…Scuigin!"

Mackenneth found himself lying on the floor of the cabin of the wrecked ship. He had left one dream for another. He rubbed his eyes and struggled to stand. Scuigin pulled him up by his arm grinning from ear to ear. The Sagart shook his head.

"How in God's name did you get here?" Mackenneth was almost glad to smell the old drunk.

"I was saved by the main mast what carried me overboard, but kept me afloat. I've been washed ashore beyond the jaw of this harbor. I knew if anyone survived sir, would be you."

Mackenneth frowned as he walked out on the deck looking for some way to float out. "How'd you manage the current?"

"I tied the rope from the sail around my waist and let myself get washed in. The mast is stuck in the rocks on the other side." Scuigin was right proud of himself.

"Yes well…well done Scuigin, but now we have to get back out." Mackenneth surveyed the wreckage. A small boat secure on the ship's deck inspired him. He motioned for Scuigin to help him lift the skiff into the water. "We'll use your rope to pull ourselves free of this current. Once beyond the opening we can head back to civilization."

Mackenneth grabbed his knife, the Bible, and the barrel of pork. Together they got the boat into the water. Scuigin pulled the rope through the forward gunnels and braced his feet on the gunwales. This way he drew them closer to the mouth, a foot at a time. All seemed to go well until they heard a commotion back on the shore. The natives were screaming and shaking their spears. Miol shrieked above the rest, as his patience was at an end and he would be feasting on Mackenneths burnt flesh for his next meal.

Mackenneth shouted at Scuigin to pull faster. Spears spiraled accurately close within range and slammed into the water only inches away.

"We've got to jump in Scuigin! Tie off the boat so she doesn't drift back!" The Sagart shouted.

Scuigin protested but Mackenneth based his next move on one hopeful possibility. "Dive in and descend as deep and fast as you can Scuigin, you gonna have to hold your breath longer than you ever have. Remember, you're better to drown, than to burn alive!" Mackenneth threw off his heavy coat into the sea and dove in. The horrified Scuigin followed.

Deeper and deeper they went, until the mechanism the Sagart counted on began. Almost twenty feet down they were grabbed by an undertow heading for the gap in the teeth. Once in the tow, both became helpless to do anything else. Seconds turned into minutes, and Mackenneth passed the opening as his lungs screamed for air. Scuigin grasp his ankle, causing the process to take longer than he had thought. He slowly let his air release to ease the pressure in his chest. He prayed for an end, because in another minute, he knew he would inhale the sea. He clenched his mouth as he thought his resistance could hold no longer. The current released him and he floated to the surface. His head cleared the surface. He gulped the air his body was dying for, and some water got sucked in. He coughed and retched. Scuigin did likewise.

They swam for the rocks where the mast was locked. Once they regained their strength, they pulled the skiff past the wall, clearing the jaws. Mackenneth secured it alongside the mast. He gathered what they needed, using part of a yardarm, with some sail, to catch the wind. The one paddle he had, he fastened for a rudder.

"Our first mission is to find fresh water. How did you manage all this time Scuigin?" Mackenneth asked.

Scuigin grinned as he pulled a small canteen from his pocket. "Whisky... just enough to wet ma whistle every day..." He opened the flask and offered it to Mackenneth.

"You're a very strange man Scuigin." Mackenneth pushed it away.

They headed north toward Muireann. Their makeshift sail and rudder proved up to the task, keeping them within sight of the shore. After several hours of tacking, the mountains began to recede. A wind from the south pushed them towards the old harbor. By morning of the next day they passed ships moving out to sea.

"Aye Scuigin, we have to keep our heads low when we get to port. There'll be some who might ask questions if we're spotted. We'll stash the boat in the reeds south of the harbor. There's an old rumrunners route around the back of the harbor. It strays unpleasantly close to 'Sliabh Dubh'. We'll have to choose our path northwest at the appropriate time or risk having to cross the dark wood."

Scuigin shuddered at the thought. "If ye's don't mind me asking, where are we going? We can't stay in Muireann, the village up north wants to hang us, and we got no money. Shouldn't we keep sailing past this place and find safer harbor?"

Mackenneth couldn't believe his ears. Scuigin almost sounded as if he had thought something through. 'Must be the lack of excessive drinking' Mackenneth concluded.

"Scuigin, you and I are on a quest to finally attain what many have searched for over the centuries. Yes we are wanted men, but riches and power are obtained for a price. I've had a divine vision that compels me to return to BlairMor. I can speak no more, except to say our destinies are about to change abruptly. You shall have what you deserve as shall I." Mackenneth smiled at Scuigin for the first time since they had met. Scuigin shuddered again.

It was after nightfall when they made landing in a washed out cove a mile below the harbor. They dragged the boat into the reeds, and filled their pockets with as much pork as they managed. Mackenneth discovered the path. With only a half moon to light their way, they pushed into the wood surrounding the cliffs.

After Mackenneth circumvented the town, he came upon a clearing, where he decided to rest until morning. Scuigin found a dry piece of dirt and quickly fell asleep.

Mackenneth lay awake planning how he would finally acquire this, which had for so long eluded him. Scuigin began to snore so Mackenneth pelted him with a rock. Scuigin rolled over. He didn't wake. Mackenneth cursed him under his breath before he went to sleep as well.

At first light Mackenneth kicked Scuigin. "Get up you fool, we need to move on."

Scuigin sat up, stretched, and reached into his pocket to produce his cherished flask. He methodically unscrewed the top to take his morning refreshment. "Ahh, be the breath of angels. I'm ready when you are sir." Scuigin stood up smiling his toothless smile.

"You know Scuigin, the time at sea, being endlessly saturated with salt water, really improved your demeanor." Mackenneth remarked.

"Thank ye sir, I do feel better. Must be true what they say about the salt air!"

Mackenneth shook his head. "No...I think it was the water...never mind...let's push on."

First day, they covered more than a third of the distance. They turned west to find the river pass. It was well into the evening before they broke through to the main road. This time of night, the roads were soulless, and the approaching winter made encountering travelers unlikely.

The two of them walked northward in silence. The cold wind began to blow in from the northwest and chilled them because they had no heavy coats.

Several hours before morning, Mackenneth agreed to stop and rest. Scuigin said nothing. He fell asleep as soon as they sat down. Mackenneth pulled his knees to his chest using Scuigin's body to block the wind. The effect of the salt water was wearing off, so Mackenneth chose to find better accommodations upwind.

With only three hours sleep, Mackenneth woke Scuigin. They pushed on.

The road was completely devoid of any travelers. This day they made it to within half a day's journey to the BlairMor. Mackenneth decided to rest at dusk with no quarrels from Scuigin. At midnight he awoke the old drunk, making clear they would travel to, and through the village, before the sun came up.

When they crossed the bridge with hardly enough light to stay on path, the two outcasts maneuvered the sleeping streets of BlairMor. Only the distant bark of some penned up dog broke the silence. The strong smell of smoldering wood and peat hung in the air suspended by a mist, which soaked their clothes as if raining full on.

They passed the mercat cross. Mackenneth increased his pace toward the farm on the hill. Scuigin kept up because this town put a strong fear into him, and he did not care to linger within its boundaries any longer than he had to. Mackenneth did not show it, but his anxiety was also rising into his throat.

They approached the house of Arthair Odhar, strangely silent, with no smoke from the fireplace. The Sagart wondered if maybe the father had left in pursuit of himself or the wayward daughter.

'It doesn't matter because either way he was to be rid of them both, and the sooner the better.' Mackenneth thought.

They walked past the outer fence nearest the barn. Mackenneth listened intently if anything stirred. He wasn't going to chance meeting up with Arthair. He kept well away from the house and its outside buildings.

The North Mountain rose from the valley behind the Odhar farm. Its ice covered peak glistened in the moonlight. A gray sky began to emerge at the dawn with flakes of snow.

Mackenneth and Scuigin had no choice but to continue on until they reached some form of shelter near the foot of the mountain. The wind picked up. Both men were struggling to keep their feet in motion. The cold had numbed every part of their bodies. Mackenneth no longer felt his legs or hands.

Scuigin stumbled several times before he succumbed to the winter storm. Mackenneth fell by his side. He made a feeble attempt to rouse him, when he too crumpled into the snow. His thoughts convinced him he was falling asleep, so he relinquished his grip on reality.

The dark world of unconsciousness seemed docile enough with its endless void of nothingness. Mackenneths mind embraced the calm senseless domain as he sank deeper into a black grave called his extinction. When his life force heard the final ping of blood freezing in his veins he thought no more.

'Eggs…bacon…coffee…' the world was rushing back like a tidal wave and the pain of all in his head. He opened his eyes and found himself looking up at a timber roof. Somewhere near he could hear the crackle of bacon frying in a pan. He tried to rise but he had no strength.

The head of a bearded giant came into view over him. "Aye, there you are. The other fellow has yet to awaken, I'll venture to say he'll be right as rain soon enough. Do ya understand me?" The giant face smiled.

"Ah…yes…thirsty." Was all Mackenneth could manage.

"No problem…we'll try some water first … see how ya do with that." An enormous hand lifted his head and ladled the liquid into his mouth. "Easy now…don't do too much."

Mackenneth drank and coughed. He sat up looking around him. Scuigin was lying near an open fire covered in blankets. The giant seemed harmless enough. Mackenneth took another drink.

"I had ta wash yer both in cold water to get yer blood moving again. That'en there needed more than one bath before I could bring him in. He's the only man I ever smelt frozen like that. No worries…yer clean … yer clothes are soon dry. You'll both be right as rain before you know!" He stood to his full height beaming a giant smile. "Some breakfast here when you feel up to it."

"Your hospitality is mortally appreciated sir. My companion and I owe you our lives to say the least." Mackenneth scanned the room.

"Nonsense…weren't much…neither of ye's were more than a handful for 'ol' Wullie.' I happened ta find ye before the wolves did. Yer welcome ta stay as long as needs be…I've no boarders or neighbors to speak of…yer company will serve as payment enough. They call me Wullie…what do they call you?" He extended his hand.

Mackenneth weakly shook the mammoth paw offered him. "My nom de plume is…'Breugaire'…and my friend…'Amadan'. Mackenneth though through his lie as he spoke.

The giant regarded him suspiciously.

"Those be different names to my ears, no matter, a person can't choose their own name now can they? Please try to have something to eat." Wullie pulled a chair from the table.

"Aren't you going to have some breakfast too?" Mackenneth tried to seem cordial.

"Me? Oh heavens no, I'll be having ma oats as usual. If the angels come fer me after I've finished a hot bowl of steaming porridge, I'll go a happy man and none the worse fer it." He smiled and began to whistle some tune he obviously made up as he went.

"Looks like yer friend may be coming around."

Mackenneth quickly moved to Scuigin's side pretending to show concern while pinching him to get his attention.

"Are you alright Amadan? This kind stranger who has given us a shelter from the elements has rescued us. Rise Amadan and give thanks for your life." Mackenneth added extra stress when he called Scuigin by the strange name.

Scuigin opened his eyes and looked around the room not understanding what was about.

"Father, where is we?"

"Father... are ye a priest?" The giant frowned.

"No...no...not at all sir...he's a bit belligerent from the cold...must think I'm his papa. No Amadan, it's me. Breugaire, your companion since this long journey began. Look at me friend don't you recognize me? Are you alright?" Mackenneth drew him close and made sure the giant could not see him wink.

Scuigin finally took the hint.

"I am damit! Oh yeah, I forgot, Bruger, we's lost in the snow."

"Bruger?" Wullie asked.

"It's a name between friends. He calls me Bruger. I call him Damit, we get along, and that's what counts." Mackenneth feigned a weak smile.

"Doesn't matter, yer welcome to call yerselves whatever suits ya. Best be eating that food before it gets cold. I'm going to check on the animals. Make yerselves at home. I'll be back soon." Wullie's demeanor had changed. Mackenneth sensed it.

The door shut. Mackenneth pulled Scuigin to the table. They finished off every last morsel of food, and drank their fill of coffee. When the Sagart had eaten, he berated Scuigin.

"Bruger? Are you trying to get us handed over to a lynch mob? Pay attention, we've got to find a cave marked by three rowan trees. That giant may know exactly where it is. Now...when he returns we tell him we came from down south to dig for gold. The mine was suggested to us by a 'lorgaire' we met at the harbor. We have to convince him, or our journey will end up at the end of a rope. Do you think you can handle that?" Scuigin nodded his head when the door burst open. The giant returned. He was carrying some logs for the fire.

"The air is colder than a witches behind out there lads. Better get them clothes on. The winds are terrible and the snow ain't letting up anytime soon. If ye's don't mind me askin, where were you two gentlemen traipsing off to in this weather?" Wullie threw the wood on the stack by the fireplace and proceeded to add more to the blaze.

"My friend and I were looking for a cave at the foot of the North Mountain. We planned to dig for gold on the advice of a lorgaire we met down south." Mackenneth studied the giants face wondering if he accepted the lie.

"Gold…in these hills? I'm afraid someone has had you on, there's no gold nor anything else to be dug from this mountain, besides, what were you planning on digging with, yer hands?" Wullie walked to the table and sat down on his giant chair. He leaned on his elbow, waiting for an answer.

"You see, kind sir, we got lost from our packhorse some miles back. I'd wager he's returned to the harbor before long. We were preparing to put on our heavy coats when a wolf howl spooked him. He ran off with everything we had, you found us at nature's mercy. We can never thank you enough." Scuigin listened intently so as to back up the story if asked.

"Well I guess luck has gotten you this far, but I'm afraid you're chasing a wild goose for gold. Yer best bet is to travel to BlairMor and wait for the weather to clear. This mountain will be frozen solid in a week's time, neither man nor beast are able to find much to live on. I've got some old coats small enough to suffice ta get you home and maybe a bit of dried meat with hard tack. I've a skin of water you're welcome to, although I think Amadan prefers something stronger judging by his breath. Either way, you'd be better getting on as soon as you feel up to it. The conditions outside are going to get worse quickly." The giant seemed less cordial than before.

"For the sake of knowing, and since we traveled so far, is there a cave with three rowan trees blocking the entrance you know of?" Mackenneth asked calmly.

"Aye, and as well you didn't find it. No one has ever returned from that cave. Men have gone to it and none have returned. It's cursed. The trees were intentionally planted there to keep the evil from getting out. Your luck saved you from freezing, but no amount of fortune could retrieve ya from that place" The giant placed both his hands on the table.

"But I can tell by the look in yer eyes yer gonna go there with, or without my help, so I'll tell ye's how to get there. But know this, I want yer solemnly sworn oath you relieve me of any blame in yer horrible demise in that cave. Swear it or try yer own luck finding it!" He extended his hand, and with a small blade, he cut his palm.

Mackenneth did not reply or hesitate as he pulled up his sleeve, took the knife, and sliced his own hand. Scuigin appeared horrified. He tried to slink away before Mackenneth grabbed him stabbing his shaking finger in quick motion. They dropped their blood together on the table and with a stick of yew the giant stirred it.

"Ye's swear by yer eternal soul ye's won't hold ol' Wullie ta blame fer yer actions when ye's meets yer doom. Agreed…say Aye!"

"Aye." Mackenneth shouted.

"Aye." Scuigin muttered.

"Done. There's no backing out now. The cave is about two miles due northwest from this cabin. You keep an eye on the growth of larch within sight. Once you get to the trees, a creek will guide you to the foot of the mountain. The creek turns east. When it does, you'll be standing in front of the rowans. You'll have to cut a path through them to enter the cave. I'm agin the idea I'm sending anyone to their certain death, but I don't think you would take my advice anyway."

He stood and reached into a cupboard, producing two candles and a small axe.

"Ain't much but you'll need this to get through and find yer way." He walked to another closet and removed two thick shabby coats.

They waited until about midday and decided they were ready to leave. Wullie reached into the hearth and grabbed a log flaming on one end. He handed it to Scuigin. "This will be yer only source of fire between here and the cave. Keep the flame alive or you'll die."

"I'll guard it with my life sir, if needs be I'll stash it under my coat!" Scuigin beamed at the giant.

"No, I wouldn't, just try to keep the wind off should do." Wullie shook his head in disbelief.

"Again we thank you sir. Our expected good fortunes will be your good fortunes." Mackenneth bowed and walked out the door.

"Come on Damit!" He shouted at Scuigin.

They headed for the grouping of larch near the foot of the mountain. The wind had died leaving the faggot of fire untouched. It took most of an hour before they actually approached the forest. These pine-like trees changed colors, unlike their evergreen cousins. Orange, yellow and brown larch trees spotted the base of the hills

There was no scrub or undergrowth to deal with, so the walking was easy. The sky remained gray with only a peak of sunlight casting shadows on the snow. Another hour's walk and the creek crossed their path, which they followed out of the forest until turning abruptly toward the west at the foot of the cliffs. Here, across the bank, stood three ancient rowan trees intertwined within each other's limbs. Their root system weaved a tight blanket of wooden lattice above the ground, leaving nothing visible beyond their branches. After several hours of vigorous hacking, they finally got a glimpse of the stone behind. Mackenneth tried to burn his way through, but quickly found out the tree did not ignite. He gave the flaming log to Scuigin. He renewed his efforts at cutting.

It was almost nightfall when he finally broke through with a gap large enough for them to squeeze through. Mackenneth went first, handing the torch to Scuigin. Scuigin passed the flame back, and pulled himself past the trees. The fire illuminated a cave entrance marked with unknown runes. Mackenneth made no sense of them and decided to go in. He pushed Scuigin in first, following with the torch.

Once inside, the flame came to life, increasing its fire by more than half. Scuigin lit his candle. He was scared beyond anything he had ever known.

The single hall stretched more than a mile before coming to an intersection of three. One path led up, one continued straight, and one descended. Without hesitation, Mackenneth walked to the one going down. Scuigin reluctantly followed. The flame seemed less infused as they descended. Slowly the light diminished, until it only glowed and finally died altogether. Scuigin's candle did the same.

They stopped blind in the darkness, until faintly; they began to perceive a silver blue glow coming from somewhere further down. Mackenneth increased his pace, until he rounded the last curve.

Before him, a clear brook illuminated the entire chamber. He walked toward the far wall. The deep end of the water flowed under an outcropping of rock some sixty foot distant, accessible only by climbing up onto its plateau.

Mackenneth began to climb when he noticed Scuigin was no longer moving.

"Scuigin get up here! We're almost to it!"

Scuigin bit his lip. He stalled as long as he dared before Mackenneth shouted again.

"Scuigin if you don't come here now, I'm going to abandon you once and for all in this God forsaken labyrinth!" He shouted.

Scuigin climbed reluctantly to the top alongside Mackenneth. Mackenneth stared into the deep pool and pointed at a green gem lying alone on the bottom.

"That's what we came for. That stone is our destiny." Mackenneth was beside himself.

"How are we to get it Sagart?" Scuigin feebly asked.

"You're going to dive down and bring it up Scuigin." The Sagart replied.

"Why me sir? My heart feels as if it's going to jump out my chest any minute. I don't think I'd survive." Scuigin pleaded.

Trust me Scuigin; you're going to live forever once this stone leaves the water." Mackenneth smiled.

"Really sir? Me live forever?" Scuigin relaxed at the thought.

"I guarantee Scuigin. It's part of the endowment of removing the gem." Mackenneth motioned for him to jump.

Scuigin removed his coat and dove in.

The pool exploded in color as Scuigin broke the surface. He swam down until his hand touched the stone, which reacting to his touch, gave off a blood-like secretion when he lifted it. The red trail followed him to the bank. He offered the stone to the Sagart but Mackenneth instructed him to lay it down on the bank. Scuigin did so and pulled himself out of the water.

"Amazing sir, it wasn't cold at all, and had a sweet taste. I don't feel any different; you think I'm immortal now?" Scuigin grinned.

"I've no doubt Scuigin. Put the stone in this bag for me." Mackenneth open a cloth sack. Scuigin dropped the talisman in.

The pool of water was slowly altering color. The blue was giving way to red. The light glow was changing to an opaque dull blood-like substance.

"What do you make of that sir? The water looks like blood now," said the ol' drunk.

Scuigin didn't see the hand that grabbed his shoulder pushing him helpless into the bubbling cauldron of pus and goo.

Mackenneth wrapped the stone with Scuigin's coat and hurried out of the chamber. He ran until he could see a faint sliver of moonlight slicing the darkness. He found the entrance and crossed into the night.

The rowan trees were now dried up. Mackenneth kicked away the dead wood. He stepped across the threshold.

Somewhere back in the cave he heard a bloodcurdling scream.

"You see Scuigin; I didn't lie to you after all". Mackenneth laughed to himself as he made his way towards the cabin.

Aigéad- acid

Airgead- silver

Alba- Scotland

Arsanaic- arsenic

Baile- Small dwelling

Bana-Bhuidseach – The most powerful sorcerer of all

Basilisk- a legendary reptile reputed to be king of serpents and said to have the power to cause death with a single glance

Bean-Sith- The bean-sith or bean-sidhe (banshee) is rarely seen, but her mournful wail is said to be heard when death is near. She either wears a grey, hooded cloak or a grave robe meant for the unshriven dead

Burn- Stream

Cailleach- also known as the Cailleach Bheur, is a divine hag, a creatrix, and possibly an ancestral deity or deified ancestor

Cariad- Unrequited love

Ceannard Diabhal- King of the Demons

Clampróir- The ship of the 'Beast' Brúid

Crags-Rugged projecting cliffs

Cruithne- The Cruithne were the first Celtic racio-tribal group to come to the British Isles, appearing between about 800 and 500 B.C.

Doppelganger- Exact double; Twin

Dorchadas- Darkness and obscurity

Fair Dues- Equal standing; what's good for one is good for the other

Hermitage- a <u>National Trust for Scotland</u>-protected site in <u>Dunkeld</u>, <u>Perth and Kinross</u>. Located just to the west of the <u>A9</u>, it sits on the banks of the <u>River Braan</u> in <u>Craigvinean Forest</u>. It is home to <u>Ossian's Hall of Mirrors</u> and <u>Ossian's Cave</u>, <u>Georgian</u> <u>follies</u> built by the <u>Dukes of Atholl</u>, who had their former main residence in nearby Dunkeld House (demolished early 19th century), in the 18th century to honour the blind bard <u>Ossian</u>. The Hermit's Cave was built around 1760 for the third Earl of Breadalbane, who unsuccessfully advertised for a permanent eremite. The guide in 1869, Donald Anderson, dressed up with a long beard of lichens and clothes of animal skins.

Interamici- an ancient <u>Celtic</u> tribe of <u>Gallaecia</u>, living in the north of modern <u>Portugal</u>, in the province of <u>Trás-os-Montes</u>, near the border with <u>Galicia (Spain)</u>.

Gall-òglaich- Mercenary brotherhood for hire. Renowned for their blood lust and cruelty. Formed from the remnants of defiled warriors of the first Demon War.

Kraven- Warrior general that took the last great relic from the fortress of the Silver Star and fled leaving his warriors to be slaughtered.

Làrach of Corriechatachan- Fortress built before the first demon war.

Marrok- Demon general cursed as a werewolf.

Máthair Shúigh- Kraken, a large octopus like creature.

Mearcair- mercury or quick silver

Medraut- False name of a man-god intent on releasing the beast.

Mercat Cross- A mercat cross is the Scots name for the market cross found in Scottish towns and cities where historically the right to hold a regular market or fair was granted by the monarch, a bishop or a baron. It therefore served a secular purpose as a symbol of authority, and was an indication of a burgh's relative prosperity.

Míshéanmhar- The unlucky

Muireann- The very appropriate name of the 6th century mermaid caught by a fisherman.

Múscailt- awakening

Myrddin- legendary prophet and the greatest wizard of his kind.

Namhaid- Undead enemy

Peristylium- Open courtyard

Potais loiscneach- potassium hydroxide

Olc Sonnach- Ruins of The Fortress of the Silver Star

Ruairidh- The Anointed Red King of the Silver Star

Runes-Old Norse Script

Sagart- Priest

Saltus- A place of leaping and mounting

Sliabh Dubh- Black Mountain

Spàirn- a difficult obstacle

Steading- Farm structures made of stacked stone

St. Elmo's fire- a <u>weather phenomenon</u> in which luminous <u>plasma</u>
is created by a <u>coronal discharge</u> from a sharp or pointed object
in a strong <u>electric field</u> in the <u>atmosphere</u> (such as those gener-
ated by <u>thunderstorms</u> or created by a <u>volcanic eruption</u>).

Tèarmunn- Sea-locked prison

Thaumaturge- A performer of miracles or magic feats.

Traxis- A wooden staff powerful enough to
create towers of unquenchable flame.

Triùir- trio

Yggdrasill- In Norse mythology, Yggdrasil ('The
Terrible One's Horse'), also called the World Tree, is the
giant ash tree that links and shelters all the worlds.

Cailleach:

> 22yrs old.
>
> Waist length Reddish black hair.
>
> Eye color- Black
>
> Muscular
>
> Pregnant with Coinneach Odhar, supposedly by Cadno MacKenneth
>
> Daughter of Arthair Odhar
>
> Stands 5' 7" 120lbs

Arthair Odhar:

> 42yrs old
>
> Short- cropped Black Hair
>
> Eye color- Green
>
> Gentle Giant
>
> Wife died at childbirth.
>
> Inherited farm from relatives passed down hundreds of years.
>
> Farmer
>
> Stands 7' 6" 425lbs

Father MacKenneth:

> 48yrs old
>
> Long Black hair with streaks of gray
>
> Collar length black beard
>
> Eye color- Brown
>
> Sagart
>
> Father- Earl of Seaforth

Uncle of Cadno MacKenneth

Stands 5' 10" 168lbs

Cadno MacKenneth:

26yrs old

Blond hair (bowl cut just below ears)

Eye color-Grey

Drunk

Mother is sister of Sagart on Mackenzie side

Supposed father of Coinneach Odhar

Stands 6' 1" 195lbs

Luthais Monroe:

56yrs old

Balding grey hair

Eye color-Blue

Ancestor of Arden Monroe

Blacksmith

Best friend of Arthair Odhar

Stands 5' 11" 210lbs

Betrain MacLeod:

38yrs old

Red hair below waist

Eye color- Lavender

Widower

Farmer

Has one daughter named Inga

Is in love with Arthair

Grandfather was a warrior

Stands 5' 7" 135lbs

Hamish (Armstrong) Anderson:

30yrs old

Very short cropped red hair

Eye color- Blue

Horseman

Trader

Mercenary

Stands 6' 3" 280lbs

Scuigin Morrissey:

42yrs old

Brown greasy neck length hair

Scraggly beard (unshaven)

Eye color- Brown

No teeth

Drunkard

Thief

Stinks from never bathing

Opportunist

Stands 5' 7" 145lbs

'Barrel' Bob Macaulay:

45yrs old

Balding Black hair close cropped

Eye color- green

Tavern owner and keeper

Stands 5' 5" 280lbs

Elrick:

Ghost of Viking

Once stood 6'8" 260lbs

Waist length gray hair

Chest length grey beard

Died at hands of Marrok

Cursed by Epona for stealing her ring

Released from Epona's curse by Nidhoggr

Has friend vs. enemy relationship with Nidhoggr

Very lonely

Loves to talk

Marrok:

One of the Demon generals

Was once human

Cursed trying to defeat Olofin and condemned to live in the body of a wolf forever

Has only one power (The proximity spell- within 60 feet of his person, magic has no effect.)

Immortal

Taliesin:

Elysian Raptor

Greatest of his Eagle kind

Friends with Nidhoggr (They indulge themselves in constant debate)

Familiar of Epona

Immortal

Eye color- Yellow iris on red

Feathers are gold and silver

Can assume human form

Hair in human form is long with blond curls

Human form is 6' 3" 260lbs

Epona:

Female goddess of Horses

Protector of all animals and innocence

Blue skin

Red hair below her shoulders

Emerald eyes

Nidhoggr:

Dragon

8600yrs old

Red and Gold scales

Guards the Yggdrasill tree (Tree of knowledge and life)

Can become invisible

Loves to talk

Stands 160' 28000 lbs

Is not immortal

Ruairidh:

    Apprentice to Myrddin the great wizard

    Age unknown

    Rumored to have been heir to the throne of the Fortress of the Silver Star

    Considered very powerful and dangerous

    Shoulder length brown hair braided into seven strands

    Chest length brown beard also braided into seven strands

    Eye color- blue

    Wears the robe of master wizard

    Hides a secret past

Eeyul:

    Queen of the Banshee's

    Scream can dishearten any and all opponents

    Curse holds her to Dark Wood

    Has ability to command wind

    Can move the earth

    Black hair

    Black eyes

    Lily white skin

    Face twisted into horrible scream like contortion

    Wears vale over her face

    Related to Arthair Odhar

    Has limited memory

    Desires acceptance

Namhaid:

    Walking dead

    Horrible stench

    Can be obliterated but not killed

    Cannot tolerate the touch of metal

    Brought from the deepest bowels of Olc Sonnach

    Stand 7' 300lbs

Stone Giants:

    Ancient slaves of warrior Gods

No intelligence

Made of granite

Stand 25' 1200lbs

Saltus:

Ancient forest sacred to the' Cruithne' people (Picts)

Home to standing stones within Ancient Oak Grove

Protected by spells and conjurations

Stronghold

Máthair Shúigh:

Keeper of the Sword

Keeper of the truth

Blue octopus

Keeper of wisdom

Abdul:

Shop keeper in Olc Sonnach

Trader of body parts

Slad:

Master thief

Stands 5' 2" 120lbs

Gold teeth

Small; almost feminine

Strong and quick

Fiadh:

Young deer with red ears

Powerful guardian

Dorchadas:

Dark cloud that provides transportation

Can carry unlimited amount of cargo

Only two known to exist

Supposedly created to carry demons to every end of the earth.

Tearmunn:

> Coastal prison also called the "Satan's Jaw"
>
> Lower west coast below Muireann
>
> Natural barriers keep prisoners inside
>
> Most inhabitants are cannibals

Muireann:

> Name came from captured mermaid who was later turned into a
> human when she was baptized.
>
> Sits at base of Mons Aquila in the Valley of Arach
>
> Established by the Normans then later by the Vikings

BlairMor:

> Established by Seanathair Odhar
>
> Stretches from the Valley of Epona to the North Mountain called
> Uamh-Puca or Starry Mountain.

Outland:

> Also called "Sanctuary"
>
> Stronghold of murderers, thieves, and outcast
>
> Located on the southern central coast of Leuist
>
> Governed by democratically chosen 'Assembly' made up of seven
> people (three women, three men, and one arbitrator chosen anew
> each month)
>
> To enter is free, but to leave requires payment
>
> Punishment for breaking any law is death.

Wullie:

> Age 36
>
> Arthair Odhar's Younger Brother
>
> Stands 12' 7" 975lbs
>
> Lives alone near the Starry Mountain in a cabin
> he built himself to accommodate his size.

Diabhal:

> God of the Demons forever chained deep within Tèarmunn

Myrddin:

    Age unknown

    Long silver hair braided in seven places.

    Long moustache and beard have grown into each other yet trimmed just below the jaw.

    Rumored to have been killed by Medraut

Scáthach:

    Female warrior and martial arts teacher.

    Age unknown

    Stands 6' 160lbs

BOOK TWO
The Gathering

Lightning Source UK Ltd.
Milton Keynes UK
UKOW03f1902260114

225281UK00001B/36/P